GODS & GANGSTERS

AN ILLUMINATI NOVEL

SLMN

Kingston Imperial

Gods & Gangsters Copyright © 2020 by Kingston Imperial 2, LLC

Printed in the United States of America

Rights Department, 144 North 7th Street, #255 Brooklyn N.Y. 11249

First Edition:

Book and Jacket Design: PiXiLL Designs

Cataloging in Publication data is on file with the library of Congress

ISBN 9780998767420 (Trade Paperback)

PROLOGUE

etective O'Brien had a *punch me* face, but Spagoli's was pure *shoot me.*

He wasn't in a position to do shit, chained to a table in the interrogation room. He had just enough chain to get a cigarette from the packet in front of him and light it. So he just told them like it was. "It's a war going on outside," he said as he inhaled his cigarette, exhaled, then added, "Nobody's safe."

Spagoli and O'Brien looked at one another, then looked back at him. "Not even you," Spagoli said with a sneer like a razor slash across his face. It wasn't a question. It was a statement of cold hard fact.

He chuckled, but not because he was happy. "*Especially* me. If niggas knew what I was doing right now..." he began to say, before his voice trailed off in shame and regret.

O'Brien was all triumph and victory. Like a hunter who has finally bagged his prize prey. "Yeah, look at you now. Big gangsta nothing! How's it feel to be a rat?" O'Brien knew exactly where in the heart to stab him.

His blood boiled and his hands made fists. There had been a time when his name would've never been mentioned in the same sentence with the word *rat*, and cop or no cop, he would've murdered anyone who did. But that was before. Now he was exactly what they said he was.

A rat.

He looked at himself in the reflection of the two-way mirror on the wall behind the detectives. It reflected the interrogation room strip lights like spotlights onto his shame. He knew she was probably on the other side watching him.

I'm doing it for you, he thought, as if it would make the guilt eating him drain away. As if it would make any fucking difference. It wouldn't. So just to let her know he knew she was there, he blew her a kiss before returning to Spagoli and O'Brien.

Fuck that bitch.

Focus.

"You know O'Brien, they say the only thing that will survive a nuclear war is the rats and the roaches. I guess that makes us both survivors huh, you fucking cockroach."

O'Brien lunged at him, but Spagoli was quicker and caught an arm that was about to send its fist, pile-driving into his nose. Spagoli pulled O'Brien to one side.

"Save it." Spagoli told O'Brien, then turned to him and said, "And you watch your friggin' mouth! If it wasn't for us, your black ass would be floating in the East River! Now tell us what we want to know!"

"What do you want to know?" he said, enjoying O'Brien's anger just enough to let it show on his face. If O'Brien's eyes were 9mm hollow-points...

"Everything!" Spagoli bellowed.

He inhaled the cigarette smoke. "Everything? Even about her?" he teased, tossing his head in the direction of the two-way mirror. "You wanna know what her pussy taste like?"

"Shut the fuck up," Spagoli hissed. Spagoli was on edge too. He smirked.

"Relax, spaghetti head. It ain't that serious, unless...you're fucking her too?"

Spagoli leaned across the table, slamming him in the shoulders and jerking him back in the chair. Many men were cold in the ground for a lot less.

"You want to play with me, you cocksucker? Huh?!" Spagoli seethed.

His eyes lit up with realization. "Oh you *are* fucking her, huh? Wow, she really does get around!"

His laugh creased Spagoli's face like an old five-dollar bill. Fortunately, O'Brien pulled Spagoli off him. "Sit down!" O'Brien yelled.

He was getting to the both of them. If he was going to be a rat, he might as well have some fun along the way. How much fun depended on how much juice he could give them. So he re-lit his cigarette and began.

"It goes like this, the start of the ending..."

TRACK 1

The MAC-II sat on Hurricane's lap. Nobody called him that. They called him "Kane." Brutal and to the point, like the man himself. A blunt burned crisply between his lips, the tip glowing dimly in the dark as Messiah drove.

Kane loaded the MAC's extended clip with hollow tips, his hands gloved to avoid leaving prints. "Then I fucked her," Kane said with a shrug, inhaling the blunt's smoke like he'd just said the most natural thing in the world.

Messiah laughed and thumped the steering wheel, his face alight. "Get the fuck outta here, thun! You ain't fuck that bitch!"

Kane tuned the MAC over and looked at Messiah with a gleam. "Nigga, I fucked her. Word on the dead homies, right there in the kitchen!"

"Yo thun, kill that bullshit! You ain't fuck that bitch mother," Messiah laughed, yet his laugh betrayed him. He knew Kane's word was truth.

Kane loaded the clip in the MAC, then cocked it back, sending one hollow head into the chamber. He drew on the blunt like a man remembering something real sweet. "Man listen thun, my bitch was asleep..."

The only sound alive was the soft tick...tick...tick of the kitchen wall clock as Kane stepped into the kitchen. Clad in nothing but his Tommy boxers, he went to the refrigerator and opened it, flooding the dark kitchen with the fridge light. Seeing the full refrigerator put a smile on his face. Growing up in the Queens Boro projects, he was always used to seeing nothing but the back of the refrigerator when he opened it. Now that he was old enough to provide, it always made him proud to see a full refrigerator, especially one he filled.

Kane pulled out the container of Donald Duck orange juice. He didn't even think about getting a glass. He turned it up to his mouth.

Kane heard Ms. Jefferson before he saw her. "Now I know you ain't got your mannish ass in my kitchen in your boxers, drinking out of the carton."

When he looked, he saw her standing in the doorway. His dick automatically twitched in his boxers, because Ms. Jefferson looked like Angela Bassett with bigger titties. She was wearing a robe, but it was open, revealing the silk top that stopped right around her upper thigh. Her legs were thick and her toenails were painted a soft pink, which seemed to glow in the dim refrigerator light.

"My bad yo, I didn't want to dirty no glasses," Kane explained, trying to keep his eyes off her cleavage – and failing.

"Mm-hmm," she replied with a smirk as she stepped into the kitchen. She grabbed a glass out of the dish rack and held it towards him. "Well I just hope you saved some for me."

He poured some juice into her cup on the counter. Their fingers touched. Kane pulled his hand an inch away, but as he poured she moved the glass so that their fingers connected again. Kane looked up. She wasn't looking at the glass, she was looking right at him. Like the glass was the last thing on her mind.

She eyed Kane over the rim of the glass. He saw her tongue moving in her mouth. The tip resting on her top lip, denting it with a glisten of saliva before she spoke. "Who can sleep with all that moaning and groaning going on? You think I don't hear y'all? Tiffany screaming like you killing her! Is that what you be doing? Killing my daughter?" Ms. Jefferson said, raising the glass to her slowly parting lips.

Kane played it off with a chuckle, but he was feeling the heat from her stare down.

"Nah, you know what I'm saying, I just do what I do." His dick had already taken on a life of its own, peeking its head out of his boxers. She looked down at it and arched an eyebrow. The tip of her tongue sat again on the cushion of her top lip.

"Damn, it's like that? No wonder she be hollerin'," Ms. Jefferson giggled. She moved closer to him, her shoulder against his as she reached across him to put her glass down on the counter with her right hand. As the glass clinked down in the silent kitchen, her left hand touched Kane's belly and slid down to grip his dick.

"I want you to do to me what you do to my daughter," she whispered in Kane's ear.

Kane needed no second invitation. He pulled her into him, peeling the robe from her shoulders. Her whole body was trembling and there was a heat coming off her that flared in his nostrils.

Bitch was in heat. And now so was Kane.

Kane tongued her neck and she tasted like cherries. He pulled her silk top up to reveal she wasn't wearing any panties. He slid his hand around and palmed her juicy ass. What started as a moan became a deep growl in her throat. It moved him on.

"Damn your dick thick," she gasped, squeezing and pulling at it.

"See how much of it you can fit in your mouth," Kane grunted while pressing down on her shoulders.

"Mannish ass," she snickered as she dropped to her knees.

As soon as she wrapped her lips around his dick, she mmm'd like it was the best thing she'd ever tasted in her life. Kane had no idea if Ms. Jefferson was getting regular dick, but she was sucking him hard enough to jumpstart a Lexus, as if it was saving her from drowning. This hungry lust excited Kane. Damn her mouth was good. Better than her daughter, dead ass. Kane grabbed a handful of her hair and began to fuck her face. "Goddamn," he breathed.

Kane thought since he had just fucked her daughter he'd be long winded, but Ms. Jefferson's deep throat skills had him ready to bust two minutes into it.

"Yeah bitch, eat that dick," he spat. Pushing harder from the hips, pulling her head on. Ms. Jefferson had other ideas. She pulled back, his dick sliding down her chin. "Uh uh! Not before I get mine!"

Kane smiled, pulling her up by the hair, and bending her over the sink. She didn't resist, but her pussy was a little ways behind... "Sssss baby, take it easy... It's been a while," she groaned, putting her hand on his stomach to stop him from going too deep. That explained how greedy she was for Kane's dick, but that only made him more determined.

"Nah, don't get shook now yo. You gonna take this dick," Kane said, with a tone as hard as what he was about to put inside her. He spread her ass cheeks and pushed balls deep with a single thrust. This pussy wasn't complaining no more.

Ms. Jefferson gasped, her hand going out across the counter, knocking her glass on its side, spilling juice. "Make me take it then! Make me take all that dick!" she begged, as hungry in the pussy as she had been in the mouth.

Ms. Jefferson wasn't lying when she said it had been a long time. Her pussy was the wettest and tightest he ever felt – the kind of pussy weak men die and kill for.

The soft glow of the refrigerator light made them shine with a bluish tinge in Tiffany's eyes. It took her a second to understand what she was seeing. She gripped the kitchen doorframe, as her world tilted. When her mind completed the jigsaw puzzle, the image played in her mind like a hologram from hell.

The glass her mother had knocked over, rolled from the counter and smashed. It triggered Tiffany's voice.

"You trifling ass bitch! My mother, my own mother?!" she screamed.

Ms. Jefferson froze, her pussy clamping even harder on Kane's dick. It felt so sweet. So tight. You don't pass up a pussy like that, whatever the situation.

So Kane kept punishing Ms. Jefferson's pussy, even as Tiffany began to beat at his back with her balled fists.

He figured he'd rather get caught for keeping it going than get caught for stopping.

Khalil Boyd was a street cop working out of the 114th Precinct on Astoria Blvd. Queens. The people who knew he was a cop viewed him in one of two ways: a brave street soldier or a total traitor. There was no middle ground. He'd been a cop for eight years — a good cop according to his Captain, and his beat included the Queens Boro Projects. He was originally from Staten Island and made the move to the Boro Projects with his parents when he was four. When he was grown and able, Khalil moved his family to Hollis three years ago thanks to his cop salary. It felt like home now, but the stain of the Boro would forever be on him. His first four years on Staten Island could have happened to someone else. There was no doubt in his mind that being a cop was what he wanted to be when he grew up. Other friends had gone other ways. Needless to say, they weren't friends no more.

Khalil had just gotten off work. It was only an hour late tonight, which was some kind of record. It was a fuck of a shift, but he cleared his paperwork and made it out the door before any major calls came in. From there he headed home through the dark wintery streets.

It was New York cold, but he didn't mind that. New York had a temperature for every mood, and Khalil's mood was chilled in a good way. The Mrs. was already surprised to hear him home before the kids made it into bed. This would be points on his score card. Misha had been bitching like crazy over how little time he spent at home, so perhaps tonight getting home before dawn would catch him a break.

Khalil's path was illuminated by the Christmas decorations that seemed to light Hollis up like a mini Beale St. Khalil loved Christmas. As a child, his mother was too poor to buy him any gifts, and now that he was the father of 3-year-old twin boys, he did what he had to do to make sure that their Christmas would always be memorable.

Khalil turned into his driveway, turned off the car, sat back and smiled. He was proud of how far he had come. At 32, he owned his own home and provided well for his wife and kids.

Life was good. Even if he spent his days in the dirt of the Boro, when he got home, just walking through the door made him clean.

"Man, get the fuck outta here!" Messiah laughed, flipping on the windshield wipers. Snow was beginning to fall in light flurries, erasing the darkness through the windshield with smooshed wet flakes.

Kane laughed, kissing his fingertips and held his palm up. "That's my word, thun. I was smashin' that old bitch and Tiff came in spazzin'! I thought they was 'bout to fight. My word, I was heated too 'cause I was just about to nut!"

Messiah thumped the steering wheel with the heel of his

hand, laughing hard. Kane had his mind on the mission. As the windshield cleared up, he said, "Make a right. Make a right!"

"You on some bullshit, thun," Messiah chuckled, turning the wheel. "This the block?"

Kane looked around carefully. The windshield was smearing quickly, obscuring his vision, but he knew Hollis because his grandmother lived there. "Yeah, yeah, right there. That's that muhfucka's house."

"You sure?"

"No doubt."

Messiah nodded; all traces of playfulness were gone. Shit was about to pop. He pulled down the block and parked the stolen Buick. They both packed MAC-11's in their goose down parkas. They got out into the chill air, their breath making clouds.

The buildings on the block all had Christmas lights decorated the windows that covered the warm rooms. Shadows moved behind the glass as TVs flickered. Somewhere, lame ass Christmas carols leaked from an open window.

They walked like Christmas never happened, pulling the masks down over their faces, heading for their objective.

The snow felt like cold kisses on Kane's skin.

"Daddy's home!" Jason shouted. He ran to Khalil as he came through the door. He bent down and scooped him into his arms. "What's up, my little soldier? You been good?"

"Yes!" he sang, like the innocent angel he wasn't.

"No," Misha said behind them as she came out of the kitchen. "Tell your Daddy how many times I had to tell you to pick up your toys."

Khalil looked from Misha to his son. "Is that true?"

Jason dropped his little head, as if his toes could tell a better story.

"You must not want the toys I asked Santa to bring you

tonight," Khalil said, putting his index finger under his chin and lifting his face up.

"No Daddy, please I'll be good! I'll clean up! I promise!"

Khalil held back his laugh. "I don't know, I'm gonna have to call Santa and see what he has to say. You go to your room."

He put Jason down and he trooped off, head hung, like he had just been sentenced. As soon as he disappeared up the stairs, Khalil and Misha released their laughter, embracing at the same time.

"How long do you think before he comes back pleading?" Khalil chuckled.

"There's no telling," Misha replied.

There was a moment when this could have gone any which way. Yesterday, Misha was breaking his balls about work, today, well...Khalil pulled Misha in gently and then kissed her softly. For once she didn't stiffen and pull away. Maybe Christmas would come early for him tonight too. Misha's eyes were big and as wide as her smile. Khalil wanted that look to last forever.

"Enough time to make the move?"

"Hell no," Misha protested, but the look in her eyes said *maybe later*. They both laughed.

It was their last joyful noise.

Kane peeped in the front window, holding his breath so not to steam up the window and saw Misha and Khalil hugging.

"He in there?" Messiah whispered.

"Hell yeah that bitch ass nigga in there. Come on..."

Kane led the walk around the side of the house, heading to the back door. The sound of carols in the air was lost as they made it into the yard. Kane toggled the gate. Unlocked.

Perfect.

The yard was full of plastic garden toys, piled for the winter. The window on the back door was dark. No lights on in the kitchen. Kane tried the knob – the door was open. His gold-grilled smile looked as menacing as a vampire. "That bitch ain't shit," he chuckled.

"QB hoes, you already know," Messiah answered.

They pushed open the door and entered the kitchen. The house was all but silent. There was enough light spilling from the living room door to light their way, and they went past the table and chairs like ghosts.

They emerged in the living room. Misha and Khalil were still in their embrace, but Misha was looking over her husband's shoulder. At the sight of Kane and Messiah, she let her hands drop and moved away from Khalil.

"Hey baby..." Khalil began to protest, but as soon as he was clear of his wife, Kane and Messiah raised their MAC's. Khalil must've heard the rustle of their clothes because he looked around then and saw the glint of the guns aimed straight for him.

Kane nodded at Khalil, like he was signaling to an old friend across the street, then the guns spat vengeance and retribution.

Brrrrrap! Brrrrrap!

Bullets tore through Khalil like a kid through the wrapping paper of a present. Holes appeared in his police shirt, popping the material and running a line up his chest, through his chin, blowing apart his nose and then smashing into his forehead. Pieces of brain, bone and skin flurried up like bloody snowflakes.

Khalil tumbled and flipped over the coffee table, spinning around and falling face first to the carpet, his hand twitching. After two seconds it stopped, and then like Khalil's fingers, everything in the room was still.

Misha's eyes watered up. Up until that moment, she hadn't realized how deep she was. Khalil had been her husband and the father of her children, but fifty grand brought a serious amount of treachery, even against her husband. She moved towards Kane and

Messiah who had dropped their guns. The air stank from blood and cordite.

"You gotta go. I gotta call the police to make it look good," Misha said, hating herself, but keeping her mind's eye on the prize.

Kane smiled.

"Yeah, but you goin' too!" Messiah spat, pointing the MAC at Misha's face point blank. This wasn't how it was supposed to be. She'd done what they asked: Left the back door unlocked, kept Khalil busy while they got into the house, and had even telephoned them to tell them Khalil was coming home early tonight. *What more did they want?*

"No! Power said he only wanted Khalil!" she screeched.

Kane shrugged. "He lied."

The MAC spoke its last story as it told Misha its unhappy ending.

Her face opened like a can of tomatoes on a firing range. This time the bullets went down, digging into her neck and damn near separating her head from her body. *A guaranteed closed casket kill,* Kane thought with grim amusement.

"Mommy?"

Messiah and Kane turned. Jason was standing at the top of the stairs. Holding a teddy bear to make himself feel braver. Jason had already wet himself at the noise of the gunfire. His pajamas were leaking and so were his eyes.

"Leave my mommy alone!" he shouted in his best tantrum voice.

Messiah and Kane looked at each other. In their gaze was one question – kill him?

Kane cracked a wicked grin. "Merry Christmas, shorty," he chuckled, then he and Messiah left Jason and his brother to be orphans.

What up kid!

I know it's rough in the bing...

Power sat back and smiled. He had been on Riker's Island for almost a year awaiting trial, but the letter just confirmed what he knew would happen if he stayed focused and his team held him down. Now, his freedom was a foregone conclusion.

Power stood up and stretched. The deferasirox he took for his thalassemia kept the crisis cramps at bay, plus stopped his hands from swelling, so he was glad to be feeling good. The best in his life, in fact. Prison kept him on an active workout regimen and he was eating right, as best as he could while living in a concrete and metal hell. The thalassemia wasn't something he spoke about with anyone. He just took his medication and lived his life, and when he needed treatment, went in to the doc for a transfusion to help manage the disease. He preferred it that way. On impulse, as if to underline how good he felt, he dropped and did 50 push-ups in one clip. Even though he hated every day behind bars, he had made the best of it, especially when it came to his physique. He was 5'9" and 140 lbs when he got knocked. Now a year later, he had sprouted three inches and his workout regimen had him a cobra-backed at 180 lbs with a six-pack that you could wash clothes on. He couldn't wait to get out and drive the bitches bonkers. He was already a green-eyed, curly-haired pretty boy, and now with the body to match, he was ready to take his game to another level.

He was about to do another one when he heard, "Ay yo Power! Peace God! What's today's Mathematics?"

It was his man C-Allah from Fort Green Projects in Brooklyn. He was facing a murder charge too. He and C-Allah bumped heads when Power first came to be housed in the infamous C-74 juvenile building on the island. Brooklyn niggas ran the building, and just because Power was from Queens, they thought shit was sweet.

Power put an end to that when he blew up on a nigga from East New York over the phone. It was about to get real ugly, but C-Allah respected Power for standing up to a potential massacre and squashed the beef. Since they were both *Five Percenters*, the lesson became the foundation to a relationship that soon flourished across the board.

"What up God, today's Math is wisdom and knowledge all being born to myself, being the maker, the owner, cream of the planet earth, father of civilization, God of the universe," Power replied smoothly, while giving C-Allah a gangsta hug.

"True indeed God, true indeed. Ay yo, you know that nigga Duppy from uptown?" C-Allah asked.

"That party promoter nigga that fuck with Global Reserve Records?"

"Yeah, him. I just got off the jack with this little bitch named Mona from around my way. She said she fuck wit' that nigga, yo," C-Allah informed him, shaking his head.

Power frowned slightly. "What's wrong with that?"

C-Allah chuckled.

"That bitch the hoe of my projects!" Power laughed.

"Don't get me wrong – the little bitch bad as fuck. I'm just saying this nigga trying to housewife a hoe."

Power and C-Allah shared a laugh over Duppy's lack of judgment before Power broke his laugh and said, "But yo, tell shorty to holla at that nigga for me. You know my shit is official."

C-Allah smiled like "I got this," and replied, "Come on God, you already know I got you. She said she gonna do that, but she wanna wait until you find out what up with your case."

Now it was Power's turn to smile. "I already know. My mans just wrote me. I'm good."

C-Allah didn't need to hear the details. One look in Power's eyes, and he automatically understood.

"That's what's up, though. Your peoples some official niggas. I'ma have to start giving you Queens Boro niggas some credit," C-Allah remarked.

"Credit? Nigga, you Fort Greene niggas wouldn't last a week on the 81st side. It's all Vietnam, God. Serious *Apocalypse Now*. Don't make me bring down the horror," Power boasted with a smile.

They both playfully got in their fighting stance and began to play box.

Someone at the cell door cleared their throat.

Power and C-Allah dropped their hands, but not before giving each other a play shot each to make it a draw.

They turned around to see Officer Kim Jones at the door. She stood with one hand on one sexy ass hip. She was a bad bitch and she knew it.

"You know y'all ain't supposed to be playing horse in here," she remarked.

Her Jamaican tongue twirled around her Brooklyn accent, making everything she said sound like a song.

C-Allah looked at Power then gave him dap because he already knew what time it was.

"Yo, handle your business, kid," he chuckled as he walked out. Kim gave him a side-eye which sliced him dead and stepped into the cell. "Cell search," she smirked.

"Didn't you just search me yesterday?" Power said, smiling and playing along.

"You a security threat, so I gotta watch you. Now, put your blind up so nobody sees what I find," she gave him that *I'ma fuck the shit out of you* look. Power knew the look well and was hard already. Power put his towel over the window on his door so no one could see what was about to go down. As soon as he did, Kim put her hand on his chest and pushed him against the wall. He didn't want to resist *this* search.

"You got any weapons on you?" she asked, kissing his neck and raking her nails over his six pack.

"You think I would tell you if I did?" he replied, wriggling his hand down the back of her uniform pants over soft, warm flesh. Kim purred and pushed out against his hand. He knew she enjoyed the rake of his nails along her skin.

Kim reached into Power's peel that was unzipped to the waist and already off his shoulders. She pulled his dick out and began squeezing it.

"Look what I found," Kim giggled, "A baseball bat."

Power nuzzled her neck, up to her ear. "Come here," he said, taking full control. He spun her around and made her face the wall. He began kissing her neck and licking the fuzz of hair at the nape. Power undid her belt one-handed, with the ease of someone who had done this many times before. Kim's pants slid down like they were cooperating fully, releasing her fat, juicy ass. Power spread her ass cheeks and slid two fingers in her pussy.

"Damn, don't tease me. Hurry up, before the Sergeant come looking for me." There was lust in her voice.

"Fuck the Sergeant."

"No, fuck *me!*" she shot back, reaching around and grabbing his dick, before cocking one knee against the wall and pulling him into her.

Power plowed into her wetness with all of the force he could find — at the same time moving Kim's mouth against the back of his hand on the wall to block the sounds that were growling there. Power did not want her to tell the whole pod how good his dick felt. She took it like a big girl, cocking her knee higher on some Spider-Man shit. His back shots had her ready to scale the wall.

"Damn, I love this dick," she hissed into her hand, coating his dick with juices, her breathing telling him she was close to cumming already.

"Throw this pussy back," Power growled, slapping her ass with a resounding smack.

"I am!"

Smack! She pushed back into him, doubling the force of his thrust. He grabbed at her hips through the jiggly fat there, pulling her back onto his thighs like a fist pounding an open palm.

"Oh fuck, you gonna make me cum again!"

Smack! Smack! The surface of her ass made waves as each blow hit home.

Kim was in a fuck frenzy, loving the pain of pleasure. "Please baby, cum please! I gotta go!" Kim pled. Grinding into him with greater urgency.

Their bodies slapping together sounded like applause as he pounded her. *The crowd goes wild!* Power's whole body convulsed and he exploded inside of her. He slid out of her. She turned, dropped to her knees and cleaned him with a greedy tongue.

"Damn," Kim said when she'd finished, wiping her mouth with the back of her hand.

She stood and pulled her pants up in one movement. As she clipped her belt buckle up she smiled and blew Power a kiss. He could smell himself on her breath. "Oh yeah, I came up here to tell you to get ready. You have to go to court."

"Do I have time to take a shower?"

"No, you gotta go smellin' like this good pussy you just fucked the shit out of," she winked as she sashayed out the door.

Power tucked his dick into his boxers and shrugged up his peel. There was no better way to get ready for the judge.

"Will the defendant please rise."

Power looked at his lawyer as he stood up, and his lawyer did the same. As usual Power was the only black guy in the room.

"On what grounds are you seeking a dismissal of all charges, counselor?" the judge asked, looking as if he could care less. The judge was fat, white and looked down at Power and his lawyer, Cal Robertson, as if they were a disease, through half-moon glasses. The judge looked like an egg with eyebrows.

Robertson, a thin New Yorker with more smarts than you could fit inside the usual white guy cleared his throat and replied, "I've talked to the D.A., your honor, and because of the tragic death of the state's only witness to this alleged crime, one—" he looked at his notes—"Khalil Boyd, there simply is no case."

The judge nodded. This was an old story. "I see. And how did this...Mr. Boyd... meet his demise, counselor?"

"Home invasion, your honor. He and his wife were gunned down."

"How convenient," the judge remarked sarcastically, before turning his attention to the D.A. "Mrs. Pointer?"

The D.A. Sally Pointer stood. She reminded Power of a teacher in his elementary school who would wear skirts that would flash her thighs every time she sat down. Mrs. Pointer wore the same kind of skirt today. Power knew he should be concentrating on the proceedings, but for a white bitch, Mrs. Pointer had fine legs.

"Yes your honor, I don't think it's in the best interest of the state to pursue charges at this time."

The judge looked at his file, then at Power. "Mr. Mitchell, how old are you?"

Power was still fixated. Robertson nudged him and the judge repeated the question.

"Seventeen," Power said, adding an extra subtle sneer to his tone.

"Mr. Mitchell, you aren't even old enough to drink and you already have several assaults, including, I might add, a *double* murder that you are currently charged with. I am inclined to believe this is a pattern," the judge said.

Mrs. Pointer was adjusting her blouse and Power had her titties on his mind. *Old white bitch always grateful for black dick.*

Power had to snap back again. "Not guilty, your honor," Power replied to a question that hadn't been asked.

"I'm not asking how you plead, young man."

"Then what's your point?" Power drilled the judge with a look that would burn stone.

The judge smirked. "Ah, I see I have a tough guy in my courtroom. My point, Mr. Mitchell, is you are a very violent young man and I find it highly fortuitous that the only witness is dead. But, as they tell you in law school, it's not what you know; it's what you can prove. I just hope I'm the one on the bench when your luck runs out."

"We done yet?" Power asked Robertson.

The judge banged his gavel with maximum annoyance. "Case dismissed! See you soon, Mr. Mitchell."

Under his breath, Power mumbled, "fucking cracker."

He turned to his lawyer as they walked into the cold marble floored corridor outside the courtroom "Thanks...for nothin'."

"Hey, I got you off." Roberson said dead pan. Like it meant something.

"QB got me off, remember that."

Sighing, Robertson handed Power over to the Corrections Officer who would take him back to Riker's for release processing.

Before they'd gotten ten yards, two men waving detective badges, Spagoli and O'Brien, called to them. The C.O. escorting Power stopped. Spagoli grilled Power hard, peeling out of the shadows to block Power's way. Power gave nothing away on his face. He made sure he didn't even look irritated.

"Do you know who I am?" Spagoli gritted.

"Nobody," Power answered without blinking.

"No, nobody you want to fuck with," Spagoli countered. "You think you're the shit because you had one of your fellow monkeys murder the witness, huh? Well, trust me...next time it won't be so easy."

"Yo, I don't know what you're talkin' about, but if someone got murdered, it sounds like you ain't doin' your job. Protect and serve, right?" Power smirked.

Power could see Spagoli wished they were having their conversation in a dark alley. Power met a lot of officers who wanted to wipe that look off his face permanently. He still hadn't blinked, not once, and wouldn't until Spagoli's eyelids gave him the win.

Spagoli blinked.

O'Brien stepped in. "Oh, believe me. You will get served...but I don't know about the protect part."

Spagoli and O'Brien walked off, leaving Power to contemplate their wake, and when they were through the doors out onto the snowy streets, he allowed his eyelids to do their thing.

"Ay yo yo yo, who got bank?"

"Fuck who got bank nigga, roll the fuckin' dice!"

"Yo, I got fifty, he has four!"

"Money on the wood, nigga!"

Their breath clouded the alley, the sodium glow of the street lights seemed to make the space feel colder. Kane crouched in the middle of the circle, shaking the dice like a voodoo doctor shakes bones ready to cast a spell.

"Come on baby, six-six-six! Mark of the beast!" he grunted, letting the dice fly. As the bones clicked and clacked together like skeleton teeth, a new, seventh voice yelled, "Freeze! Muhfuckas. Lay down!"

Nobody had seen the man creep up on them, but now that all six of them were staring down the barrel of a chrome .40 caliber with mother of pearl grip and gold accents, they knew he caught them slipping.

He was a cold man holding a pretty killer.

Kane looked up straight into the gunman's eyes.

"Nigga, this my hood! I promise you, you won't make it off this block alive!" Kane growled.

"Gimme the loot!" the masked man growled with a deep voice.

Kane was about to continue his protest and threats but stopped. He squinted. "Hol' up, I know that voice. Yo Power, I'ma kill yo' ass!" As soon as Kane said his name, Power busted out laughing.

The other five dudes relaxed as Power removed the mask, laughing hysterically. Kane started to curse him out, but he stopped, too happy to see Power back on the street. He slammed him with a thorough gangsta hug. Power put the S&W in his pants and dapped the circle.

"My nigga, God damn it's good to see you! But I should kill your ass, playin' wit' me!" Kane barked.

Power laughed.

"Fuck that, you was shook! Talkin' about 'this my hood!' I

heard your voice crack on some Minnie Mouse shit!" Power said, pushing Kane's shoulder.

The crew laughed and Kane couldn't help but crack his signature sinister gold grill grin.

"Fuck outta here," Kane said, a chuckle not far from the surface.

"When you got home, thun?" a dude named Black Jesus asked Power, giving him a pound and a gangster hug.

"Today," Power answered, scanning the faces around him, and then adding, "Yo Kane, where the twins at?"

"On a mission," was all Kane replied, but his eyes said much more...

THREE YEARS LATER

"*S* *everal members of the notorious rap group Q.B.C. were arrested today in Raleigh, North Carolina on firearms and related offenses. It began as an altercation after a performance in a local nightclub, but quickly escalated when shots were exchanged between the group and the crowd. The police found that several of the guns used in the shooting had been stolen three years ago and police say the altercation ultimately cost one man his life. The body, however, was never recovered.*"

Messiah gazed up at the screen as he stood in the day room of the Wake County Jail.

The red peel swallowed up his slim but wiry frame because they only had one that was three sizes too big for him. He also hated the fact that he had to wear cheap ass flip-flops with no socks, keeping his feet cold.

"Man, this some bullshit," he grumbled to himself, as he looked around his bullpen.

Overcrowded wasn't the word for the conditions. There were three people sleeping in a cell meant for one man — people sleeping on the floor, people everywhere. The place stank like a dirty armpit in summer all day long. The smell never got out of his nose, never went from his mouth. On some days even, the food tasted like armpits. Messiah was already pissed, but the Carolina niggas were making it worse, ice grilling him as if looks could kill.

Messiah took one look around at the squalid day room and decided a single cell in the hole was preferable to being cramped up in general population.

Besides, he wanted to release some stress.

He stepped up to three dudes standing by the phone who had been ice grilling him since he came in. The biggest dude was four inches on Messiah's six feet even stature, but size was never a factor when his outcome was to be determined by will.

"Ay yo, you know me or somethin', son?" Messiah questioned, ice grilling the dude just as hard.

"You know me?" the big dude shot back.

Messiah could see that dude really didn't want any problems, but the mere fact of having his two friends right there was putting a battery in his back. So Messiah knew sooner or later, the situation would escalate. He preferred sooner.

Shit! Messiah spat the gem star razor from his mouth.

The dudes never even saw it coming. Messiah had marveled when he came in to Wake County and the police officer who strip-searched him never told him to open his mouth. Now he was glad he hadn't.

The big dude cried out as the razor slit his face open like it had a zipper. The straight lipped line ran from his temple to his chin. Blood spitting, landing on Messiah's cheek as he ripped the big dude again across the lip, splitting it in two.

Then in the same motion, he pushed the big dude into his man on the left, who was lunging at Messiah. Cooler than new frost, Messiah slit the dude on the hand, right across the palm, wrist and forearm because he raised his arms in time to save his face.

"Oh shit."

"God damn!"

"Fuck!"

Everyone standing around jumped away as blood gushed, but

Messiah wasn't done. He went after the third dude just as four police officers burst into the pod, spraying mace and pulling out Tasers.

"Get down on the floor now!" the first officer bellowed as he reached to grab Messiah.

But Messiah was in a zone. He didn't know it was the police who grabbed him, so he spun with the razor and slashed the officer across the check and the bridge of his nose.

His flesh sliced open, yanking a bitch scream out of his mouth as blood got in his eye.

"I can't see! I can't see! My face!" he yelled.

The other officers made short work of Messiah, punching, stomping and tasing him until he went down and his lights went out.

When he came to, Messiah was laying on a cold steel slab in a solitary cell. The stench of mace was still on him, and when he tried to get up, he grimaced with excruciating pain because his ribs felt like they were broken. There was no window in the cell, so he didn't know if it was day, night or even how long he had been there.

"Ay yo," he called out, hearing only the echo of his own voice in response. "Yo!" he screamed louder.

This time he heard the jingle of approaching keys, slowly scraping into the lock. A fat redneck officer appeared in the window of the steel door.

"Get up, you've got a visitor," the redneck told him, voice dripping with contempt.

"Get up?! Man my ribs feel broke. I need to see a nurse," Messiah said.

The redneck shrugged. "She ain't here. She's busy stitching up the officer you cut. Maybe you can see her tomorrow...or the next day. Maybe. Now get up or I'm coming in there to get you up," the redneck growled.

Messiah knew he was in no shape to buck, so he struggled... painfully...to his feet, walking like an elderly man, gritting his teeth and holding his ribs with every step.

The redneck opened the tray slot in the door.

"Turn around and put your hands behind your back to cuff up," the redneck's orders were like snot sneezed onto a hand.

"This some fuckin' bullshit," Messiah mumbled, as he turned his back to the door.

When the redneck snatched his arms behind his back, the pain was so intense that Messiah saw stars, but he refused to give the satisfaction of hearing him cry out, so he bit his lip until it bled.

"Open 211," the redneck squawked into his walkie-talkie. The steel door slid open as smoothly as the rock in front of Jesus' tomb. Messiah stepped out, eyes red with pain, but a smirk on his lips. "QB we take it and smile."

The redneck shoved him forward. "Just walk!"

He led Messiah to an interrogation room. As soon as he walked in, the first thing he noticed was the two-way mirror that covered the entire right wall. He hadn't even noticed the two detectives sitting at the deck, until Spagoli remarked, "Remember us?"

Messiah turned his head to the sound of the voice and his heart sank. He knew the game was over. O'Brien read his expression.

"No smile? And here I thought you'd be glad to see us, after we came all the way from New York in your honor," O'Brien remarked. The redneck sat him down hard. He grimaced.

"What's the matter? You don't look so good? But then again, you never look good," Spagoli cracked.

"Fuck you. I need a doctor, my fuckin' ribs are broke," he seethed.

Spagoli shrugged. "Imagine how it feels to be buried alive, suffocating, begging for air. Did you let him see a doctor?"

He glared at Spagoli.

"I don't know what you're talking about."

"*That's* what I'm talking about!" Spagoli shot back, slapping four 8 x 6 glossies on the table in front of Messiah. He refused to look.

"Look at it," Spagoli ordered in a menacing tone. He shifted in his chair, refusing to look.

"I need a doctor!"

"Look at it!" Spagoli spazzed, grabbing him by the neck and forcing him to look at the photo.

The body was sprawled out on the ground beside the hole he had been buried in. The body had decayed badly, maggots having eaten away at his face, but he knew exactly who he was...Tyrone.

THREE YEARS EARLIER

"Yo Messiah, you ain't gotta do this!" Lil' Earl pleaded.

"Man shut the fuck up and just dig!" Messiah ordered, his gun held down by his side.

Lil' Earl chopped down with the shovel, lifting another chunk of earth, and flopping it down onto the growing pile, but Messiah could see his heart wasn't in it.

Knowledge, Messiah's twin brother, sat in the passenger seat of the rented Taurus smoking a blunt, leaning out of the open door. Messiah got his name because he was the first twin. The King Twin. The One and Only First Power. His brother called himself Knowledge because his wisdom was knowing who was the best. Both of them claimed superiority over the other for different reasons. Everyone else just called it a draw.

There was a steady bumping noise coming from the trunk. Lil' Earl paused and leaned on the shovel.

"Come on, cuz! I swear we ain't got to worry about Ty," Lil' Earl repeated for the thousandth time.

Messiah stepped up to Lil' Earl and put the gun to his forehead for extra encouragement. "You damn right we don't, 'cause that's exactly why you diggin'...cuz. I don't give a fuck about that nigga.

He fucked up. We told him not to take that shit and he took it anyway! You think I bailed that nigga outta jail 'cause I like him? I bailed him out to keep him from rattin' us out! You my cousin, and blood mean something to me, but don't get it fucked up and make me choose blood or money, E.," Messiah spat coldly.

The whole time he spoke, he had the gun pressed to Lil' Earl's head. Every word made the gun metal press into his flesh, and despite the cold wintery night, Lil' Earl was starting to sweat like a nun in a cucumber field.

Tyrone laid in agony, stuffed in the trunk of the Taurus. His whole face felt like it was bashed in. He could hardly breathe because the blood had caked up and congealed in his nose. Deep down, he knew he was about to die. He felt it the moment he walked out of the county jail and found Lil' Earl outside waiting for him.

"I told you I got you, my nigga," Lil' Earl said with a smile.

He had known Lil' Earl ever since first grade, but something screamed at him *don't get in that car!* Now it was too late to listen.

Tyrone cursed the moment he saw the gold nugget watch. He had to have it. Messiah had told him, "No, we here for the guns," but Ty couldn't resist. He used the butt of a magnum .357 to break the counter and in the process, cut his hand on the glass. The police used his DNA to trace the robbery back to him. Now, he was about to pay for his greed with his life.

"Dig!"

Lil' Earl was bone tired when Messiah, looking down into the crazy edged hole, finally told him, "Aight, that's deep enough."

Lil' Earl crawled out of the hole. By the time he had finished, Knowledge was knocked out, the extinguished blunt stuck to his bottom lip.

Messiah hit his leg. "Man, wake yo' ass up! We gotta get this nigga out the trunk," he said.

"Man, fuck that nigga!" he replied, then went back to sleep. Their Momma had to get Knowledge out of bed with a glass of ice water sometimes. It got him up, but it rarely got him all the way to school.

Messiah gestured to Lil' Earl. "Open the trunk."

Lil' Earl laid the shovel down and took the key from Messiah.

Messiah stood with his gun at ready. Sure enough, as soon as Lil' Earl opened the trunk, Tyrone lunged at him with all the strength that he had left, which wasn't much. He managed to knock Lil' Earl to the ground before Messiah was on him, pistol-whipping him with the gun. The cold cracks of the metal against Tyrone's skull echoed through the trees.

"Please, don't let me die, Lil' Earl!" Tyrone begged, as fresh blood spewed out of his cranium by Messiah's blows.

Lil' Earl's eyes were guilt ridden and his mouth speechless as Messiah dragged Tyrone's limp body to the hole, then dumped him in. Messiah picked up the shovel and handed it to Lil' Earl.

"Now cover him up."

"Cover? But...he's still alive," Lil' Earl pointed out. Tyrone's hand moved slowly up to protect his skull from Messiah's assault twenty seconds too late.

Messiah laughed. "This ain't just punishment; it's a lesson. Give him something to think about."

Lil' Earl shook his head. "Man, cuz, th-that's cold-blooded! At least kill the nigga."

Bloc! Bloc!

Both shots flew by Lil' Earl's ears so close, he felt the heat. "Bury him or join him," Messiah said, with no heat in his voice, just promise. The look in his eyes let Lil' Earl know he was dead ass.

Slowly and with shaking hands, Lil' Earl began to dump dirt on a man he had grown up with. He couldn't even look at him as he did it.

Such is life.

As the dirt slapped into Tyrone's dazed face, and covered his mouth with earth Messiah could see Lil' Earl maybe regretted ever bringing his twin cousins down to North Carolina...

Messiah wondered how long it would be before he'd have to make Lil' Earl feel it for real.

TWO WEEKS EARLIER

"I told you shit was sweet!" Lil' Earl exclaimed as he, Tyrone and the twins pulled up behind an abandoned warehouse.

It was after midnight, and like most small southern towns, Goldsboro had tucked itself in. Few cars were driving around, and the ones that were had the same criminal intent they did.

They drove past the warehouse to the back of the pawnshop, a small brick building about the size of the average convenience store. The face of the store fronted one of the busiest streets in town, but the back was totally obscured by the leftover pallets and an old rusty bread truck. Perfect for a robbery.

"Man, they get every gun on earth in there," Tyrone remarked, with his smooth country accent.

Messiah eyed him in the mirror hard.

"Ay yo, shut the fuck up! I'm tryna think!" he hissed.

He wasn't feeling bringing Tyrone along from jump. It just didn't sit right with Messiah. But Lil' Earl had vouched for Tyrone, and since Lil' Earl was family, he trusted his judgment. Mistake number one.

Knowledge cut through the tension in the car, when he said, "Fuck that bullshit. Let's get this money!"

"Everybody know what we gotta do, right? No mistakes," Messiah warned, as he opened the door.

The rest of the team filed out behind him. Knowledge popped the trunk; inside were four sledgehammers and a coiled rope. Messiah, Power, Tyrone and Lil' Earl grabbed one a piece.

"Let's go!" Messiah said, amped for the action at hand, took the rope and the last hammer. The weight of it in his hand felt good. He felt like the black Thor.

Messiah climbed up onto the rental car and grabbed the roof of the pawnshop. He threw the rope and hammer up, and when he heard them clatter down, he pulled himself up. Standing on the roof made climbing up like doing one pull-up, something Messiah was used to. So was Knowledge and Tyrone. They came up easily. The night was warm and there were no homes nearby, the strip was all businesses. Across the parking lot, Messiah scanned roofs and windows of the nearby businesses. A Wells Fargo office, with windows all dark. A tire and auto repair shop across the street, quiet as a grave. All the way through the trees out to the huge blue mushroom of the Goldsboro water tower by the railway track, everything was silent and sweet.

"H-h-help me up," Lil' Earl strained, holding on by the grip of his fingers. Being little, it made it hard to grab, jump and pull.

Messiah laughed. "Man, pull yo' little chubby ass up."

"I...can't," Lil' Earl wheezed.

Messiah relented and pulled him up. Once he was up, Messiah handed him back his sledgehammer. "Get to work."

They each wrapped their sledgehammer in a towel to muffle the thud of each blow.

The streets may've been empty, but the silence would only make the noise carry further. They also coordinated their blows to strike at once, so there wouldn't be a cacophony of impacts.

It had only been a half hour, but they had banged open a hole large enough to go in through the roof. Messiah looked down and from where he stood, he could see the alarm beeping red, still engaged because it wasn't connected to the roof in any way.

Stupid muhfuckas, he thought to himself. If you had the balls and the brains you could get into anywhere.

Knowledge tied one end of the rope around an iron pipe sticking out of the roof, then knotted the rope in several places so it would be easier to climb down.

"Ay yo Lil' Earl, stay yo' fat ass up here. I ain't tryin' to have to pull you up," Messiah remarked playfully, but he was dead ass. Tyrone laughed.

"Man, fuck y'all," Lil' Earl chuckled.

One by one, Messiah, Knowledge and Tyrone descended the rope, and Lil' Earl was alone with the night.

Once they were down, they were like kids in a candy store. The counter was full of guns; the display on the wall was full of riot pumps, AK47s and rifles.

"God damn! Jackpot!" Knowledge whispered excitedly, giving his brother a loud smack of a handshake.

"Yo, here go the duffels," Tyrone called out, as Lil' Earl stuffed them through the hole. Messiah and Tyrone caught the bags, but Knowledge was distracted. He fell to his knee behind a display case of pistols.

"Yo, police!" Knowledge said, somewhere south of a shout, but well north of a whisper.

They all ducked and looked as the police car drove by without even looking.

"Man, they ain't even look. This time-a night in this one camel town, po-po just want their donuts and coffee. They ain't lookin' for or expectin' missions." Messiah retorted, upset with his brother for scaring him for no reason.

They forced the door into the warehouse, and it was like they'd woken up in a fairy-tale. It was all boxes of guns. Messiah almost cried tears of joy.

"We 'bout to get rich!" Tyrone cackled. "It must be at least a thousand guns!"

There were actually 1200: nines, four-fifths, .40 calibers, revolvers, .38's, .357's, 44's, all shapes and sizes down to pink derringer .22's.

"This for my bitch!" Knowledge laughed, kissing the gun's box like his girl.

Then there were the bullets. There were so many, they filled a duffel bag the size of a body bag. Bag after bag went up the rope; so many that Lil' Earl yelled he was getting tired of pulling them up. In all, they filled 8 full-sized duffel bags.

That's when Tyrone saw the watch.

The rest of the jewelry on display was pawnshop-typical: thin ass herringbones, pinky ice rings and a couple of cheap tennis bracelets. But the watch stood out.

"Yo, I gotta have that watch!" Tyrone's voice was full of lust.

"Yo, we out. Fuck that watch. You can buy a hundred of them cheap ass shits," Messiah replied, taking hold of the rope now that all the bags were on the roof with Lil' Earl...

But Tyrone was too locked in. He used the butt of the gun to break the glass...and sealed his fate.

"Shit fuck and day-um!" Tyrone hissed as the glass from the display case bit into his palm. He held up his hand for them to see the fresh wound, gripping his wrist hard, red blood running over his sleeve. "Fuck, look at that!"

But Messiah wasn't looking at the cut on Tyrone's palm. All he saw was the blood on the glass, the blood in the case and the blood on the floor.

In some ways he wished he'd shot Tyrone in the face right there.

PRESENT DAY

"**W**hat kind of mission?" Power questioned, once he and Kane were driving along Merrick Boulevard, smoking a blunt.

"Guns, my nigga. Guns. They got a cousin in Carolina that turned them onto a sweet ass pawnshop lick. Shit official," Kane explained. Kane passed Power the blunt.

"Ay yo, I got some official shit, too."

"What up?"

"That nigga Duppy."

Kane scrunched up his face. "The rap dude?"

"Yeah," Power replied, exhaling smoke. "His Brooklyn nigga back on the island got links to 'em."

"So what, we gonna stick that nigga? God damn thun, pass that shit."

Power hit the blunt once more, then passed it back. "Nah, yo. We gonna get dude to put us on."

"Man, ain't no money in that rap shit. We see more dough than them," Kane replied dismissively.

"That's 'cause they ain't us. Nigga, our weight up! That Q.B.C. shit we on is murder music for real. All we need is the plug,"

Kane flicked the roach out the window. The night, lights and cars streamed by. He couldn't see it. "Man, that rap shit is a pastime for me. But fuck it, you wanna see this nigga? I'm wit' you."

Power smiled, a dragon's breath of smoke blooming from his mouth and nostrils. He passed the blunt back to Kane. "Yeah, 'cause if he don't put us on, we can always rob his punk ass," Power said. He said it like he was joking, but deep down they both knew he was dead ass.

———

"What you call yourself?"

That was the first thing Duppy asked Power and Kane once they introduced themselves at the club. Power wasted no time getting in touch with the chick Mona that C-Allah had told him about, and she shot straight at Duppy. He'd told them to meet him at club Vertigo in Manhattan, where he was having a showcase for an R&B group he was planning on signing.

Kane and Power looked at each other, then back at Duppy. "Call ourselves?" Kane echoed.

"Yeah, the name of your group."

"Q.B.C.," Power replied without hesitation. It had always been their crew's name, so he just went with it.

Duppy nodded thoughtfully. "Q.B.C. What it stand for?"

"Queens Boro Crew."

Duppy sat back and swigged straight from the magnum of champagne he had in his hand. Power watched him with amusement. Power could tell Duppy was the type of dude they used to chase home from school and rob in the cafeteria; the type of dude the rap game would elevate into shine status and who would act like they were really street dudes.

He looked at Duppy's two bodyguards standing close to him, creating a false sense of security that could easily be shattered.

"You know that street shit don't be sellin', right? You gotta make that smooth shit for the bitches. That's where the money at. Y'all got some smooth shit?" Duppy asked.

"Nah," Power answered simply.

"That's too bad. Don't get me wrong, I like that street shit. I mean, I'm a Harlem nigga for real, but business is business. Hol' up, they about to intro my new group. Watch these bitches go crazy!" Duppy said, his arrogance screeching like fingernails down a blackboard.

They turned towards the stage, Duppy's bodyguards on either side of him scanning the crowd like he was the President of Shit.

"And now, Duppy presents his latest discovery: Exclusive!" the emcee announced, and the crowd reacted with frenzied applause.

"Watch," Duppy said, his eyes lighting up like neon dollar signs in a cartoon.

Three dudes dressed exactly alike in rhinestone-covered jean suits and Timberland boots hit the stage. They all looked like pretty models, and just as Duppy had predicted, the bitches screamed with abandon. Power looked across a sea of gyrating pussy. Hands in the air, asses working like dryers in the laundromat. Power liked the look of the crowd, but was not impressed by the lame ass niggas on the stage.

"Yo, this nigga a clown, thun," Kane agreed with Power's expression of disgust, as he shifted his weight from foot to foot like he was ready to see it.

"No doubt, but he our connect to that industry dough, my nigga. Check it. I got an idea," Power replied slyly, then began to approach the stage.

Kane fell in behind him. They maneuvered through the crowd, then disappeared through a side door, and saw a short set of five steps leading up to the stage. Kane looked at Power. "Fuck you thinkin' about doing, thun?"

"I'm on my KRS-One shit tonight," Power cracked, and they both laughed.

They grasped hands and gangsta hugged, then hopped up the steps to the stage. Exclusive was still doing its dance routine, sparkling like some Vegas act. The group was putting it to the crowd as if they were already worth a million dollars and were going to be drowning in the pussy sea tonight. They had no idea Power and Kane were behind them and walking forward.

Duppy looked on. When he saw Power and Kane, his whole face scrunched up. "What the fuck is these niggas doin'?!" he barked, jumping to his feet.

"What you want to do, boss?" the head bodyguard Jaylan asked, ready to rush the stage. Before Duppy could respond, Power had snatched the mic from the lead singer and mushed him over, sending him toppling into the crowd, just as Kane pushed the alto and knocked dude out cold. The third dude dropped the mic and ran. The crowd went from crazy to bananas, screaming so loud for that real shit, that bitches was getting nosebleeds.

"QB in the house!" Power bellowed.

"Buck! Buck! Buck!" Kane barked, stepping over the sprawled body of the sleeping singer.

"Yo DJ, fuck that corny smooth shit! Gimme that real shit!" Power demanded.

The DJ in the booth looked at Duppy. He was fuming, but he could see the energy in the room was on a thousand. He reluctantly nodded. The DJ cut in the boom bap with a thunderous scratch, then the beat for Wu-Tang's "Protect Your Neck" exploded like a terrorist bomb in the club.

Kane set it off, spitting about growing up in Queens Boro and the way that makes you into steel, forged in the city's fire.

Then Power took over. Doubling down on Kane's line. Murder and terror just a way of life. You fight back or die.

The crowd lapped it up like thirsty bitches on a dry day. The DJ clicked hard with Power and Kane's attitude, and gave them the sickest beds on which to lay their lyrics. The club rocked, the bass boomed. Even Duppy's head bodyguard was nodding along like this crazy shit was getting inside his head.

Duppy finished the last dregs of champagne from the bottle and then popped the cork on another from the ice bucket. One more look at the madness in the room and his eyes were counting gold bars.

Q.B.C. were definitely moneymakers.

TRACK 2

"And that's how it started."

"I'm more concerned with how it ends."

"Make up your mind. You said start from the beginning," he reminded Detective Spagoli with a swarthy smirk. Spagoli sat back in his chair.

"Q.B.C. is responsible for several murders and the distribution of tons of cocaine up and down the east coast, correct?" Spagoli questioned.

"Indeed," he confirmed.

"So what in the hell makes you think I give a fuck about when they started rapping?" Spagoli hissed like a boiled kettle. Leaning on the table, he looked him deep in the eyes.

He took his last cigarette and crumbled up the pack. He held up the pack and looked at O'Brien.

"I'm out of cigarettes. Maybe you can get me a fresh pack? Or maybe she can go," he remarked, then looked at the two-way mirror. "Baby, can you handle that for me?"

"You're cute. I bet the booty bandits in Leavenworth will feel the same way," O'Brien sniped.

"Well, that's why I'm here, correct? So I don't have to go to Leavenworth, right?"

"As long as you tell us what we want to know," Spagoli reminded him.

"Then it's time we talk about her…"

———

"Guitar Jimmy, stick wit' us 'cause you 'bout to hear that murder shit," Power bragged as he and Kane walked out of the engineering room and headed for the booth.

Once inside, Kane pulled out the bottle of Henny he had inside his bubble goose.

Jimmy gave them a disapproving look.

"Chill, Guitar Jimmy. This the magic potion right here! Start the track," Power told him.

"Yo, I'm goin' in there wit' them!" Messiah announced, once he saw Kane turn up the Henny bottle.

The whole clique followed suit and Jimmy breathed a sigh of relief.

While in the booth, the buzz sounded like the block.

The beat kicked in, Power swigged from the bottle, gripping it by the neck like a broad he just bagged, bobbed to the beat and began:

As Power and Kane went back and forth over the track, Jimmy could only bop his head. He had never heard a sound so street get so melodic, almost hypnotic, at the same time. Just when Jimmy thought he had heard one of the realest rap records ever, Kane blurted out, "Yo, yo, turn that shit off! Turn it off!"

Power looked at Kane himself. "What up, thun?"

Kane shook his head. "Yo, who did that track?"

Jimmy answered, "DJ Diamond. Hottest producer on Duppy's team."

"Man, that shit is wack as fuck!" Kane blasted. The whole time, only Power and Kane could hear the track, so Messiah stepped forward and said, "Let me hear it."

He took the headphones from Kane and Jimmy played the track. After only a few bars, Messiah took off the headphones and announced, "Yo, that shit is ass!"

Jimmy looked pissed as fuck. "You think you can do better?" Jimmy challenged Kane.

Kane hit the Henny and glared at Jimmy. "You God damn right."

"Come show me."

Kane didn't hesitate to do just that. Power knew Kane had never made a beat in his life, so he wondered what made Kane so confident that he could. It didn't take long for him to find out.

"Yo, the bass line is pussy. It needs to be like the pulse of a killer at midnight," Kane said.

"At midnight?" Jimmy echoed. "I have an idea what you're talking about."

"Like this," Kane replied, then verbalized what he meant.

Jimmy used the keyboard to emulate it.

"Darker," Kane said eyes closed. Feeling it deep.

Jimmy, understanding Kane's visual better, dropped the key an octave. Kane smiled his sinister grin. "Yeaaaah," he nodded.

Power watched as Jimmy and Kane went into a musical zone that had them both focused. Every suggestion Kane visualized, Jimmy was able to bring out. When they put it all together, it was a certified hood banger. "God damn, you did your thing, God," Power exclaimed, giving Kane dap.

Kane smiled cockily. "Told y'all I could do better."

Jimmy face was impressed. He hadn't expected this, and Power could see it in his eyes.

"Man, you're a fuckin' genius!" Jimmy said with feeling. He picked up the phone on the mixing desk and dialed a number, smiling and shaking his head at the same time.

"Yo, you need to get down here ASAP," Jimmy said, then hung up.

"Who you just call?" Power questioned.

Jimmy looked at him. "Duppy."

Duppy hung up the phone and looked at the woman sitting in front of his desk. He had seen plenty of beautiful women before, exotic beauties of every ethnicity, but he had never seen one so mesmerizing. Her mother had definitely named her right...

Egypt.

She had the natural cat-eyed look that most women need eyeliner for. Her skin tone was the color of an Arabian sunset. She was slim, but statuesque and shapely. She could've been Greek, Latin, Italian or a mixture of it all.

But she was a black woman through and through, and she had the voice to prove it. Her voice was just as beautiful as she was. It was as soulful as Alicia's and as strong as Whitney's — she was the truth and Duppy knew it.

"So you want to be a star, huh?" he asked.

Egypt smirked, crossed her legs and the sun through the window lit up her hair like a spotlight. "I'm already a star, I just want the world to know it."

Duppy chuckled. "Confidence. I like that in a woman."

"Thank you. I come from a long line of confident women. My great grandmother punched Al Capone in the face."

"Get the fuck outta here," Duppy said, covering his incredulity with a snicker. This woman was a fine thing, but he didn't want to give too much away about how much he wanted her as an act in his growing stable. Business first. Pleasure later.

"True story. She worked at the Cotton Club in Harlem, you know, back in the 20's. She was a dancer and a singer. She could've been a headliner, but she was darker than a paper bag," Egypt explained.

"Darker than a paper bag?" Duppy hated showing there was shit he didn't know.

"It was a Cotton Club thing. If you were darker than a paper bag, you couldn't perform. My grandmother was an exception, but they still wouldn't let her headline. Anyway, Al Capone wanted her to come back to Chicago with him and work in his club. 'To headline?' she'd asked. He said, 'No, but you'd make a good whore.' So she punched him in his face," Egypt shrugged.

Duppy laughed. "Word? Your grandma was ill. What did Capone do?"

"He bought her a drink, and when she died, he sent a hundred roses. You want to know what the card said?"

"What?"

"You'll headline in heaven."

Duppy nodded. "Classy move."

"Classy lady."

"I see the apple doesn't fall too far from the tree," Duppy complimented.

Egypt smiled. Duppy had to forcibly lift his eyes from the stretch of blue jean material across her inner thigh. She was beguiling him with looks and personality, and Duppy was drifting. It would be easy to get lost in the notion of this woman. Very easy indeed.

"So does that mean I get to headline your label?"

They looked at each other across the desk. Duppy's wolf-eyed look said everything his words didn't — *I've got a whole lot more in mind for you.*

Egypt's face said, reading him perfectly — *whatever it takes.*

"I need to run down to the studio. You wanna ride with me?" Duppy inquired, getting up from behind the desk, coming around and offering his hand like a Knight to a Queen.

"I'd love to," she said, taking it.

———

"Aight, let's take it from the top," Kane said into the mic as he adjusted his headphones. The booth was full of smoke and magic.

He passed the blunt to Power, exhaling hard. The screw turned to the max inside him. This was living.

There was smoke everywhere by this time, because Jimmy was totally caught up in the vibe. All rules were out the window. It was hot and dark in the studio. Just a lamp over the mixing desk, the glow from the LEDs hitting Jimmy's face and turning it into a Halloween mask. In the booth, all lights but a tiny spot were off. The studio was as dark as the beat, and the beat was lower than Hell.

The beat cracked open and filled the room like poison gas. Everyone jerked and bopped uncontrollably. This wasn't music, this was voodoo that the street melted down and poured into your ears.

Kane ripped through his verse while Power chugged Henny, bobbing his head like his neck was broken. He was just about to kick his verse, when light from the studio door spread across the room as it was opened. Power was about to throw down at whoever had spoiled the atmosphere, breaking the mood, until he saw who had come in. It wasn't only Duppy who had invaded — if it had, Power would have torn him a new asshole — but it was who was with him that drained the anger from his lips.

Power passed the Henny to Kane, and just stared through the glass. The woman with Duppy was like something from a fever dream. If you put all the best aspects of the opposite sex into one body, and then made her walk like she owns the whole damn joint, then she would look like this.

Her eyes caught Power's across the studio and through the glass. This was the kind of woman who knew exactly the effect she had on men. And she was working it like there were no more Saturday nights left in the universe.

Power stepped out of the booth and gave Duppy a base-level head nod out of respect. Then he took the woman's hand.

And that's when time stopped.

The night was thick, layered around the dirty streets.

Her way into the alley was lit from above, only by the yellow windows of the tenements around her. Her every step was firm but cautious. She knew her life depended on each eye movement and swing of her gaze.

A lid from a trashcan clattered to the ground. She spun her head, just in time to see a scrawny cat slinking into the shadows with its fish-head prize. Sirens wailed in the distance and the city seemed to breathe darkness along the lonely streets.

A white man with a knife jumped out from an alley. His eyes were wild, his face set. The knife glinting as he scythed it down through the cold air.

Buck! Buck!

She put two in his face, and the knifeman spun away, crashing into the cat's trashcans.

She kept it moving. This was the worst part of town for a woman to be out in at night. The walls of the alley seemed to move in. She went forward on hurrying feet, hearing the click of her heels. At the junction she paused, not sure which way to go and then she heard a squeal of brakes and the rumble of a powerful engine. The car skidded up, the driver hanging out the window with a MAC-11.

Buck! Buck! Buck!

Her first shot cracked his skull, the last two exploded his face all over the dashboard. The body fell back, spurting blood.

Should she take the car or keep running?

She ran, aware that the street, slick with rain, could hold anything ahead. Or anyone. Her nerves sang, her heart beat.

A white light to the left. The dazzle of the pistol flashlight?

Buck!

Egypt's heart sank. She'd just put a .45 caliber bullet into a six-year-old's forehead.

"Fuck!" Egypt yelled as she snatched the virtual-reality headset off.

No longer alone in the dark virtual street. She was in the media room of the Chicago Police Department's 14th District, Shakespeare station. The room was bright from strip lights and from the windows looking out on North California Avenue. Cars whooshed by; just another day in the city.

For Egypt it was anything but.

Egypt's eyes took a second or two to adjust, and she was feeling the first splinter of a headache coming on from her thirty minutes in the VR training simulator.

"Run it again! Give me one more chance," Egypt requested, looking at Sergeant Malone.

Malone sighed. He was a twenty-year veteran of the force, built like a linebacker. He looked like Ray Lewis with less hair and a badge. A good cop, but his limp from a liquor store bust that went south fifteen years ago would have made him a liability behind the scrimmage. He had seen it all and liked telling Egypt that he had, but she always assumed he thought she wasn't cut out to be a police officer.

"Let's take five, okay?" he suggested.

Reluctantly, Egypt answered, "Okay."

They went to his office, along the long-carpeted halls. His office looked out over the parking lot, and she got the impression he'd rather it overlooked the trees running the length of the avenue. His office was full of potted plants to compensate for the lack of greenery in the view. It was like walking into a greenhouse.

Egypt took a seat while Malone poured them both a cup of coffee. He sat them on the desk, then pulled out a small bottle of brandy from his desk drawer. He held it up, raising his eyebrows in a questioning expression.

"Just a splash," Egypt said. It might help the headache.

"A splash is all you were getting anyway," Malone smiled. "This shit's expensive."

Malone handed her a cup, sat on the edge of his desk and sipped his brew.

"Good stuff," he commented.

"You should be a bartender," Egypt cracked.

Malone wasn't in the mood for joking. He cut straight to the chase. "Moore, can I be straight with you?"

"Definitely."

"You're too dam pretty and too trigger happy to be a cop. What the hell are you doing here?" he asked. Egypt knew she was a conundrum no one had yet solved in the Chicago Police Department.

"I want to make a difference," Egypt replied without hesitation. She knew it sounded lame, but it was the best she got.

"Join the Red Cross." Her falling face made Malone soften some. "Look, Moore, I don't know what's driving you, I –," he began to say.

Egypt sighed, holding up her hand. If she was to escape the lame ass reply of a typical Beauty Pageant air-head she'd just given, she might as well go the whole nine.

"My great grandmother."

"Huh?"

"You said you didn't know what was driving me. Well, it's my great grandmother. She... she was a God-fearing woman. Never drank, never cursed, and never lied. All she did was go to church, until one night coming home from worship, she was gunned down in a drive-by. Senseless, random violence and she was the victim."

The headache was replaced by the prickle of tears in the corner of her eyes. She wiped them with the heel of her hand. "It's for her. If I can stop that happening to someone else, just one person, then it would be worthwhile."

"I get it, but grief isn't the reason to own a uniform, and neither is revenge. You're wild, Moore. Too wild. Giving you a badge is like throwing gasoline on a fire. How do I trust you on the street, when you screw up so easily in the simulator?" Malone said. He wasn't being an asshole for the sake of it, she could see in his eyes he believed what he was saying.

Egypt was furious, but she kept her composure. "Sarge, with

all due respect, I think that's bullshit. I graduated at the top of my class in the academy, my psych report gives no indication of this wildness you claim..."

Malone cut her off abruptly.

"Fuck the academy! I know a wild card when I see one, and I'm looking at one right now!" he bellowed. He took a breath and a slug of coffee. Egypt wondered how far he'd got counting to ten in his head before he spoke again. He sighed. "Look, I could easily stick you behind a desk and bury you, but you'd probably transfer to another precinct and get assigned a beat anyway. My point is, I've seen your kind before."

"I'm going to be a cop, Sarge," Egypt replied firmly. He shook his head, went around the desk and sat down. "Suppose there was a middle ground."

"I'm listening."

"How do you feel about undercover work?"

This, she wasn't expecting. This felt like a reprieve, a chance to prove herself to Malone and all the Chicago PD cops who thought she was all heat and no fire. "Whatever it takes," she said finally.

Malone leaned forward. "What do you know about the music business?

"Ay yo, step up! That was your cue," Kane said to Power, bringing him back to reality partially.

Power glanced at Kane, but he was still conscious of the beauty sitting in the corner of his eye. Damn, even this woman sat like a queen. If she'd walked in with a leopard on a leash instead of Duppy, Power would not have been at all surprised. Power jumped tracks in his head and came back to the now.

"Yeah yeah, my bad. Go back and I'm on it."

The beat broke in.

On her part, Egypt was just as struck by Power, but she was much subtler about it. She was aware that when she was looking anywhere other than at Power in the booth, that Power's eyes were hot on her. Normally, she'd feel sorry for the guys looking at her who were so far out of her league, but Power was anything but. It wasn't just the way he looked, although he made pleasant tingles in all the right place. It was the way he moved—liquid yet sharp, all attitude, but with a smile that could kill at a hundred yards. Even the way he walked, all lopsided shoulders and gangsta sway, made her heart skip a little.

Lust at first sight.

Duppy didn't even notice her sudden infatuation with the green-eyed bandit in fatigues, rapping the sound that would soon rule the streets. Only when Power rhymed did he lock eyes on her, and she in return looked right on back.

His style sent chills through her. She licked her lips in anticipation of what the future might bring. Shifting positions in her seat wasn't helping cool the fire any. Power was *burning* her.

When Kane and Power entered the engineering room, Duppy gave them a pound and a gangsta hug. "Yo I can't even front, that was the illest shit I heard in my life! Yo Jim, how come I never heard that beat before? When did Diamond do that?"

"He didn't," Jimmy replied. "Kane here did."

Duppy looked at Kane wide-eyed. "That's you?"

"You already know," Kane's arrogance made Egypt smile behind Duppy's back. Kane wasn't as much to Egypt's taste as Power, but there was a dark intensity to him that she really appreciated.

"We definitely need to talk," Duppy responded. He was about to say more, when he saw that Power was all but ignoring him, and only had eyes for Egypt. Duppy moved into both of their eye lines, and trying to catch the situation early said, "Oh my bad, fam. I didn't introduce y'all. This beautiful woman is about to be the first lady of Notorious Records. That is, if she can handle the pressure and prove her position. Egypt, this is Power and Kane, also known as Q.B.C."

Egypt looked at Power. "What does Q.B.C. stand for?" she questioned.

"Real niggas everywhere," he replied.

She was about to get confused, then her expression showed she understood. "I mean the letters."

"Queens Boro Crew. So what you do? Rap?" Power probed.

Egypt smirked mischievously. "You want to *see* what I do?"

"Seein' is believin', right?"

Oh I wanna show you, her face said as she sashayed through the studio, and into the booth.

Egypt put on the headphones. The room smelled of blunt, Power and Kane. There was electricity in that smell. It was all potential. She looked through the glass as Kane and Power sat down, swapping the blunt. Power never took his eyes off her.

"Give me something clubby," Egypt requested.

It took Jimmy a minute to find an appropriate track, but when he did, Egypt's nod told him he found the right one. She dug into the track with a joint she knew they wouldn't be up on, an old Chicago house classic.

From the moment she opened her mouth, she saw that first note grabbed every man in the room and wouldn't let go. They swayed like a nest of cobras around a mongoose.

There was no denying her talent.

Power got up, and spoke in Duppy's ear. Egypt could read his lips easily. He was saying, "I want to do a joint with her," but all the while never taking his eyes off her.

Egypt could read Duppy's face just as easily. He was hearing the words, but knew Power wanted to do a lot more...

"Yo, the world's about to feel us, thun! They all gonna be tryin' to speak the thun language. What the drilly wit' that tho!" Ty Five$

laughed as he washed his tongue down with hundred dollar Moët.

"Yo thun, that bitch had you fucked up," Kane teased with a knowing laugh, as he passed the blunt to Power.

He, Power, Messiah, Ty Five$ and Lil' Earl were on top of Kane's building in QB, getting their drink on and smoke on. The evening was falling towards night. Across the river, the Boro was lighting up and the city beyond was shadowing against the orange sky. The sun looked like it was rolling down the cheese cut edge of the old Citicorp Center, and the air around them was cool and comfortable. The whole city was making them feel like they were on top of the world, so they went to the top of the world to celebrate.

"Man, you buggin' the fuck out, God. That bitch was checkin' *me* out," Power retorted cockily, as he took the blunt.

"Bullshit! I seen you, yo. I just ain't say nothin'. She is a bad bitch though, yo. I ain't gonna front," Kane admitted, giving Power dap.

Power hit the blunt.

"Yo, I gotta hit that," he rolled. "Word."

"Fuckin' the boss' bitch? If we lose our deal over that ho, I'ma fuck you up!" Kane laughed.

"Fuck Duppy, that nigga soft. Besides, we the best thing that ever happened to him. Without us, he'd still be scrapin' Exclusive off that stage," bragged Power.

"Word," Kane cackled, giving Power a heartfelt dap.

Lil' Earl looked like the only one who wasn't feelin' it tonight. He stood in the corner, leaning against the overhang of the building's masonry, looking out over Queens Boro Park. He wasn't smoking, he wasn't drinking. Messiah peeled away from the others and went over.

"Ay yo Earl, the fuck wrong wit' you?" he asked, eyeing his cousin skeptically. Lil' Earl was shaking. Ever since witnessing and being made to participate in Tyrone's murder, he had been progressively getting worse. He'd told Messiah last night that at the beginning, he heard Tyrone calling him, then he thought he had begun to see shadows in the dark. "It got to the point where I couldn't sleep with the lights off, but that made it even worse..." he said. *Because he started seeing Tyrone,* Messiah had thought. *Fuckin' pussy.*

Lil' Earl had described that he'd see Tyrone's body decaying and all he could smell in the dream was the rotting stench of his flesh. "I-I-I'm sorry, Ty. I swear I didn't mean to do it," Lil' Earl told Messiah he said in the dream. "Tyrone never opens his mouth, but I can hear his words, *Tell the truth.... Tell the truth.... Set me free.... Tell the truth.* Those words haunt me, cuz...They were in my mind like a song stuck in the brain."

Messiah had spanked Lil' Earl's face hard and told him to put that shit behind him. He didn't want to hear none of that stuff no more, yet here was Lil' Earl again taking the shine off the whole situation.

Messiah didn't have to say anything; Lil' Earl knew just by looking at him how angry he was. "Man, I can't take this anymore."

"We dealt wit' this nigga. You some noid ass crazy," Messiah hissed, so the others couldn't hear over the laughter and smoking. He didn't want Lil' Earl killing the buzz.

Messiah kept an eye on Lil' Earl since the murder, but hadn't realized how fucked up his cousin was until last night. Messiah was glad he had brought Lil' Earl back to New York with him.

Lil' Earl looked up at him, his expression on the verge of tears, his posture was bent and broken. "Tyrone...he...he still speakin' to me," Lil' Earl admitted.

"No he isn't, cuz. That's just shit in your head. Jus' the chocolate you been smokin'." Messiah said, staying firm.

The whole time they were talking, the rest of the crew were oblivious to their conversation.

Lil' Earl shook his head.

Messiah gazed down at his little cousin, his mother's sister's son; his little man that peed the bed whenever he stayed with him. He loved him, but he loved himself and Knowledge more. There was no question Lil' Earl would tell. The only question was when.

He reached his hand down to help Lil' Earl up.

"Don't worry about it, cuz. We'll take care of it," Messiah assured him.

Looking into his eyes, Lil' Earl saw it, but at that point, he was too gone to care. "O-okay," Lil' Earl replied, as he reached up and took his cousin's hand. Messiah pulled him to his feet and then without missing a beat, he shoved Lil' Earl's head and sent him toppling over the side of the roof.

Power caught the moment out of the corner of his eye. "What the fuck?!"

In that last instant before he fell, Messiah and Lil' Earl's eyes met.

On Lil' Earl's face was an expression of relief. He knew what his cousin was going to do, but deep down he thanked him because he knew he didn't have the heart to do it himself. His arms flailed around as he felt the pull of gravity, making his heart pound — but then he looked down and saw Tyrone smiling up at him, no longer rotting, but whole and glowing.

Then his arms went from flailing to embracing as his body sped downward, faster and faster, until he hit the pavement. The crash taking out all the lights on the building, the Bridge, and the city from his head. Last of all, the light in Lil' Earl's eyes went out.

Messiah looked over the edge at the broken bird of his cousin, spread on the ground, arms and legs doing impossible things. In seconds, there was screaming and running footsteps. A woman fell to her knees by the body, her hands useless. There was nothing she could do. She looked up at Messiah.

Messiah shook his head moved back from the edge to face his crew.

All conversation on the roof had stopped. They all knew what happened, but none of them knew why. Messiah looked at them — at their questioning eyes and simply said, "He fell."

And that became what happened.

THREE YEARS LATER

"He fell?" O'Brien echoed with a disbelieving smirk on his face. It was the smirk you'd paint on if you'd just been told a stupid joke or read a lame meme on Facebook. It wasn't the face you made when you heard someone had become pizza on a project pavement. Or, looking at Spagoli and O'Brien, perhaps it was.

"He fell," he repeated with a shrug, then lit a cigarette.

"Bullshit," O'Brien spat. "You killed your own cousin because he knew about the murder in Goldsboro. Admit it!" The detective banged the table to hammer home his point, but it didn't startle him. All O'Brien got out of him was a shrug. "Yo, if you believed that, I'd be under arrest. Like I said earlier, my fuckin' ribs is killin' me. I need a fuckin' doctor!"

"You think you're hot shit, don't you?! Running all over the world with that nigger rap shit. Well, let me tell you, I'm not fooled! You're not a rap group, you're a fuckin' drug-dealing hit squad!" Spagoli bellowed in his face as he pulled out a stack of glossies, slapping each photo on the table one by one. "Cincinnati! Houston! Miami! Hawaii!"

Each picture showed a different dead body, headless or

grotesquely disfigured. Spagoli and O'Brien had thrown out the nice and nasty cop interrogation handbook. This was all nasty. They paced the room in front of him, like tigers in a crammed cage at the zoo.

"You better hope, no, you better *pray* that none of these murders can be traced back to those stolen guns, Spagoli threatened, "because if they are, I'm going to squeeze you until you squeal like a bitch."

He just laughed at Spagoli's see-through tactics. "The last time you heard a bitch scream was when she caught you trying on her underwear."

Spagoli seethed. "You're just a piece of shit. We're gonna take you down so hard we'll be able to roll you up, put you in a tube and post you to Riker's Island."

PRESENT DAY

The city streets of Manhattan rolled by as smooth as silk on a virgin's thigh. Duppy and Egypt rode in the back of his stretch Maybach, sipping champagne. He glanced over at her crossed legs, a Louboutin red bottom dangling from one sexy toe. She looked as fresh as a new plucked rose, and he wanted to get tangled up in her thorns.

"Damn, you a bad bitch," Duppy said, whistling and shaking his head.

Egypt giggled, and made a face like the compliment hit the correct target. "I'm glad you were smiling when you said it."

"Nah ma, believe me – I mean it. Trust. The world is going to love you," Duppy replied, eyeing her thighs, like they were answering instead of Egypt's mouth.

Egypt knew that with just one little push, she could have Duppy falling. "I'm not wearing any panties," she informed him nonchalantly.

She saw the bulge in Duppy's pants thicken and he moved to a more comfortable position. "Really?"

"I never wear panties..."

Hook.

Line.

Egypt took a sip of champagne.

And now the sinker, "...you want to see?"

Duppy eyed the back of the driver's head. "Now?"

Egypt flashed her eyes. *And why not?*

"Come on, Duppy. You mean to tell me you've never had sex in a Maybach? I find that hard to believe."

"Nah, I mean, yeah," he lied, clearing his throat. "I just – I don't mix business with pleasure."

Truth be told, Duppy had never been good with women.

Growing up in Harlem, females saw him as average and seldom paid him much attention. Now that he had money, he could buy good looks. His s-curl, veneered teeth and permanent contacts gave him an air of pretty boy swag, but deep down, he was intimidated by beautiful women.

This bitch was on the launch pad offering him a damn moon shot, and he still felt that hesitation that came with a lack of confidence. All the possibilities of being made to look foolish ran through his brain like a crazy cartoon.

He looked again at the driver. Jaylan was tight, he wouldn't say anything to anyone if things didn't work out.

Duppy glanced at the Hublot on his wrist. They had time. He had time. And Egypt's countdown was already on go for the main engine start.

Egypt sensed Duppy's apprehension, so she went in for the kill. "First time for everything, huh?" she replied smoothly, hiking up her skirt and straddling his lap. Duppy's eyes bulged like the dick in his pants, and she could see he was struggling to keep his cool. She took his hand, guided it between her legs so that he could feel the wetness there. She knew her pussy was so wet, it would make a stain on his crotch.

"Mmm," she purred, feeling his dick instantly rock up. "I think you like me."

Egypt began kissing his neck and unbuttoning his pants. "Y-you don't mind Jaylan?"

"I like when people watch," she whispered.

She slid his rock hardness inside her slippery wet pussy and cocked one leg up on the seat, giving him a full view of himself pumping in and out of her gripping tightness.

"Fuck, your dick feels so good," she rubbed at her clit with her own fingers, bringing her on because Duppy on his own wouldn't have got her close. Thinking about Power taking her from behind, yanking at her hair made Egypt cream around Duppy's dick. Making sure her moans sounded as sweet as her singing voice.

Egypt knew exactly what she was doing to Duppy. She wasn't just fucking him, she was opening up his head and climbing inside.

Duppy moved like he had never felt a pussy so warm and wet in his life. Every pump had his heart racing, the pulse in his neck was raging. He grabbed her by the hips, scrunched down in the seat and began bouncing her on his dick.

"Yeah baby, take control of this pussy," she moaned, bracing her hands on the ceiling.

After just a few pumps, Duppy couldn't control himself, and he came before two minutes did. "Ay yo, God damn...that shit never happened before!" he stammered, embarrassed by his short performance.

Egypt leaned down and kissed him passionately. "It's not your fault, baby," she soothed his bruised ego. "I came real good already."

She reached underneath his nuts and applied pressure to a spot at the base of his scrotum, while using her pussy muscles to massage his dick head. Before he knew it, he was hard as stone again. He had never cum so quick then gotten erect again so fast. His mind was doubly blown.

"Damn, you a beast," Duppy grunted, watching her grinding motion as he spread her ass cheeks to get deeper.

Egypt licked her lips and replied, "Tell me how this pussy feels."

She began gyrating her hips and squeezing the shaft of his dick at the same time. It felt like her pussy was sucking his dick. His toes curled in his Gators.

"Uh, sir," Jaylan reluctantly interjected, "We've arrived at our destination."

Egypt wondered if Jaylan's dick was hard too because all she could see in the rearview was his eyes staring back through the car as she jumped up and down on Duppy's dick.

"G-g-go around the block," Duppy stuttered.

Egypt smiled, looking at Duppy's face showing an intensity like he had taken an Ecstasy pill. "You like that, baby? Tell me you like it," Egypt moaned her lies.

"I love it," Duppy huffed, their skins smacking together like slapped faces.

Egypt felt the sensation rumble through him. Like she was dragging the orgasm outta him with a chain-fall, making him arch his back and cum for the second time inside of five minutes. His breathing was hoarse, eyes blurred. Duppy threw his head back and it thudded against the window. "Fuck," he gasped.

Egypt smiled down on him, caressing his cheek and thinking to herself, *Mission accomplished.*

She climbed off, digging his cum from her pussy and then sucking her fingers clean, never once breaking eye contact with him, or stopping thinking about Power. Duppy's eyes were wider than the Grand Canyon.

Egypt looked out through the window, straightening her skirt and then running her fingers through her hair, making the change from *just fucked* to *fuck me later* with practiced strokes of a woman used to balling in unusual environments. "We're here," she giggled, her words making a cute double entendre.

Duppy looked up and saw that they were parked outside of the small Italian bistro, which was indeed the destination.

"I, um..." he cleared his throat, trying to get himself together. "Let's go inside."

They were met at the door by two bodyguards built like vending machines, who wasted no time shaking Duppy down. One turned to Egypt, took one look at her dress and smirked. Egypt smiled back and quipped, "What you see is what you get."

He motioned her to go on in with a nod of his head. They took their time with Duppy making sure he knew the score, then eventually let him follow Egypt in.

The bistro was empty except for the bodyguards and the smell of Panini sandwiches. The man they had come to see sat at a back table, sipping espresso and smoking a cigarette.

This had only been the second time that Duppy had been in his presence, and he was still struck by his looks. Duppy knew he had real difficulty admitting to himself that another man struck him as pretty, he wasn't gay by a long shot, but this pencil-mustached, wide-faced dude made Prince look like a hunch-backed gorilla. There was a column of projected cool around him that moved as he stood to greet them. His suit was so sharp you could shave your face on it, and he had a smile that could throw a spotlight up the Empire State.

His name was Xavier and he was Colombian, or as Duppy knew him, *The* Colombian. It was rumored that he was the richest man in Colombia. He had diplomatic immunity, so American laws were something he treated like youthful curfews. They were bound to be broken.

Xavier opened his arms wide as Duppy and Egypt approached.

He shook Duppy's hand, then looked at Egypt, struck equally by her presence as much as by her looks.

"Duppy, you flatter me. Who is this?" he said, soaking in everything about Egypt.

Egypt offered her hand. "His first lady," she playfully replied with a wink. Xavier chuckled.

"The first lady to make Mi Corazon skip a beat, eh?" he replied, and kissed her hand. "Welcome."

"Thank you."

"Please, sit," Xavier offered and they complied.

"So, have you thought about our last conversation?" Xavier asked, getting straight to the point.

Duppy glanced across the table. "You're asking a lot."

"Yes, but I'm giving much more. I'm willing to..." Xavier paused for a moment, looked at Egypt and asked, "Forgive me for asking this but...are you a police officer?"

FIVE YEARS LATER

"Yesss," Egypt purred, as she luxuriated in the feeling of Vanya's tongue all over her clit. "Yes I ammmmmmm..."

Vanya smiled up at her, Egypt's juices an invisible moustache on the peach fuzz over her upper lip. Her horizon was an expanse of belly, breasts and open mouth all the way to Egypt's impossibly beautiful eyes.

"I know, so am I," Vanya replied, but Egypt was too gone to care. Her palm slapped back onto the wall as another wave hit.

Vanya slid her hands under Egypt's voluptuous ass and feasted on her pussy like a condemned prisoner devouring a last meal on death row. Egypt arched her back and cocked her legs back even further.

"Yes...there!" her moans rising and her pussy melting all over Vanya's tongue.

Egypt was hit by another spine cracking rush, then immediately another. As her body jerked, her legs shook continually on the unending wave.

"Damn," Egypt gasped as the convulsions subsided. "If you're trying to turn a bitch out, you're too late."

Vanya giggled. "No, mon cheri, not turn you out – turn you *on*," Vanya replied, snuggling up next to Egypt and kissing her ear, then adding, "Now tell me – what is this investigation about?"

TWO WEEKS EARLIER

"What do I know about the music business?" Egypt echoed.

"Well, at least I know there's nothing wrong with your hearing," Malone was famous for his sarcasm, but Egypt didn't bite. This was an opportunity not to pass. "Whatever I don't know, I'll learn. I catch on quick."

"That's not what I asked you."

"Nothing. I don't know anything about the music business," Egypt admitted.

Malone nodded. "Good," he said, then got up and went around his desk. He picked up a manila envelope and put it in front of Egypt. She picked it up and took out the pictures inside.

"That's James Manifred, aka Baby J."

"I know his face, Sarge. He owns a record label here in Chicago. He's a legend," Egypt explained. So she knew more than she said she knew. Perhaps Malone wouldn't think she was such a fuck-up after all. She hid the smile of self-satisfaction with the edge of her hand.

"Exactly. Do you recognize the girl?"

Egypt looked at the second photo. It was of a female about her complexion, but looked like a turbo charged version of Alicia

Keys. She was breathtakingly gorgeous, so much so that Egypt remarked, "My God, she's beautiful."

Malone nodded. "Didn't know you went that way."

"I don't," Egypt answered firmly, unaware of her future self. She looked at Malone. His eyes showing, he understood he'd overstepped a professional line. Egypt felt she was getting the upper hand at last.

"It's said that she is the American liaison for The Colombian," Malone explained.

"The Colombian?"

"Now that Escobar is dead, there's only one: Xavier Montenegro. We believe he is investing in rap labels across the country to launder his drug money and tap into the power structure of every major city."

"Sounds like a plan," Egypt said, looking closely at a grainy long-range telephoto lens shot of a too pretty man on the lower deck of a super yacht. All she could make out was that he was wearing sunglasses above an open shirt and was holding a fluted glass up to his mouth.

"Yeah well, we've got a better one to stop him. You want to be a cop, here's how you pay your dues."

Egypt nodded. "What do you want me to do?"

PRESENT DAY

E gypt replied without hesitation: "As a matter of fact I am, and you're under arrest for being so damn fine."

Xavier threw his head back with laughter. "Flattery will get you everywhere! I'll take that as a *no*," he said to her, then turned to Duppy. "I am offering free money to invest in whatever you so choose, as well as a nationwide network. You will never get your hands dirty."

Duppy had the sweat on his top lip that told anyone who was looking that he knew he was in over his head, but his eyes were a Vegas jackpot and he couldn't help himself but nod. Egypt knew that Duppy had gotten involved with Baby J without knowing who really backed him, but she could see now that Duppy couldn't say no. Whatever the risk. Nobody said no to The Colombian.

"Let me think about it," Duppy replied, trying to disguise the eagerness that was showing like a big neon sign above his head.

Egypt could see that Xavier was smiling because he knew Duppy was just trying to save face and make the decision seem like it was his own. It was clear Xavier was operating on a whole other level. Xavier stood up and extended his hand.

Egypt slunk to standing as Duppy shook Xavier's hand.

"Then I hope to hear from you soon," Xavier said.

"As soon as I can," Duppy assured him.

Xavier turned to Egypt and kissed her hand. "You can arrest me any time," he winked.

Egypt giggled. "I'll keep that in mind."

When they got outside, Egypt asked, "Is he...gay?"

Duppy shrugged. "This is only my second time meeting him. Why?"

"Ain't no nigga 'posed to be that pretty."

TRACK 3

"The Colombian?" Spagoli spat like it was a germ in his mouth. "Who the fuck is The Colombian?"

The room was getting hotter. He knew they'd turned off the air-conditioning to make him uncomfortable while they were sweating him, but he was still cool as a fan. The detectives on the other hand had to take off their jackets and loosen their ties.

That fat fuck O'Brien looked like he was in a sauna, just waiting for a delivery of birch twigs. Spagoli was just the oily WOP he always was. He liked watching them losing their cool in more ways than one. "I just told you," he replied.

"Never heard of 'em," Spagoli retorted, then looked at O'Brien. "You ever heard of Xavier Montenegro?"

O'Brien shook his head with a face like a slow kid in the wrong math class. He wiped his hand across his forehead, soaking the cuff of his shirt.

He looked to the one-way window, imagining he could see her shadow behind the glass. He looked hard at the glass and he fanned his face with his hand, nodding toward the detectives and giving his best *I don't give a shit* smile. He knew if she was there, she'd know exactly what he was up to with the detectives. The detectives were too stupid to realize. They were getting no satisfaction from him. If he was going to have to rat to save his ass, then he was going to make Spagoli and O'Brien work for it like bitches.

"Maybe you two need to get out more," he suggested, lighting another cigarette just to add to the claustrophobic atmosphere in the room.

Spagoli pointed at him. "Don't get fuckin' cute. If I look up this fuckin' Xavier character and he ain't who you say he is, the deal is off," Spagoli threatened.

TEN YEARS EARLIER

"You doin' good in school?"

"Yes, sir."

"Sir? Who the fuck is sir? I'm your Daddy not a goddamn cracker in a suit!"

"Yes, Daddy," Power corrected as he glanced out of the car window, as the landscape of Long Island fizzed by. The harsh winter sun made everything more real, as the green girders of the overhead railroad flashed by like the backbeat to the city's rhythm. The music of the metropolis, all brutal angles and tempo. The click-track to Power's childhood, on which to build a new sound one day, in a future that right now was as uncertain as hell.

"I want you to stay out of trouble, you hear me? Stay away from that bullshit and keep your nose clean, you dig?" His father Buddy fluffed, whipping the car expertly lane to lane, constantly checking the rearview.

"Yes, sir. I mean yes, Daddy."

Power glanced up at his Daddy. He liked he was growing into the spitting image of him. Buddy caught his son looking at him, took his hand from the steering wheel and turned Power's eyes back to the windshield. "You be a lady's man, son. Never look at a guy like that, even yo Daddy. *Want* the ladies, don't be one."

Power forgot himself. "Yes, sir."

Buddy thumped the steering wheel and took the car into another lane, pushing between an MTA bus and a black BMW.

"Is that all y'all say? Yes, sir. No, sir? What is you, a punk?"

"No," Power barked like a puppy at a pitbull.

"Then let me hear you curse! Say, hell no!"

"Hell no!" Power bellowed, happy to oblige his father in rebellion. They both laughed. Buddy checked the rearview, the view drying up his smile like sun over a puddle.

"You know this the last time I'ma see you right?"

Power looked up at his father, face full of innocent ignorance. Buddy's face showing the look tore through him like shrapnel. The tears in his eyes fell freely. Power had never seen his Daddy cry before. It confused him. Momma cried a lot. At the TV, and the songs on the radio, when Daddy and her had their *arg-U-ments*. Power had only recently learned how to say *arg-U-ments* correctly and although he liked the feel of the word in his mouth, he didn't like what situations between his parents had made him learn it. But Daddy crying...that was new. He wanted to hug his Daddy now, like how his Momma hugged him when he was a little kid. Make the tears go away.

"Why this the last time, Daddy?"

"Because of that," Buddy spat, gesturing over his shoulder to the police cars closing behind, sirens wailing.

They had been behind them for a while at that point, long enough for there to be a whole line of police in pursuit while a helicopter hovered overhead. Buddy was an expert driver so he effortlessly avoided them so well that Power's young mind didn't know it was any more than a Saturday morning drive. But the dragnet was closing in.

"Daddy, I don't want you to go to jail again," Power cried, tears bursting from his face.

"Hush that goddamn fuss," Buddy demanded, even though his

tears were twice as thick as Power's. "Shut it up! I ain't going to jail ever again. I'm tired boy—tired as fuck. Tired of runnin' in place and calling it hustlin'! Tired of these crackers on my back, tired of sticking this shit in my veins," Buddy hissed, his voice cracking.

He opened the bag on the seat between them. Inside it was full of money.

"Here, quick, hurry up. Stuff as much as you can," Buddy instructed.

Power didn't hesitate to comply. He began to stick bands of money in the elastic of his Superman Underoos.

"Take off your shoes, hurry up!" Buddy barked, seeing the road block up ahead.

Power put a band a piece in his Kangaroos, making him instantly three inches taller. Buddy took off his crucifix and gave it to Power.

"That money you give to your Momma, but this is for you. That Jesus shit is some bullshit, but maybe it'll bring you luck."

Buddy stopped twenty yards from the police blockade. They were surrounded—half a precinct behind him, the other half in front of him, a helicopter hovering above. Buddy took one look at it all and then cracked a bittersweet smile.

"You take care of your Momma, ya dig?" Buddy told Power, looking him dead in the eye.

Power, too crushed with emotion, yet realizing the solemnity of the moment, met his gaze and nodded. Buddy kissed his forehead, took two .44 magnums from his waistband, and got out.

"Welcome to my world!" he cackled at the police with manic glee.

"Get down on your knees!" A policeman shouted back.

"Tell that to your goddamn Momma, cracka!" Buddy barked back, and then the fireworks began.

Power peeked over the dashboard and watched as Buddy single-handedly went to war with the police, killing two officers before they filled Buddy full of holes, his brains misting the air.

It wasn't just the sight of his Daddy dying that moved Power the most; it was the sounds. The music of the sirens, the bass of the helicopter's engine, the drums of the guns...

PRESENT DAY

"Wow," Egypt remarked as Power concluded. "I'm sorry you had to see that."

They were sitting in the lounge area waiting for Duppy to arrive in his office. They were relaxed on the plush, leather couch sipping on Hennessy, Egypt's legs curled up under her like a cat.

"That was my pops," Power shrugged, swigging the Hennessy to push back the tears.

Egypt fingered the crucifix around his neck. "And here I was thinking you wore this because you were a good Christian," she giggled.

"Yeah, I'm a regular choir boy," he winked.

"Did the police find the money?" she asked.

"Hell no! I gave most of it to my mother."

Egypt arched an eyebrow. "Most of it?"

"I've always been greedy," he replied, eyeing her like she was breakfast. They both laughed, but their eye contact said something more was simmering.

"Did you know he was going to rob the bank?" Egypt asked, putting her knee against his thigh.

"Nah, I didn't even know we were at a bank. Pops stopped, said I'll be back, and went in. I was too busy unwrapping Now & Laters to give a fuck," Power explained.

"Oh, I used to love those! Which was your favorite?"

"Banana."

"Ill! Watermelon," she shot back. "Least favorite?"

"Chocolate!" They said together. They laughed again, the chemistry building. The atmosphere was easy and chilled, but the underlying tension was there in every look, every new point of contact. His eyes were saying, *I wanna fuck you*, and Egypt's were saying loud and clear, *I'm gonna let you.*

The elevator door opened and Duppy got off, his face looking like he had caught them fucking. Power laughed inside. Dude better never play poker.

"Ain't this crazy?" Duppy quipped sourly.

Power smiled with his mouth, but there was a smirking glint in his eye. "Just waiting on you, big bruh!"

Egypt put her glass on the table, got up and gave Duppy a hug. "Hey baby, Power was just keeping me company," she cooed.

Duppy had the look of a man who knew he was being played, but Power knew he wasn't man enough to do anything about it.

Power stood up. "I don't know about you, Duppy, but I'm ready to lay some hot shit. Like you always say, time is money," he winked as he walked by Duppy on his way to the studio.

Duppy followed his movement with his eyes. Egypt directed his face back to hers with a gentle gesture with her index finger.

"If we don't have trust, we don't have anything," she gamed.

"I trust you," he replied. "It's him I don't trust."

"Then trust me," she mocked gently, then headed in the studio.

The sway in her hips and the bounce of her ass beckoned for him to follow.

* * *

. . .

78

Her sound was undeniable.

The song Power and Egypt were working on was called "Ride Forever," and it was a hit from the first note. Kane laid a track so sinister that Power's lyrics ricocheted like hot lead, while Egypt's angelic, yet dagger-edged hook put the icing on the cake. The studio went crazy as Kane played it back. Even Duppy couldn't help but smile.

"Yo, I can't front. That's the hottest joint I've ever heard. This one has Grammy written all over it!" Duppy admitted.

Power looked at Egypt. Duppy didn't miss the glance.

Kane raised his half-empty bottle of E&J.

"To Power and Egypt, may they ride forever!" Kane toasted.

Everybody cheered—except Duppy.

"Yo, thun, I already told you, you can't be fuckin' the boss's wife," Kane grinned as he drove back to Queens Boro. Power reclined in the passenger seat.

"Fuck that nigga. He the boss for now. Plus, I ain't even fuckin' her yet," Power said with a slice of side eye at Kane while puffing the blunt.

Kane glanced at him. "You ain't fuck that bitch yet? Damn, you slippin'."

Power laughed, but wished it wasn't true. "Nigga, I'm a bitch bagger, you know it's a wrap!" The brag was legit, because Power was used to getting what he wanted. He hit the blunt deep, the glow matching the lights sliding by through the window. The reflections of the city coming off the river danced in his eyes. He wanted to get off the subject of Egypt. When he'd fucked her then he'd talk about it all with Kane, but until then..."Ay, yo, Messiah told me you said you fucked Tamika's mom."

"I did!"

"Fuck outta here! That uppity holier-than-thou bitch? Hell no!" Power protested.

Kane kissed his palm and held it to the sky. "That's my word, thun!"

They both laughed together. Power passed Kane the blunt.

"But on the real, you never told me how you got that triflin' bitch to set her man up," Kane remarked.

Power smiled mischievously. "Check it out..."

"Ay, yo L! L! What up, thun, hol' up!" Power yelled across the 12th street courtyard.

It was almost two in the morning and Power had just emerged from his jump off Vanessa's apartment. He had spotted L sliding through, his shadow like a ghoul on the wall trying to avoid detection, but he was too late.

"Damn," he hissed to the crackhead chick he had with him. L put his hand on the butt of his .32 revolver in the waistband of his Guess jeans.

Power pulled up his pants as he bopped over to L's position, which happened to be right under a street light.

"What up, thun. I ain't seen yo ass in a week," Power remarked, his half chuckle masking seven days' worth of frustration.

"Nah man, shit been crazy," L stammered and then started mumbling, shifting from foot to foot.

"Bitch ass nigga, you don't speak the thun language, fuck is wrong with you? Where the fuck is my money?!" Power growled, taking a menacing step closer to L.

Out of reflex, L stepped back and put his hand on the butt of his pistol. The crackhead chick nervously fluttered like a scared bird.

"Oh, you gonna shoot me now?" Power's face was wide with scorn.

A cold flash of realization shot through Power when he remembered he left his gun on Vanessa's nightstand, but the cold flash quickly turned to lava as his anger dared L to be the man they both knew he wasn't.

"Nah, Power, I'm just sayin' you ain't got to talk to me like that," L replied, trying to stand firm, but backing up as he said it.

"Baby, let's just go," the crackhead chick suggested. Power was oblivious to her presence as he stepped toward L again, totally closing the distance and giving L no room to pull out the gun.

With Power breathing down his grill, L's muttering machismo went mute. "Bitch I said shoot," Power bassed, feeling like fucking Supernigga.

L couldn't even look him in the eyes. "I—I'ma get your money, Power!"

"Nah, nigga, you was gonna shoot me, fuck that! Pull it out!" Power demanded.

"My word yo, I wasn't. I was just..."

Power smacked L so hard the crackhead bitch recoiled like he'd smashed them both with the same move. "Pull it out!" Power commanded.

Tears of fear streamed from L's eyes. "Come on, Power!"

Power was in a zone of menace; his ego had him so fucked up that he was slipping and this coward could've had the one up on him if he had the balls. In a rage, he grabbed L's gun and without pulling it out of his waistband shot L in the nuts twice.

L folded like a flimsy house of cards in a puddle of pain on the ground.

"My nuts!" he screamed.

"You ain't need 'em anyway, pussy!" Power sneered, then raised up the gun and finished the job.

Bop! Bop!

Both shots blew off a small chunk of L's head, turning his final thought into macabre graffiti that hit the wall with a cartoon splat.

The crackhead ho screamed. Had she kept silent, Power would've let her live. He looked at her with the grin of the grim reaper.

"Power, wait! I—"

Bop! Bop! Click!

Power blew two holes in her chest, the first exploding her heart, killing her instantly. The other, uselessly cracking her sternum. He would've kept firing but the gun was empty.

That's when everything changed.

"Freeze! Drop the gun!"

Power heard the words and his heart dropped at the same time he dropped the gun. He thought it all was over... until he turned around and saw that it was Khalil. He raised his hands and smiled.

"What up, officer," Power said with all the derision he could stuff in his mouth.

Khalil kept the gun on Power. The Cop's adrenaline was high, so high the gun slightly shook in his hands, a fact Power noticed instantly.

"Don't move! Get down on your knees and cross your feet at the ankles," he commanded, but he was cut off by Power's chuckle.

"Don't move or get down? I can't do both."

Khalil reached for his walkie-talkie. No one had come out of the block, no one was looking out of windows. This was a play with an audience of one: one shaking, pussy ass cop. Power saw his opportunity and took it.

"I wouldn't do that if I were you," Power cautioned. "Right now, this is between me and you, but if you radio it and make it official, it's going to be between you and Q.B.C. Is this dead pussy worth your family's life?"

Khalil cocked back the hammer. "Nigga, are you threatenin' me?!"

"Nah," Power replied. "I'm promising you. Lock me up and you'll never be able to work around here again."

"Nigga, I'm from the Boro, too!"

"Yeah, but you a fuckin' cop! You no longer count."

Khalil seethed. "Get down on your knees now! Or I swear I'll put you on your back!"

Power smirked a kiss of death at Khalil. "Your funeral," Power said quietly. He slowly lowered and assumed the position.

As soon as Power laced his fingers on his head, Khalil bowled him over, making his face slap the broken glass-dusted pavement. Then Khalil put his knee in his back.

Power was so hot his red complexion seemed to glow like fire. "My word, nigga, you and your family won't see Christmas!" Power vowed.

Khalil hit him so hard Power slipped towards darkness, Khalil's voice just a buzz like an annoying fly caught in a bottle. And right now, *caught,* was what the officer entirely was.

"Unit six to dispatch, officer needs assistance. I repeat, officer needs assistance. I'm in the courtyard on 12th Street. Over," he tuned into his radio.

"Ten-four, unit six, assistance en route. Over."

Khalil cuffed Power's unconscious body, then looked at it.

A wave of sweet satisfaction washed over him because he felt vindicated for once in his life. He had been taunted all his life in Queens Boro. Bullied by the legends of QB. Power was younger than him, but Power's uncles had tortured Khalil when he was cutting up and now he finally felt like he had gotten some get back.

He had an incredible urge to spit in Power's face, but the units arrived just in time to stop him. As they got Power to his feet, he was coming to, shaking his head as he tried to get his bearings.

"Yeah, take a long look around because you won't be seeing this place for a long time," another officer cackled.

Khalil laughed, but his joy was cut short when Power looked him in the eyes and smiled. Even cuffed, Power seemed like a threat.

"Get this piece of shit out of here!" Khalil barked.

As Power was being led off, he looked at Khalil and remarked, "Merry Christmas, bitch."

Khalil took it as an idle threat.

But he didn't know what Power did.

Khalil was sleeping with his enemy.

SIX MONTHS EARLIER

"Welcome home, girl!" Kiara squealed, enveloping Misha in a full-bodied, sisterly hug.

Kiara and Misha had grown up in the Boro, best friends since ponytails. Misha laughed and replied, "Girl, I only moved to Hollis."

"I know, but it ain't like you invited a bitch to your house," Kiara sassed playfully, hand on her hip. "How is married life treating you?"

Misha shrugged. "*Bore*-ring. I'm so sick of that slow ass shit. Khalil don't never want to do nothing but work," she complained.

"At least he payin' the bills," Kiara riffed.

"You ain't lyin'," Misha seconded, thinking that's exactly why she married him.

Misha was a hood bitch through and through. She came up fucking men and fighting women over the men she was fucking, but once she hit 18, she was burnt out and wanted something more. She knew Queens Boro couldn't give it to her. She was tired of loving thugs, only to have them cheat on her, beat on her, get locked up, or worse, killed. The death of the love of her life was the last straw.

His name was Yamit. He was originally from Brooklyn but had moved to the Bridge. He was a golden glove boxer, brown cocoa skin and fine as hell. Misha fell in love with him. He cheated on her religiously, but she knew he loved her. In the hood, Yamit was feared, and as they say, a scared man will kill you quick. He was hustling out of town in Albany when a drug dealer he had previously knocked out caught him slipping and bashed his skull in with a bat. He was on life support for a week before they pulled the plug.

When Misha found out, it had broken her into a million pieces. She couldn't eat or sleep. The recovery was slow, the pain cut like a razor for what seemed half a lifetime. But when she could confidently say she was on the other side of the grief, she told herself she'd had enough.

That's when she set her sights set on Khalil.

To put it bluntly, Khalil was a lame. He didn't play sports, he wasn't popular in school and he didn't hang out. He just hung out in his room. But Misha's mother and his mother went to the same church, so she would see him in church. She approached him, came onto him, and controlled him. When she got pregnant, they had both just graduated. He got a job with the NYPD, they got married, and eventually they bought a house in Hollis, Queens. It wasn't much, but it was hope. But square, married life wasn't Misha's forte. She missed the gangsta shit.

Six months later, she was creeping back to the Bridge.

"So what's poppin' tonight?" Misha questioned while snacking on chips in Kiara's living room.

"Let's go to Darryl's," Kiara replied, suggesting a local bar where hustlers were known to frequent.

"Shit, let's go!" Misha seconded.

Darryl's was packed outside.

The street was lined with fancy, exotic cars, souped up hood-style. Inside the bling was brighter than Broadway. Game was so thick in the bar it seemed to be a virus affecting everyone as soon as they stepped through the door.

Misha and Kiara were at the bar throwing back Amaretto Sours, bought and paid for by hungry hustlers with more money than game. They were both bad bitches. Misha was short, bow-legged and dark skinned with brown eyes and juicy thighs. Kiara was taller and just as chocolate, but with a fatter ass, so they both could command attention, and were doing so with ease until Q.B.C. walked in.

Kane, Messiah, Power, Five$, and Money walked in, and all eyes were on them. Not because none of them were old enough to be in the bar, nor was it because their bling was outshining half of the hustlers inside. It was because they were known around the Boro for laying niggas down. Their hammer game kept lames on edge. Live niggas respected them and got respect in return, but suckers started tucking hustlers' jewels and quietly made for the door.

Misha spotted that the dudes buying them drinks started to ease off. "Leaving so soon?" She quipped.

One checked his phone, even though it hadn't rung. "I gotta handle somethin' right quick," he replied.

"I'm sure," she laughed.

Once they left, she asked Kiara, "Who that fine nigga there?"

"You don't remember Power, Lenny's nephew?" Kiara asked.

"Little Power?"

"Hmph, he ain't so little no more girl, trust me," Kiara answered.

By this time, Power had noticed her at the bar. He loved dark skinned women. He made his way over.

"Kiara, what up?" Power greeted, kissing Kiara on the cheek. "Who's your friend?"

"Her friend can speak for herself, *little Power*," Misha sassed playfully, looking him up and down. *His young ass can get it.*

Power chuckled. "Oh, word? You gonna play me with my government? The least you can do is tell me yours."

"Oh, you don't remember me? Misha Grant from the five building?" she said.

"Damn, ma, my bad. You use to fuck with Yamit. Yeah, I remember. Long time no see."

She held out her left hand, showing off her wedding ring. "I got married."

Power glanced at the ring and scoffed. "Where he get that shit, the bubble gum machine?"

Misha felt played and was about to spaz, but Power added, "Nah, ma, no disrespect to you. I'm sayin' yo' man gotta step his game up. A bad bitch like you 'posed to have a Flintstone rock on her finger, yo."

She blushed at the compliment. "You owe me a drink anyway," she remarked.

"How you figure?"

"'Cause you scared the dude off who I was drinkin' on."

Power bust out laughing.

Three drinks later, Power was in her ear. "So you bouncin' with me or what?" He asked, his hand on her elbow. Stroking.

She pulled back with her face scrunched. "Leave with you? You too young to handle this," she replied, as if the thought hadn't already crossed her mind.

Power pushed up on her so she could feel his dick on her thighs. "Do that feel young?"

Surprised at the size, but keeping her composure, she replied, "And? I know plenty of big dick niggas who don't know what to do with it!"

"Only one way to find out."

"Oh yeah? What's in it for me?" She asked, peering at him with glittering eyes over the rim of her glass.

"A good time," Power chuckled. "'Cause I can tell your husband ain't fuckin' you right."

Her face gave enough away for Power to add with maximum arrogance, "Your pussy twitching right now. Tell me it ain't so. Testify."

"I can't stay long."

"You ain't gotta stay long if you cum quick," Power winked.

Misha was hooked.

———

Power was making the hotel bed sing a song of mercy as he drilled Misha's pussy like a jackhammer, her legs thrown over his shoulders, her knees bracketing her titties, and Power in a push-up position. Misha felt every stroke in her spine.

"Oh, fuck, baby. It's in my stomach," she moaned in surprise.

"Nah, bitch, don't run now," Power grinned, sweat dripping. "Remember, I can't handle this pussy, right?"

"No! You can, you can!" She cried, clawing at the headboard frantically.

"Whose pussy is this?"

"Yours, baby, yours!"

"Say my name!"

"Poooooooooower!" Misha squealed as she creamed Power's dick for the third time, making her body tremble uncontrollably.

From that moment Misha became Power's jump off slut. He fucked her in cars, in Khalil's bed, and once in the basement of her home while Khalil made dinner for the kids. Power loved the fact that he was fucking a cop's wife. Every time he saw Khalil, he would smirk at him or say something slick. Khalil never caught on, but the comments and smirks only fueled Khalil's hatred of Power, that is until L owed Power a thousand, and he put his hand on the gun in his waistband when Power called him out.

———

Misha was sick.

Kiara told her the next day what happened to Power. Now, seven days later, she was craving his young dick. She took her misery out on Khalil, who had no idea where the attitude was coming from.

All she knew was Khalil wouldn't be getting' any pussy from his wife.

"What's wrong with you?" he questioned.

"Nothing," she spat coldly before slamming the bathroom door.

She was fuming, her hormones raging, and her mind torn up. Over the course of the affair, she had convinced herself that Power had feelings for her. In her mind, she felt like Power wanted more, he wanted *her*. But now, Khalil had ruined that by getting him locked up.

Her phone rang. She was about to call Kiara and cry on her shoulder, so when she saw the strange number, her womanly instinct told her it was Power.

"Hello?" she answered.

Power peeped out his clique, scanning for any piece. Then he covered his head and the cell phone he had Officer Jones smuggle in. "Misha."

Just hearing the sound of his voice made her heart race and her pussy cream up.

"Baby!" She exclaimed a little too loudly. She lowered her tone. "Where are you? I thought you were locked up."

"Where the fuck you think I'm at. I'm on the Island," Power spat back, keeping his tone low.

"You're on a cell phone?" Misha inquired.

"Stop asking so many goddamn questions and listen. I need you."

Hearing those three words out of his mouth made her knees weak. "Anything, baby," she gushed.

Power smiled to himself because he knew the bitch was gone.

"Your man is the only witness—his word against mine. I need you to get that nigga to say it wasn't me," Power explained. She heard the words, but it took time for the realization of what Power was saying to sink in.

"Oh my God, Power, I wish I could, but I know Khalil; he's a cop first. He'd never agree to that," she answered.

"Then he gotta go," Power said bluntly. The thought made her heart jump.

"Go?" she echoed.

"Ma, these muhfuckas talkin' about 25 to life—I ain't tryin' to do no time like that. Plus, I ain't tryin' to lose you. You know I love you, girl."

The words radiated all over her body. She didn't hear the lie in those words until the night it was too late to check them for the truth.

"For real, Power?" She asked, sounding like a naive little girl instead of a grown ass woman.

"Of course I do. Now look, I'ma take care of everything, just let me know when to come through."

"O-okay," she answered, signing Khalil's death warrant. "I love you," she said.

"*I love you, too,* I said. Dumb bitch believed it. I had to hang up before she heard me laughing!"

Kane slapped his thigh and hit the blunt, passing it back to Power as he exhaled smoke like a horse on a cold morning. He steered the late model BMW smooth along the L.I.E. off-ramp and eased the car into the sparse night traffic.

"Ay, yo, bitches are dumber than a muhfucka," Power laughed, giving Kane a pound.

"For real, thun," Kane seconded, making a right turn.

"She really thought I was gonna catch a body with her loved-out ass! Like I'm giving this bitch a chance to burn me and go to the po-po as soon as she catch my dick in Kiara's mouth," Power said, shaking his head.

Kane shook his head too. "When these bitches gonna learn?"

"Hoes should know they can't trust the God,"

Kane looked at Power. "Nigga that bitch Egypt got you cock-eyed," Kane teased, as he stopped at a light.

Power threw his head back laughing. "Get the fuck outta here! I'ma break that bitch like I do all the rest!"

"We'll see, thun!"

Both of them were so busy joking and smoking that they didn't pay attention to the white van that pulled up on Kane's driver side until it was too late. The side door slid back in a near slow motion, the gap was only inches when the first shots burst from inside.

As the metal around Kane and Power sparked, the side windows frosted and smashed. Kane hit the accelerator and tried to take the car through the red light. The van followed smooth as a shark. They knew that he'd try to drive out of trouble, and they were ready.

The shooters wasted no time throwing back the sliding door, fully opening fire with two automatic sub-machine guns. The bullets tore through the back window, running a line of holes through the roof. The cold air swirled in from the new ventilation as the car sped forward.

"Fuck!" Kane screamed, slamming the gas even harder and

making the stop light fall further behind. Had he not punched the car forward, the gunfire might've cut them into pieces. Power snatched his pistol from his waist and fired back as they screeched away. He didn't bother with his door. He just shot through where the back window used to be.

Buck! Buck! Buck!

The van's headlights popped and two hollow points buried themselves into the radiator. Several cars in the intersection barely missed the swerving BMW as Kane made the getaway.

Then it was over. The van didn't pursue. It backed up, pulled a sick 180 and sped in the opposite direction.

It took two blocks for their adrenaline to finally subside. Kane wanted to go after the bastards and take them out for even imagining shooting them, but Power said no. This wasn't the time. "Who the fuck was that?!" Kane huffed.

Power thought he had a good idea, which was another reason he didn't want to track the shooters down right now. He didn't want to alert the main suspect that he might have those niggas squeal before he shot them in the face.

"Nah, the question is who sent 'em?"

FIVE YEARS EARLIER

E gypt rolled over on her side and looked at Vanya. It was in that moment that Egypt understood what people saw when they looked at her. Vanya was beauty personified. She had a lighter complexion, but a man would be hard-pressed to choose between the two goddesses.

"Investigation?" Egypt echoed.

"Don't be coy," Vanya returned. "Who's the target?"

"Baby J."

"James Manfred? He's local. Small potatoes," Vanya said, tangling her finger in Egypt's hair. Rolling it around the skin.

Egypt looked her in the eyes. "He is. The department's in for you."

"Me?" Vanya chuckled. "Little ol' me?"

Egypt sat up, pushing her hair out of her face. "Little ol' you has quite a hustle. You speak seven languages."

"Eight. I just learned Cantonese."

"I stand corrected," Egypt winked. "You have ties to Russian gangsters, Bulgarian sex traffickers, Indonesian drug smugglers, and you are reported to be the American liaison to Xavier Montenegro, a.k.a. The Colombian. Did I leave anything out?"

Vanya sat up Indian-style and lit a cigarette. "I was once a Girl Scout."

"Duly noted."

Vanya hit the cigarette. "The Colombian, huh? What do you know about him?"

"Nothing, that's why I'm here," Egypt admitted. Vanya exhaled. "Would you like to meet him?"

"Again, that's why I'm here."

Vanya laughed. "It can be arranged. First, let me tell you what I know about you."

"I'm all ears," Egypt responded.

Vanya hit her cigarette, eyed Egypt curiously, then exhaled and said, "You're not a cop."

PRESENT DAY

"Who the fuck was it?" Five$ bassed, once Kane and Power explained what happened.

Five$, Power, Kane, Messiah, and Knowledge were sitting in Money's apartment trying to figure out what happened. The air was thick with smoke, but the atmosphere was thicker with anger.

"Muhfuckas just came outta nowhere, thun! Shit was crazy!" Kane spat.

"Word, if they woulda been better shots, we'd be dead now," Power added as he paced the floor, hitting a bottle of Henny with one hand and taking a blunt from Knowledge with the other. The attempted hit had been two hours ago, but Power and Kane were still wired.

After looking like he was in deep thought, Messiah suggested, "Maybe it was them 4s Side niggas, Lil' Jah and them."

"Who?" Power probed.

"The niggas we kidnapped," Knowledge reminded him.

"Or what about that nigga from Far Rock we slumped. His fam mighta found out," Five$ said.

"How you figure that bullshit, Fi? Nah, it definitely wasn't

96

them, but it could've been them Jersey niggas we robbed," Kane replied.

"Man, goddamn, who we ain't got beef wit'?" Power barked, but his tone made the room crack up, easing the tension. Power didn't know what to put to his mouth next, the blunt or the Henny, but as he was cracking up too, he thought the better of either. He slumped down in a chair.

"Word, thun, the whole world got a vendetta against us," Knowledge laughed.

"Whoever it was, we need to be on point so they don't get a second chance. Any bitch you fuckin' anywhere...pick they brain, see if anything come up. Feel me?" Power instructed.

Everyone nodded.

"Damn, I can't wait to find out who it was!" Kane exclaimed, ready to set shit off on the spot.

"We will, thun, we will," Power replied.

FIFTEEN YEARS EARLIER

"Daddy's home!" A 10-year-old Egypt exclaimed as she jumped in her father's arms.

It was way past her bedtime, but she had been playing like she was asleep, awaiting his return. It wasn't every night that Egypt got to see her father, so this night was special.

What she didn't know then was it would be the last time she would see him alive.

Tony smiled and scooped up his stampeding daughter as she neared him. Tony told her he loved his daughter like there was no tomorrow. He had his four other children by four other women, but Egypt was definitely Daddy's little girl. *Maybe it was the fact that she looked so much like him*, she thought years later. Tony was definitely a lady's man with natural wavy hair and a cinnamon brown complexion. In the dim lights of a club he'd often been mistaken for a celebrity, Egypt's Momma had told her growing up. It was what had attracted her to him in the first place.

Egypt's Momma came in right behind her.

"Egypt!" she scolded, wearing a light grin. "What are you doing up?"

"My Daddy!" she pouted, wrapping her arms and legs around

him even tighter and burying her head in his chest. He always smelled good, warm like a man should, but with an under-tang of honey.

Tony laughed. "She good, Alicia."

"Hmm, good for you. She's a holy terror when you aren't around," Alicia replied.

Tony tickled Egypt. Egypt wriggled and protested, but she didn't want to let go and was only protesting because it was expected. "Is that true, baby girl? Are you a bad girl?"

Egypt laughed so hard she couldn't catch her breath. "I'ma be good! I'ma be good!"

Tony put her down then kissed her on her forehead. "You better. Now go on to bed and if you're a good girl we'll go to the zoo on Saturday," he promised.

"You promise, Daddy?" Egypt asked, because Tony wasn't always good in the promises department.

Egypt realized as she'd grown up, it wasn't that Tony did it on purpose, but he was one of the biggest heroin dealers in the city. He ran with The Council, a group of the city's heaviest gangsters, so the demand on his time was sometimes too much for him to keep every promise. A fact he often regretted.

"I promise, baby girl," Tony winked, then hit her little bottom. "Now, listen to your Momma."

"Okay, good night Daddy!" Egypt said gleefully before skipping up the stairs heading for bed.

Egypt couldn't be happier. She ran to her room giggling the whole way. She started to jump straight in bed, but then she remembered her prayers. Egypt got down on her knees and said the two words she would never say again.

"Dear God..."

Buck! Buck! Buck! Ka-boosh! Ka-boosh!

The sounds of handguns and sawed-off shotguns shattered her childhood instantly.

Buck! Ka-boosh!

Her whole body froze, so tensely that Egypt peed herself on

the spot. She was scared to death, but she had her father's instincts that willed her to move. Egypt ran to the window and threw it open. Her window let her out onto the side slant of the roof, then she hid behind the chimney, pushing the window nearly closed, but leaving enough of a finger space to get it open again. All she could hear was the song of her own nervous breathing and the cold winter wind whistling through the trees.

"No, no, no," she whispered feverishly to herself, her young mind rushing with terror and cold thoughts that made the air around her hiding place seem like it was blowing in from midsummer.

Egypt heard muffled voices in her room and she sucked in her breath. The voices got louder until she could see a man's head stick out of the window.

"The little bitch jumped out the window! She might be callin' the police right now. Let's go, yo," the man said before ducking back inside.

Egypt didn't breathe for damn near a minute. She held it until she heard the sounds of car doors slamming and engines hauling the cars off into the night. Her little feet felt like bricks of ice as she carefully maneuvered the slant and re-entered the window. The first thing she smelled was beer, as if it had been heavy on the dude's breath.

It would be a repulsive smell to her for the rest of her life.

She stepped gingerly across the soft carpeting of her room. The smell of gunpowder punched her in the nose. The space between her room and the stairs seemed to take forever to cross. It would be this walk that she would come to have nightmares over and over about.

She hesitated. Maybe the shooters had left someone behind to catch her just like this. Egypt wavered at the top of the stairs, wanting to suck her thumb so badly, but remembering all the times her Momma scolded her for *doing baby things.* You gotta grow up now. Get that thumb out of your mouth!" And so Egypt didn't suck her thumb, she placed her hand on the bannister, and by the time she had descended the stairs, she was no longer a little girl. She had grown. And now, it went like this...

Three steps down, the smell of fresh blood made her sick to her stomach. Four steps down, she saw her mother's foot in a pool of blood. Five steps down, she froze. The image seared itself in her mind, and bore a hole into her soul. Egypt saw her mother and father, bodies covered in blood, damn near headless from the point-blank shotgun blasts to the head. Blood and what she would later know to be brains, splattered the floor and walls.

"Nooooo!" Egypt had bellowed, the depth of pain in her stomach almost made her voice sound mannish.

She jumped down the remaining steps and ran to her dead parents. Blood covered her feet as she padded across the floor.

"Momma!" she cried, putting her head in her mother's warm chest. The taste of her mother's blood in her mouth instantly stopped her tears.

The taste of blood.

It hit her like a baby pitbull and gave her such a hunger for revenge that would never be quenched until she tasted the blood of their killers.

Blood of their killers.

Egypt turned to her father's body. Soberly, she kissed his hand.

"I love you, Daddy," she remarked calmly, then stood up and went to the phone. She didn't call 9-1-1 because there was no need. She didn't call the police because that was blasphemy to her father. So, pajamas wet from her terrified peeing, her feet painted in red, and on her lips the taste of her Momma's last heartbeats, she called her Uncle Joe.

"Hello? Auntie, is Uncle Joe there? Okay, I'll hold," Egypt said, her eyes focusing on the bloody scene. Her uncle came to the line.

"What's up, Niecey?" Uncle Joe picked up, calling her by the nickname he had for her. Hearing his strong voice brought the tears tumbling back to her eyes.

"Uncle Joe..." was all she got out before she broke down. He knew why instantly. "I'm on my way."

Egypt put the phone down and stood rooted in the spot, not wanting to waste her Momma's precious blood on footprints. The TV was still playing a game show. It was throwing out happy music, the audience was cheering, and the host had the biggest smile. Egypt didn't look at her parents' bodies, couldn't look at them. But the TV, it connected with her. It told her there was another world outside this room of death and misery, a world that she could find where people smiled and cheered, and where life was simple and nobody's parents' lives were ended in their living room by gunshots.

Her parents dying was not the end. It was the start of something new for Egypt. There was no doubt in her mind. *Keep your eyes fixed above the death, child. Look to the light. Look beyond.*

Twenty minutes later, Uncle Joe and several goons arrived on the scene. Egypt ran into his arms, the TV's spell over her, broken at last.

"It's going to be okay, Niecey," he soothed, all the while the lava tears of rage rolled down his face as he looked at his dead brother and sister-in-law.

The music and audience applause from the TV continued, as Egypt pulled him as close as she had pulled her Daddy.

Egypt sobbed pointing to her temple, keeping her eyes off the bodies. "I love my Momma and I love my Daddy, but they only dead in the house. I'ma never gonna let them die in here."

All Joe could do was hold her.

TEN YEARS LATER

Vanya stubbed her cigarette, blowing out the last of its smoke as Egypt finished telling the tale about how her parents had died. The afternoon was moving on, but they were not moving from the bed. What had begun as a joyous meeting of mind and body had taken on a sadder, almost sour note. Egypt was silent, the last of the story on her lips and it seemed Vanya couldn't find any words to respond, and so in the end, just hugged Egypt instead.

"Thank you," Egypt replied, tears brimming her eyes.

They held that embrace for a while. Just feeling the breath going in and out of each other's bodies. After near two minutes Vanya pulled away and asked, "How old were you?"

"Ten."

Vanya sighed. There was compassion in her eyes and Egypt felt it fully. She wiped her cheeks knowing she had to get her head back in the game. Vanya had said something earlier that didn't compute, and however hard she was feeling about dragging up those memories, she couldn't let it slide. She had to know what Vanya had been talking about. "But why did you say I'm not a cop?" Egypt asked, when her head was as composed as her face.

"I think you know the answer already."

"If I did, I wouldn't ask," Egypt said, trying hard to keep the urgency out of her tone. She already felt exposed having to admit as much as she did, and needed something back from Vanya if she was truly going to trust her.

Vanya shrugged apologetically and nodded. "You're good, I'll give you that. But we both know as poignant as that story is, you're leaving the best part out," she said.

"Which is?" Egypt questioned. Thinking, *dammit, she's got me opening up even more.*

"The conversation you and your Uncle Joe had at the cemetery."

The revelation hit Egypt so hard she snatched the pistol she had stashed under the pillow and put it to Vanya's forehead, seething.

"Bitch, who are you?" Egypt growled.

Vanya just smiled in the face of death.

EIGHT YEARS LATER

M essiah pushed the picture of Tyrone away from him. "Never seen him before," he spat calmly.

"No?" Spagoli whipped, then snatched the picture up and shoved it under Messiah's nose. He could smell the detective's garlic breath this close up. "Well, take a closer look!"

Spagoli smushed it up against Messiah's mouth. He thought about taking a bite out of the photograph, but instead he squirmed and tried to turn away. Every sudden move made his ribs feel like they were breaking all over again, but his rage wished he wasn't cuffed so he could make Spagoli eat the picture himself.

"See it now, huh? Huh?! Look again!" Spagoli taunted.

"Get the fuck off me!" Messiah shouted, his wrists pulling against the cuffs chained through the restraining bar. They'd been in the room a good two hours now. Messiah wasn't giving anything up, but they just had to keep digging. *They don't know jack shit about this nigga.*

O'Brien chuckled. "Okay, Spags, get him up. I think he gets the point."

Reluctantly, Spagoli let up, putting the picture back in the folder and straightening his tie.

"You eggplants always get under my skin," Spagoli hissed. Messiah hated WOPs just as much, but he said it with his eyes, not his mouth.

O'Brien sat on the corner of the desk closest to Messiah. "Now that you've...seen the picture again, are you sure you've never met Tyrone Braswell?"

"I want a lawyer," Messiah growled, still looking at Spagoli, not willing to break eye contact until the detective did.

"Lawyering up only makes my point, Edwards. Only guilty people need lawyers. Now hear me out. We know Braswell was involved in the pawn store heist in Goldsboro three years ago. We also know a few of those guns from the shoot out the other night were obtained from that haul. We also know from Tyrone's girlfriend at the time that he was last seen with, Lil' Earl's cousin from Queens. Your twin to be exact. That would be you and your brother. Ring a bell?" O'Brien explained.

"What part of I want a lawyer don't you understand?" Messiah spat.

Before O'Brien could reply, they heard a knock on the door. O'Brien and Spagoli exchanged glances, looking as deflated as month-old birthday balloons.

"Yeah," Spagoli answered with all the reluctance of a man who didn't want to know what was behind the door.

An officer stuck his head in the room and informed them "Edwards' lawyer just got here."

Messiah guessed that they knew this was a possibility and had worked on him as hard as they could until the last second. But the time had all run dry.

"Damn, Edwards. You got a phone in your ass or somethin'?" O'Brien wisecracked.

"Nah, just a helluva team," Messiah said, feeling the first moment of relief since they'd brought him into the interrogation room.

The lawyer, Mr. Gould, walked in. He was a short, but dapper man who looked like someone had awakened him in the middle of the night, which they had.

"Francis Gould, detectives, and Mr. Edwards is my client," the lawyer explained from a suit that looked like it had been put on in more than a hurry than he was used to. He met the detectives' gazes and sat down next to Messiah.

Messiah smiled at Spagoli with maximum arrogance.

"That one there assaulted me," Messiah told his lawyer.

"Good to know you've got a little rat in you," Spagoli quipped, "Maybe when you're begging us to plea, we might ask for your memory to improve."

"Eat my rat dick, pussy," Messiah spat back.

"Mr. Edwards, I'll handle this," Gould told Messiah holding up his hand. He turned to the detectives. "Now, as I understand it, you two detectives came down from New York, correct?"

"Well we're here, aren't we? I don't think we're holograms." Spagoli answered sarcastically.

"Obviously not," Gould sniffed, not playing. "So, I assume you have an arrest warrant?"

Spagoli and O'Brien looked at one another. "We...uh, no we don't," O'Brien admitted.

"I see. Then I assume you have no more questions?"

"Yeah, we wouldn't want you to miss your flight back up your Momma's ass!" Messiah cackled.

The detectives knew the interview was at an end, and they'd failed to get what they wanted from Messiah. Spagoli fumed. "We'll see you soon," he snapped.

Both detectives begrudgingly got up and walked out. Gould turned to Messiah and said, "You'll be free in 24 hours. Mr. Mitchell sends his best."

"Word! Tell the God good look!" Messiah exclaimed.

———

Power hung up the phone and smiled.

"Messiah'll be out in the morning," he told Egypt.

They were laid up in his presidential suite, ass-naked, basking in the glow of a good fuck. Egypt had her head on his chest, playing with his nipple. She couldn't help but admire the way Power handled his crew and looked out for them. The Q.B.C. were tighter than tight for their leader, and he was for them too.

She saw that Power trusted and needed Messiah enough to make sure he got him out of any hole. She wondered if she'd be able to have Power feel the same way about her one day.

The conflicts that the mission and her attraction to Power personally brought up could be sidestepped, she knew. Power was not the target. He was incidental to the mission, but was not at all incidental to her. She didn't think she'd fall this far this hard so soon. The young rapper with the gangsta life was already under her skin so deeply, that she didn't think she'd ever remove him.

Or even want to.

Egypt rolled into Power's arms, he looked and smelled like addiction, and she knew then that she needed another hit.

She reached for his dick...

PRESENT DAY

Duppy stopped jogging when he saw the unmarked detective car parked behind his armored Escalade. His driver and bodyguard Jaylan was standing next to two white detectives. Duppy and D-Praved, another thug turned rapper on Duppy's label, had ended their run about a hundred feet away, then walked the rest of the way to the truck. Shameek took the door on the far side of the Escalade. The detectives didn't seem interested in him at all. Duppy took the towel that Jaylan handed him and wiped the sweat off his face.

"Duppy, I presume? I'm detective O'Brien," O'Brien said, flashing his badge.

"And I'm Detective Spagoli," Spagoli added, flashing his as well.

Duppy frowned. "Spagoli? I know that name from somewhere. Have we met?

Spagoli looked at Duppy like he'd just fucked his sister. "If we had, I would've made sure you remembered me," Spagoli scoffed.

Duppy chuckled "No disrespect, just know that name from somewhere. Nevermind, nice to meet you," Duppy said, then started to turn towards the Escalade. O'Brien put a hand against the roof of the car in front of Duppy's chest, stopping him from going through the door Jaylan was holding open.

"Do you mind if we have a word with you?" O'Brien requested.

Duppy gently lifted the detective's hand, with a smile and climbed into the smooth leather seating in the back. "You just did," he replied.

Before he could close the door, O'Brien put his hand on the door, holding it open. Jaylan looked at Duppy.

Duppy nodded that it was ok and his chauffer took his hand from the door but stood ready in case the situation changed and Duppy wanted the door closed.

O'Brien looked Jaylan up and down, and then returned his attention to Duppy. "I'm sure you're clean, Mr. Duppy, but can we say the same for your guys? You think they can stand warrant checks?"

To Jaylan's credit, he didn't flinch at the detective's threat. The passengers in the car might be a different matter. Inside Shameek was already dry from the run and was now all gold and mirror shades. Shameek was sitting with Duppy's other two bodyguards. They were crammed in the space like a bad play at Tetris.

Duppy knew Shameek had two warrants out for him under an alias and that Jaylan did too. He chuckled, "Who says the cops ain't on the job, huh? Okay, what's on your mind?" he said, relenting.

"C-Allah," said O'Brien.

"Who?"

O'Brien smiled at his feigned ignorance. "You an owl or something?"

"Nah, just at a loss as to what you talkin' about," Duppy replied, keeping his cool outwardly, but inside he could feel the heat rising. Shameek shifted uneasily in his seat pretending to check his gold Rolex.

Spagoli handed Duppy a sheet of paper and said, "Maybe this will jog your memory."

Duppy took the paper, but looked at Spagoli curiously.

"Spagoli, right? You got a brother or something? I hate when I can't figure something out."

"Just read the fuckin' paper," Spagoli spat. Duppy looked at the text on the sheet.

"It's just a bunch of phone numbers."

"It's C-Allah's phone record. Yours is highlighted," O'Brien informed him.

Duppy shrugged and handed the paper back to O'Brien. "Okay, so what?"

"So what? That's your number, which means you know the fuckin' guy well enough to have spoken to him on numerous occasions!" Spagoli barked.

Duppy was shaking on the inside now, and his composure was dissolving into a rash of sweat on his forehead. "Look, I run a label. I talk to people all the time. Promoters, producers, wanna be rappers, who knows? You got a picture of him or something?"

"I just happen to have one," O'Brien replied, pulling out a picture of C-Allah with half his head blown off.

Duppy took one look and remarked, "Looks like he's seen better days."

"You think?"

"I don't recognize him, detective. Maybe if he had a whole head instead of a head with a hole?"

Duppy paused to appreciate his own joke. The detectives sighed. Duppy held up a hand. "I'm sorry I can't help you, but I've got some things I need to handle. So if we're not finished here, call my lawyers, set up something more official than harassing me in the park," he said dismissively.

O'Brien smiled and let go of the door. "Sorry to disturb you, Mr. Duppy."

Duppy looked at Spagoli. Twisting his neck around as Jaylan steered the car away from the sidewalk

"Spagoli...that name's gonna be stuck in my head all day."

After they had silently watched Duppy ride off into the sunset, Spagoli turned to O'Brien and said, "He knows something."

"I agree. Did you see the way he looked at the picture?" O'Brien added.

"His face! He couldn't hide a pussy in a girl's school."

"Might be fun searching for it though," O'Brien chuckled.

"I think we need to apply a little more pressure to Mr. Duppy." Spagoli said, shielding his eyes against the setting sun as the Escalade made the on-ramp to the L.I.E.

"You took the words right out of my mouth," O'Brien seconded.

As they made the short walk back to their car, the discussion was all about how to turn Duppy's screws, but in the back of Spagoli's mind, all he could think of was, *How does that shithead nigger know my name?*

TRACK 4

Spagoli thought back to that moment outside Duppy's office. He'd been unsettled for the whole week. That nagging doubt at the back of his mind. He knew he'd never spoken to Duppy before that day for sure. He'd even spent a night when O'Brien thought he was out at a reunion with his buddies from his first precinct, in the office until well after midnight. He'd been searching through the archive of rap sheets looking to see if he'd crossed paths with Duppy in the past. But there was nothing... nothing at all.

So there was only one possible answer, and now that he knew the truth, it smashed into him in the interrogation room like a wrecking ball. Spagoli's stomach contracted as he tasted the hot bile of fear and anger in his throat. He hid it well, except for a flash of lava in his eyes, which O'Brien and the informer easily caught, when the revelation had hit him.

"You okay?" O'Brien asked with sincere concern.

The informer smirked. "Need to take a break?"

"Fuck you," Spagoli growled. "Just finish snitching you rat."

The rat chuckled. "Sticks and stones, Spagoli, sticks and

stones. You know, when we first started I did feel like...a traitor. But now as I purge my sinful soul, I feel like I'm doing my civic duty to society. Because as we both know, I'm not the only criminal here today."

Spagoli couldn't take anymore. He punched the informer in the mouth, drawing blood. O'Brien snatched Spagoli off him.

"He fuckin' hit me!"

"Shut up!" yelled O'Brien. "Now you know, stop poking the bear!" He turned to Spagoli. "And you, you're out of line. Walk it off!" he ordered Spagoli.

Spagoli kicked over the chair as he walked out and slammed the door.

O'Brien turned back to the informer, who was leaning his head forward enough for his chained hands to wipe at his bloodied chin.

"Look at my fuckin' lip!" he spat, eyes drilling into O'Brien.

"You'll live. Continue."

"This is bullshit! I told you I'd cooperate, but I won't be abused! I didn't sign up for this!" he ranted, glancing at the two-way mirror and imagining her laughing at him.

"Look," O'Brien began as he sat on the edge of the desk. "Spagoli is a good cop. He may be somewhat...compromised, in regards to you."

He smirked. "Are you sure? I meant, aren't you starting to see the bigger picture? Don't you see where I'm going? No one is innocent."

"I'll be the judge of that. I want to go back to North Carolina. What happened at the club that night and why," O'Brien demanded.

The informer spat blood from his split lip onto the table, making O'Brien inch away.

"It should be obvious by now. But, since I see it's not, I'll spell it out for you. It goes back to Goldsboro and the reason Q.B.C. was down there in the first place. Pay attention, because this is why shit got hot..."

FOUR YEARS EARLIER

"What time is it?"
　　　　"Like three."
"I thought he said 2:30."
"Yeah."

The twins sat in the front seat of Messiah's late model Camry, the sounds of Raekwon's the Purple Tape playing low underneath the fog of smoke their blunts were creating outside, providing the perfect camouflage for their murderous intent.

"Why you keep playin' wit' that shit?" Knowledge asked his brother aggressively, tired of hearing the click-click-click of his safety being kicked back and forth by his thumb.

"My bad." He stopped.

Five minutes passed.

Click. Click. Click.

"Yo!"

"I said my fuckin' bad!" Messiah growled.

"But you doin' it again. Ay—oh shit, here they come," Knowledge peeped that the other car was a Cadillac with two dudes inside. They pulled up to the driver's door and put down the window. Messiah did the same.

"What's up? Y'all good?" Messiah questioned. The other driver nodded.

"Yeah, you?"

"You already know."

"Follow me."

"Nah, follow *me*," Messiah insisted, then put up his window, ending the conversation.

He pulled off. The Cadillac busted a U-turn and followed them. Messiah glanced back in the rearview.

"You think they straight?"

"They better be. Where's my gwop?" Messiah laughed.

Knowledge unzipped the book bag, revealing bundles of money all wearing big faces, then zipped it back up.

Messiah pulled into the parking lot of an old abandoned school. Messiah and Knowledge got out, guns tucked, with Knowledge carrying the book bag.

The two dudes in the Cadillac pulled up, sloshing watery sludge from a deep puddle in the cracked concrete. Neon sizzled and reflected from the tall gas station sign across the street. Pop and Jay hopped out into the thin drizzle, pulling their parkas around their shoulders. They had a book bag of their own.

"What up, my nigga, how you?" Pop greeted, as if they were long lost friends.

"I'm good, but it's rainin'. Let's get this over with," Knowledge replied.

Jay eyed them evenly. Knowledge eyed him back as he handed Messiah the book bag. Messiah opened it and gave Pop a glimpse of the money.

"You straight?" Knowledge asked.

Pop saw all the money and looked thirsty. He opened his bag and flashed two bricks of coke.

"You gonna let me test it?" Messiah requested.

"In the rain?" Pop said, nodding to the sky and the squalling drops illuminated in the light from the gas station sign. Wind lifted the hoods of their parkas. Messiah was feeling the chill too, but not just from the weather. "Let's get in my car," he offered.

"Nah, let's get in mine," Pop countered, shaking his head.

The situation was suddenly getting tenser than was healthy with that much money and coke in play. Eight eyes darting around, with droplets of rain blowing into unflinching faces. In the distance they heard a siren start up. That broke the mirrored stares as all four heads cocked to work out if the siren was getting closer or going further into the distance.

Pop dropped his gaze first and opened his palms out. "Come on fam, we been peoples. What up? You coppin' or what?" Pop urged.

It could have gone one of two ways: relent or go tighter. Messiah decided to keep that screw turning. "Not without a tester," he repeated.

No one wanted to move first. Trigger fingers itched, shifty eyes still unblinking.

Then in a split second, the order of operations flipped because then everybody wanted to move first. Not for the coke or the money, but for the guns—four pistols were aimed by four greedy, not-giving-a-fuck ass niggas, and the bullets spoke in deadly conversations. This wasn't a shootout, not with everybody less than foot from one another. The parking lot echoed with ricochets and the thud of bullets ripping through clothing and smacking into flesh.

Knowledge caught a slug from Jay as he dove behind the trunk of the Cadillac, but not before he put three bullets in Jay's chest, killing him.

"It burns!" screamed Jay, his last words before he toppled.

Pop had the drop on Messiah, causing him to see his life pass before his eyes. But Pop had grabbed the wrong gun that morning. He had the tech-nine, which was notorious for jamming.

And at that moment, it lived up to its reputation.

"Fuck!" Pop spat, trying to unjam it, smacking it with the heel of his hand to shift the mechanism.

"Nah, fuck you!" Messiah cackled, feeling like he hit jackpot in the life lottery. He raised his chrome Colt and had all the luxury of time to aim.

Buck! Buck! Buck!

Pop was lifted off his feet as the three shots kicked in his face like a door slamming into his body. It smashed his very last thoughts out of the back of his head, to where they splashed down into the puddle by the Cadillac's front wheel. Pop dropped to his knees then fell flat on his face. The rain fell into the mess of the back of his head, running pink over his ears and down onto the concrete.

"Shit! Muhfucka! You ok?" Messiah yelled, running over to Power. Knowledge was holding his shoulder, he wasn't concerned about the injury.

"I'm good! Get the coke!"

Messiah grabbed both book bags, then helped Knowledge back to their car.

The back tires screamed and the trunk fish-tailed on the wet pavement as they made it out of the parking lot, and back onto the highway. For a moment, Messiah wasn't sure which way they were heading, but the lights of the city on the horizon told him all he needed to know as his breathing slowly returned to normal.

"Yo, them niggas though, they were live!" Knowledge laughed and grimaced at the same time. His fingers came away from his shoulder glistening.

"Don't laugh, don't laugh. I'ma take you to Jersey for the hospital," Messiah said.

Knowledge wasn't even listening. He had the coke book bag open. There were three packages, and he pulled one out, smearing the outside with his leaked blood as he ripped the plastic open.

One look, and he knew something was wrong.

"Ay yo," Knowledge started to say, but his voice trailed off in disbelief. He ripped opened one of the other packages and the smell that hit him was wrong. He tasted it then bust out laughing.

"What?!" Messiah barked, taking the ramp to the expressway and heading for Jersey.

"Goddamn cake mix, thun, cake mix!"

Then Messiah understood. While they were planning on robbing Pop, Pop was planning on robbing *them*. Now that was fuckin' majorly *uncalled* business. But deep down he had to admire their balls. Even if he had just shot them off.

"Them bitch ass niggas, word?" Messiah laughed.

Knowledge opened the book bag containing the money and began to pull the single big face that covered the rest of the stack, which was only paper cut to the size of money.

"Fuck them niggas! That's what they get for being on that bull-shit!" Knowledge cackled, forgetting they were on that bullshit too.

He tossed the cake mix out the window, heading towards Jersey.

Ring...ring...ring.

"Yo," Kane answered.

"What up, thun. Shit went left."

"Word thun? You good? Knowledge good?

"We in Jersey. He got hit. We out. One goin' down south, nah mean?"

"Indeed, thun. Be easy."

"Word, temperature risin'."

"Peace."

Click!

Bang! Bang! Bang!

"I'm coming! Wait!"

Bang! Bang! Bang!

"For the sake of Christ! I'm coming! Wha...who the..."

"You the doc?"

"It says Doctor on the sign doesn't it? Hey! Wait, you can't just…"

"You want me to shoot you in the face?"

"No."

"Then we're coming in."

———

Doc Simpkins wasn't used to stitching bullet wounds with a Colt sticking in his ear. His hands shook, and droplets of sweat bulbed on the end of his whiskey-red nose. The surgery light made the wound look sick and torn. Knowledge winced as Simpkins brought the two lips of the wound together and closed the hole.

The slug from Jay's gun lay squashed, gray and smeared with Knowledge's blood in a steel tray next to his ear. Messiah checked the clock on the wall and pushed the colt harder into the side of the Doc's head. "Better speed up, Doc, or they gonna be washing your brains off that wall."

"I'm going as fast as I can!"

"Go faster."

Messiah knew Pop and Jay's crew would already know about the turn-over and the corpses. They had to get away from the city as fast as if their asses were burning. This old, drunk of a Doctor had been their best bet, but bootleg docs were not easy to come by, and Pop's people would be here sooner or later to check out if Simpkins had been doing business with them.

Simpkins wound the last stitch around the forceps and cut the twine.

"You know Pop and Jay?"

Simpkins hands shook even more as he placed a wound pad on Knowledge's shoulder. "No, never heard of them," he said.

His hands were telling Messiah a whole other story.

———

"I gotta piss."

"We just stopped."

"I ain't have to piss then," Knowledge retorted.

"Man fuck that, I ain't stoppin' again," Messiah refused.

"Stop the fuckin' car, thun!" Knowledge sassed, wanting to smack the shit out of his brother.

"Yo, hold that shit. We dirty as fuck, we can't keep stoppin'. Piss out the window!"

"Stupid muhfucka," Knowledge spat back, wincing because of the pain in his shoulder, but he hung his dick out of the window all the same.

"Don't piss on the car," Messiah chuckled.

"Fuck yo' car," Knowledge spat back. He pissed on the car on purpose.

The deeper south they went, the hotter it got.

"Where we goin'? Hell?" Knowledge cursed, wiping the sweat from his brow and turning on the air conditioner.

The "Welcome to North Carolina" sign slapped a smile on Messiah's mug and had him feeling like he had crossed the finish line. He leaned the seat back a bump, lit a blunt, and put the car on cruise control.

Twenty minutes later they were headed towards Goldsboro on a back road surrounded by cotton fields. Messiah scanned the land in disbelief, watching a bunch of black people picking the crop as the sun came up.

"Yo, they still got slaves down here?" He asked, eyes wide.

Knowledge damn-near choked on the blunt, laughing hard.

"Yo thun, you dumb as fuck! Ain't no slaves no more!"

"Who the fuck else would pick that shit then?" Messiah countered, like it was obvious.

Knowledge just shook his head.

Then Knowledge howled. Messiah looked at him. "Yo pussy. You want more painkillers?"

Knowledge shook his head. "No man. Fuck! Look!"

Messiah followed Knowledge's finger down into the foot-well.

He was pointing at his sneakers. They were covered in Doc Simpkin's brains.

Messiah shrugged. Shouldn't have lied.

Back in QB, shit was shifty because the block was hot and the whispers was all about the double murder in the school parking lot. Cops were asking questions, but receiving few answers. The answers they did get couldn't be trusted because the snitches knew nothing.

Kane stayed off the radar as much as possible, but his name was too well-known for staying incognito for long.

"Up against the wall!" the police officer yelled, his hand hovering inches from his pistol.

Kane sucked his teeth and reluctantly complied with the order. One officer frisked him while the other kept his hand on his gun.

"What do you know about the murder at the school house?"

"What murder?" Kane replied, playing dumb.

"Don't fuckin' play with me, Kane. That's what they call you right?"

"Nah yo, you got the wrong man."

"Yeah, well word is you did it."

"Then why I ain't in jail?" Kane spat.

The officer grilled him hard. "Don't be smart. Be careful," the officer warned him, then slid off like a lizard.

Kane's phone vibrated and he looked at the screen. It was Messiah. He laughed, watching the police drive off.

"What's up, thun?" Messiah questioned.

"Shit fire, stay where you at. You good?"

"No doubt, yo that shit was a trip. I'll tell you about it later," Messiah laughed.

"One, thun," Kane chuckled, then disconnected the call.

Messiah hung up and then looked at Power. "Shit, hot."

"Figures. Fuck it, we good. Pass that shit," Knowledge replied, getting the blunt from his cousin, Lil' Earl.

"Yo, I'm glad y'all niggas came down here. It's mad money 'round heah," Lil' Earl said in a smooth, southern drawl.

They were relaxing at Lil' Earl's apartment, weed smoke filling the air.

"Word? Add on," Messiah urged him.

"Man, me and Ty be goin' all over robbin' niggas: Wilson, Raleigh, Rocky Mount. Ere' where."

"What's your heat like?" Knowledge questioned.

"Heavy. We got two techs, three nines, and a 38mm. But yo, we got a power move we schemin' on," Lil' Earl explained.

The brothers looked at each other like hungry wolves.

"Speak on it," Messiah told him.

Before Lil' Earl could answer, his girl Dee Dee came in the room. She was definitely a big girl, but she wore it well and knew it. She was heavy-chested, wearing a tight t-shirt and cutoff jeans that showed her thick, brown-sugar thighs.

"I need some money," she announced without introduction.

Lil' Earl looked at her in aggravation. "Bitch, don't you see we talkin'?"

"You wanna eat tonight, don't you?" she sassed, cutting her eyes at Messiah. He couldn't help but eye her thick, but well-shaped frame.

Lil' Earl grumbled, handing her some money. "I'ma smack the shit out of you."

Dee Dee kissed her teeth and then walked out, throwing her wide, but not very fat ass. She was definitely showing out.

"Now like I was sayin', the pawn shop," Lil' Earl said.

"The pawn shop?" Messiah echoed.

Lil' Earl nodded. "I'm tellin' you cuz, the shit sweet! See, down here a lot of pawn shops keep mad guns up in there. I'm talkin' about big shit, too! It's at least a thousand guns!"

The twins were damn near salivating. They knew guns in New York sold for a least $500 a piece, which made the lick $500,000.

"Where at?" Messiah asked.

"George Street."

"Nah, I mean where. Big Street, little street, what?"

"George a main street, but the back side is an old warehouse. It's perfect," Lil' Earl explained.

Messiah nodded. "Take us over there."

"We gotta holla at my man Ty."

"Why?"

"That's my man and he set up the lick," Lil' Earl replied.

That was the first time Messiah thought about murdering Tyrone. Five hundred grand between three people is a lot more than between four, especially when the fourth isn't family.

The twins had come to the same conclusion without a word passing between them.

"I feel you, thun. Let's meet the nigga," Knowledge suggested.

As they walked out, Lil' Earl asked, "What's thun, thun?"

Tyrone Bramwell was the epitome of a southern street nigga. Black as coal, but with Cherokee Indian wavy hair that had the bitches going crazy. He was a true hustler, and his gun bust crazy. The twins liked Tyrone from jump, but not enough to give him $125,000.

"Yo, Ty, what up? Meet my cousins from up top," Lil' Earl announced proudly as they stepped inside the pool room.

The others inside stopped and looked, too. The dudes were giving them standoffish grills, and the chicks were openly flirting.

Ty looked up from the pool table, mid-shot, a toothpick hanging from the corner of his mouth.

"Hol' up, cuz," he drawled, then proceeded to bank the nine ball into the side pocket.

He stood up and bopped smoothly over to them, clapping Lil' Earl's hand and giving him a gangsta hug.

"What up, players?" Ty greeted, dapping the twins.

"What up, thun," Messiah returned.

"Ain't nothin'. Yo, Lil' Earl said you a nigga we need to know," Knowledge added.

Ty smiled, revealing his gold tooth. "Straight to business, huh? Yeah, player, I like you already. Come on, let's dip and I'll tell you all about it."

When they got in the car, Messiah slid in the backseat with Lil' Earl behind Ty, while Knowledge drove. It was something they always did with a strange nigga in the car; never let him sit behind you.

"So what up, thun. Talk to me," Knowledge began as he drove.

Ty lit a cigarette.

"Make a right. I'ma let the situation speak for itself."

Three blocks later they were at the stop light across the street from the pawn shop. It sat at a major cross section, but the back side was bordered by an abandoned warehouse, just like Lil' Earl said it was, which gave them unlimited access to the rear—totally concealed from sight.

"Damn, that shit look sweet," Messiah admired. Ty smirked.

"It gets sweeter."

Knowledge pulled into the parking lot and then they all went inside. It was your average pawn shop, aisles and aisles of people's broken dreams, stolen goods and deferred plans. But once they reached the counter, Messiah saw the layout. The entire back wall was covered with guns. AK47s, MAC-11s, pumps, rifles, hand guns and shotguns. In one of the display cases there were enough pistols to make a man shed gangsta tears. Shit was heaven, for real.

"Yo, look at this shit!" Knowledge exclaimed, but he wasn't talking about a gun.

He didn't want the owner seeing them sweating the guns. He played it off and focused on the display case right beside it, filled with jewelry.

"Damn, look at that herringbone, yo," Messiah marveled, while cutting his eyes at the Desert Eagle .45 in the gun display.

"My man, how much for the bone?" Knowledge asked.

"Thousand," the salesman answered.

"That much? Fuck outta here."

Ty scanned the display case until his eyes stopped on a gold nugget ring.

"Now that's what I'm talkin' about," he smiled, loving the way the ring would look on his hand.

Messiah glanced over and chuckled. "Damn, thun, you on your eighties shit huh?"

"Nah cuz, shit like that never go outta style," Ty replied, slightly offended.

"Come on yo, let's get outta here," Lil' Earl suggested.

Once they were back in the car, Lil' Earl asked, "So what y'all niggas think?"

"It's nice, but I'm sayin', we runnin' up in there robbin' scrams or what? I know he packin'," Messiah surmised.

Ty chuckled like Messiah was missing the obvious.

"Nah, yo, we ain't goin' in the door; we goin' through the roof."

Knowledge cracked an evil grin and replied, "Yeah, I'm feelin' that. Damn, that's ill!"

"I told you my nigga had the ill lick," Lil' Earl nodded, lighting a blunt.

"It's like this. The roof ain't got no alarm system attached to it," Ty explained.

"How you know?" Messiah asked.

"We been on the roof banging hard cuz, no alarm," Lil' Earl affirmed.

"So why you ain't already make it happen?" Messiah probed.

"That's a million-dollar lick, yo, and I wasn't about to fuck it up. Once it's done we can't have the shit around here. We needed an up top connect we can trust," Ty told him.

"How many people know?" Knowledge asked. Ty looked at him like he had two heads. "Nobody. Believe me, ain't nothing slow about me but my walk."

Messiah gave him dap. "Yo, I'm feelin' you thun," he remarked truthfully, even though he was picturing his head with a bullet in it.

"So, when do we hit?" Knowledge inquired.

"Whenever y'all niggas ready," Ty responded.

"We need to lay low for a minute, but once shit cool off back in QB, it's on," Messiah told Ty.

Ty nodded. "Say no more. Now, let's show y'all 'Greensboro."

"Not tonight, yo. I'm tired as fuck," Messiah yawned.

"You soft as fuck," Knowledge teased.

"Fuck you, take me to Lil' Earl's crib," Messiah spat back, then laid his head on the rest and closed his eyes.

"New York...New York."

Those were the words Messiah heard as soon as he laid down. His brother and them had dropped him off at Lil' Earl's apartment in Seymour Homes. Having driven all the way from Queens Boro, he was tired as hell, but the soft female voice woke him right up.

"New York," Dee Dee repeated again, her southern accent making a mockery of the city's image.

"Yo," he croaked, without opening his eyes.

"You asleep?"

"Fuck it look like," he growled.

She sucked her teeth and fronted like his attitude wasn't making her pussy wet.

"Dag, you ain't gotta be like that. I just wanted to know if you hungry," she sassed.

"Nah," he hissed, then turned over on his stomach, thinking about pulling the pillow over his head.

There was a long pause, and Messiah could feel her eyes boring into the back of his head. Bitch wasn't leaving the room, no way no how, and that was confirmed when he felt the bed rock and shift as she sat down next to him. "What part of New York you from?"

Messiah was too aggravated to see the vibe Dee Dee was sending so flipped onto his back and spazzed. "Bitch, the fuck is wrong with you?"

It was already out his mouth before he saw that she was wearing nothing but a long t-shirt that clung to her voluptuous hips and her thick, juicy exposed thighs. She was country thick and she knew it. "You *mean*," she pouted.

Messiah had love for his little cousin, but he loved pussy more. Once his dick started getting hard, it was a wrap for family loyalty.

"Bitch, stand up."

"Huh?" she smirked, acting like she didn't understand the command, all while doing what he said.

"Take off your shirt," he told her, pulling out his long black dick. When Dee Dee saw all that dick in his hand, her mouth parted and she put the heel of her hand between her legs. It came away wet, and she showed it to him. Then she pulled her shirt over her head and stood there butt ass naked. Her titties sagged a little, but they were full and juicy with chocolate chip nipples.

"Damn, you got a big dick," she remarked, her country drawl like molasses poured over pure lust.

"Come 'ere. Let me see what that head's like," Messiah growled.

Dee Dee dropped to her knees between his legs. She ran her tongue up the full length of his shaft, then teased the head of his dick with the tip, worming it into the snake-eye and never taking her eyes off him once.

When he couldn't take it anymore, he grunted, "Eat that dick, bitch," while grabbing a handful of her weave and shoving himself down her throat.

She took it like a pro, deep throating him without even the hint of a gag, working her neck and lips until she had his toes curling.

Dee Dee was on her porn shit, sucking and slurping up his dick, but when she felt him about to bust, she sat up, waving a finger in his face.

Messiah understood, pulled her up by the hair, laid her flat onto the bed beside him, and rolled on top of her, taking her down through the groove made by her honey thighs, right into the wet warmth beneath. He started his plow slow until he got the depth, and then within thirty seconds he was smashing that pussy balls deep. Dee Dee brought up a knee, gripping the covers so that he could get in even harder. She moaned like she was singing a spiritual, and he knew right there Lil' Earl couldn't fuck her right because she was exploding and cumming all over his dick after only a few pumps.

"Goddamn, New York, get this pussy," she gasped, reaching back and holding her pussy lips open so he could go deeper.

Her pussy was the best Messiah had ever known. He was open as he long-dicked her until he couldn't hold it anymore, and he came deep inside of Dee Dee.

She collapsed on the bed.

"Damn, I needed that," she sighed contently. Messiah pulled up his pants and sat down beside her.

"You act like cuz don't be handlin' his biz."

Dee Dee sucked her teeth. "Shit, all he want to do is hang with that nigga Ty. Sometimes I think he fuckin' him," she huffed, then laid her head on his chest and added, "you gonna take me to New York wit' you?"

Messiah busted out laughing.

She propped up on her elbow. "What's so funny? I might be country, but I know I'm a bad bitch," she replied with a twist in her neck. She pulled him across her and sucked on his neck. Messiah wasn't used to a bitch making a move on him like this. He pushed her away and she flopped back on the sheets cupping her titties like she was offering him peaches. Messiah couldn't deny the fact that, despite her country thickness, she had definite potential. But still...

"Man, I don't love them hoes," he said, shrugging.

"Nigga, I ain't no ho, I'm a hustla."

"A hustla?"

"I know what y'all be doin' comin' down here and shit."

"What?" Messiah probed, just out of pure amusement.

"To rob niggas."

He laughed.

"Don't even try and lie, cause I know. Matter of fact, I know where somebody you can get right now," she told him, eyeing his reaction.

That got his attention. "Who?"

"Oh, you ain't laughin' no more, huh?"

"Bitch, don't play with me," he growled.

Smirking, she replied, "He live in Raleigh. His name is Peanut Wooten. He sell dope."

"Why Lil' Earl don't get him?"

"'Cause I ain't never tell Lil' Earl."

"Then why you tellin' me?"

Dee Dee pulled him down again, kissed his lips, looked him in the eye and replied, "'Cause I'm choosin'."

Right then Messiah knew he'd have to kill her. If he did this lick and left her behind, he knew she'd get in her feelings and probably tell the dude Peanut who robbed him.

"So you tryin' to be a nigga's Bonnie, huh?" he whispered coldly.

She nodded, her eyes gazing seductively into his.

Just the thought of a lick had Messiah's dick hard as a rock.

He pulled her on top and she gripped his dick and sat her down on it slow.

"Mmmm, goddamn Daddy, you tryin' to turn a bitch out," she moaned deliciously. Her creamy pussy made smacking sounds as she grinded on him hard. She leaned back, stretching her body out, leaning one hand behind her for balance, and putting the other behind her head, digging into her weave. She grinded down into his hips, circling like warm water draining from the bath.

What a waste, Messiah thought to himself, knowing what her destiny would be. He gripped her hips and started bouncing her on his dick.

"Oh, Daddy, right there. Right there, Daddy," Dee Dee breathed as she creamed.

Her pussy wouldn't stop gripping and shaking.

"I want to taste you," Dee Dee moaned, dismounting long enough to reposition and deep throat his big dick. It wasn't long before he was fucking her face again, then cumming all over her cheeks and chin."

"Goddamn, you a beast," he grunted.

"That's just the beginning. Let's get this money," she said, pulling him from the bed...

Peanut Wooten was one of the biggest dealers in the Raleigh-Durham area, plus his team wasn't to be fucked with. He let very few people near him, but he had one weakness—his family.

"What up, baby girl?" Peanut said as he opened the door letting Dee Dee and Messiah in.

"Hey Uncle Peanut," she sang, kissing him on the cheek.

Peanut looked at Messiah with suspicion, then turned his attention back to Dee Dee.

"So, what brings my favorite niece to see me? Let me guess, money," he laughed.

Dee Dee giggled and playfully hit him. "Like I can't come check on my Unk-Unk just because."

"Hmmm," he grinned skeptically, folding his arms across his chest.

"But a sister could use a grand or two," Dee Dee added. They laughed while Messiah only smirked.

Uncle? He thought to himself. Either this bitch cold-blooded or she dumber than a muhfucka. Peanut looked at Messiah again. "So, who's your friend?"

Dee Dee slid her arm through Messiah's. "Oh, I'm sorry Unk-Unk, this is my boyfriend Mark. Mark, this is my uncle Peanut."

Peanut shook Messiah's hand, looking him in the eye. "How you, Mark?"

"I'm good, yo. Nice to meet you,"

"Yeah," Peanut replied, coming up to his full height and leaving his arms swinging, but with fists balled. Messiah could see Peanut was someone who was ready to slam down if need be and was always ready for something out of leftfield. Peanut turned his attention back to Dee Dee. "Didn't I just give you a grand last week?"

She put her hands on her hips, one heel twisting on the wooden floor of the hallway, "To fix my car. Where Auntie at? You bein' *mean*."

Peanut pointed to the ceiling and so Dee Dee headed up the stairs, leaving an awkward silence in the hallway. Peanut led Messiah into the living room. The furniture was all white leather and there was a SONY TV like the size of a Cinema screen showing MMA with the sound off. A fifteen-thousand-dollar sound system crouched in one corner of the room like a robot from a Japanese space movie. Lights and dials were flickering. Peanut loved his input, Messiah surmised. Peanut turned to Messiah. "New York? Right?"

"Yeah," Messiah replied, feeling the weight of the gun he had tucked in the small of his back, and thinking about inputting lead into Peanut if shit got tricky.

Peanut nodded. "You like my niece?"

Messiah shrugged. "She cool."

"Don't hurt her," Peanut warned.

Messiah just smiled thinking, it's you who needs to worry. But before he could say anything, Dee Dee and Peanut's wife, Michelle, were coming down the stairs.

At first Messiah thought Michelle was laughing. Her face was contorted in an expression that defied context. It only took a second for Peanut to realize that Michelle wasn't laughing, she was crying. But by then, Messiah had his gun out and it was cold against the back of Peanut's head.

"What the—," Peanut started to say, but Messiah smacked him in the back of the head with the pistol. Peanut reeled, staggering as one leg almost gave way. Michelle still in her white bathrobe, pulled the material around her like it would protect her, and squealed as Peanut took another blow.

"Shut the fuck up and get on your knees!" Messiah barked. Dazed from the hit and already leaking from the head, Peanut dropped to his knees.

"B-b-babygirl!" Peanut stuttered, unable to believe his eyes.

Dee Dee shoved Michelle face first into the carpet, then aimed her gun an inch from Peanut's nose.

"Nigga don't Babygirl me! You think I forgot?! Huh? You think all them nights you were coming into my room, fucking my little pussy, that I'd forget? I was six, nigga, six! You know I can't have kids because you fucked my womb up?!" Dee Dee cried. Then, without warning shot Peanut in his thigh.

"Jesus fuck!" he grunted, falling on his face beside Michelle.

Messiah looked on in amazement. The situation had slid off the pile. Now he knew why she was so sharp to take Peanut's cash. Fuck, man. That was some serious sickness right there. It almost made him feel sorry enough for Dee Dee to let her live.

Almost.

Dee Dee squatted down and put the gun to Peanut's cheek. "Now you see I'm dead serious, right?"

"Y-y-yes," Peanut gasped, his whole-body creasing with the pain in his head and hole in his thigh.

"I'm only going to ask once. What's the combination?" Dee Dee said, with eyes flashing that she meant every word.

Peanut was silent.

Buck!

Dee Dee had shot Michelle in the hand. She screamed like a white bitch in a scary movie.

"I got four more to give, nigga. Where you want the next one?" Dee Dee hissed.

Goddamn this bitch gangsta, Messiah thought to himself. He was so caught up, he forgot he was involved for a second. "Hol' up, ma. I know how to make a nigga talk. Where they bedroom?" Messiah asked her.

"Upstairs, last room on the right" Dee Dee replied.

Messiah bounced up the stairs and disappeared into the shadows.

"B-b-babygirl! You ain't got to do this. I know I hurt you and I'm sorry. I-I'm a sick man. But if you leave now, we'll call it even," Peanut grimaced.

"Oh, I'm leavin' nigga, with every dime you got," Dee Dee laughed, then smacked Michelle so hard with the pistol she knocked a tooth out her mouth. Michelle flopped back onto the carpet like Dee Dee had when she had been on the bed with Messiah, but that's where the resemblance ended. Michelle's hand came up to her face without thinking, and the burnt edges of the bullet hole showed the gap in her teeth right through it. If it wasn't so crazy fucking serious, Dee Dee may have laughed her ass off.

"Oh my God! I-I didn't do nothin'!" Michelle cried, her hand and mouth drenching with blood.

"Shut up, bitch. I never liked your ol' high yella ass anyway!"

Messiah returned with a curling iron, jumping the last three stairs and skidding across the well varnished wood floor.

When Dee Dee saw the iron, she smiled. "I like the way you think, New York."

Peanut glanced up and saw Messiah, unplugging the TV. The

screen blinked out and Messiah plugged the curling iron into the socket. Peanut's eyes got as big as plates.

"Ay yo, please man!"

Messiah let out an evil cackle. "What's the goddamn combination?"

Peanut didn't answer. Dee Dee could see he still thought he could bluff his way out of this shit. "Yo, yo my neighbor. I know they heard those shots! They gonna call the police."

Messiah dragged Peanut close to the wall and snatched his pants down around his ankles.

"Hol' up, hol' up! The neighbors!" Peanut shrieked hysterically, but greed still wouldn't let him give up the combination.

By then the curling iron was heated up.

Messiah sat on Peanut's legs and without hesitation, plunged the red hot curler straight up his ass. Peanut let out a scream that would peel paint of a QB girder. It was so primal that Dee Dee rushed to cover his mouth with a pillow from the couch. But even the muffled scream bounced off the walls and rattled the teeth in her head.

When Messiah extracted the curling iron, the putrid smell of hot shit and blood instantly filled the room to a nauseating level. Green diarrhea ran from Peanut's ass like a cracked sewer.

"Nigga, talk!" Messiah demanded.

Peanut nodded his head and slapped the floor like a wrestler signaling submission. "It's...38...41...16," he confessed in a raw, hoarse whisper.

Messiah looked at Dee Dee and said, "I'll be right back."

"Okay, Daddy," she cooed, her southern drawl as sweet as syrup. "The safe's under the bed."

Messiah dashed back upstairs and into the master bedroom. He dropped to his knees but didn't see anything but shoe boxes. He swatted them aside, but it was obvious there was no safe.

He stood up and yelled, "Ain't no safe under the bed!"

"Lift the bed out of the way and move the carpet!" Dee Dee replied.

"Why that dumb bitch ain't say so in the first place?" he mumbled to himself as he snatched up the mattress and box spring. When he lifted the rug, a smile licked his face like a spark igniting a forest fire, as he stared at the enormous safe.

"Hell, yeah." he breathed.

Messiah got down and spun the dial to the tune of Peanut's agony: 38-41-16. When it opened, the smell of money kissed him in the face like a sleeping princess. He had never seen so much money at one time in his life. He knew it had to be over a million dollars easy.

"You got it, Daddy?!" Dee Dee yelled from downstairs.

"Yeah!" he hollered back, then the next thing he heard were shots.

Buck! Buck! Buck! Buck!

Messiah knew right then that she had killed Peanut and the bitch.

"Damn, she go hard," Messiah admired Dee Dee's steel, but there was no way she was leaving the house alive.

He heard her come up the stairs and enter the room. He was too busy putting more bundles of cash into pillow cases that he didn't notice her vibe until he felt cold metal against his temple.

Messiah froze.

"Nigga, the only reason I ain't gonna kill you is cause you got some good dick. Don't make me change my mind," Dee Dee spat with the grit of a female pitbull.

Messiah snarled but his fingers flexed uselessly. "Bitch, I counted four shots, plus the other two. She empty!"

"Mine is," she snickered. "But yours isn't."

Messiah had tossed his gun aside when he started bagging the money.

She had picked it up from the bed he had moved aside to get at the safe beneath.

"Nothin' beats the double cross but the triple cross, nigga," Dee Dee said triumphantly. "But I don't feel bad, because I know you were gonna do the same thing to me."

"Come on, ma. I was takin' you to the Boro with me," Messiah offered. A last roll of the bones.

"New York, I wasn't born last night. Trust me. Now. Hurry up and bag my money," Dee Dee ordered.

Messiah was seething, but he wasn't stupid. He had already seen what she was capable of, so he definitely wasn't about to try nothing. But if she slipped...

He put all the money in the bed sheet and knotted the top because it was too much to fit in the pillow cases. When he finished, he started to get up.

"No. Stay on the floor and strip."

"Strip?"

"Yes. New York. Strip. *Now* nigga."

He stopped at his boxers.

"Everything," she demanded. It was clear from her voice and face that she was enjoying the power she had over him. He stepped out of his boxers.

"Now drag the money downstairs. And New York, if you do anything stupid, I won't hesitate to drop you, got me?" Dee Dee warned.

Messiah was hot. He couldn't believe he was being robbed by a country bitch. He grabbed the money and began dragging it down the hall.

"Goddamn, ma, you could at least let a nigga get a couple grand," Messiah urged.

"I'll send it through UPS," she snickered.

He dragged the money down the stairs. The first thing he saw was Peanut's brains dripping from the curtains and Michelle's brains leaking all over the carpet. Dee Dee glanced at their bodies and whispered. "Good riddance."

Outside, Dee Dee popped the trunk and Messiah put the money in it, then turned to face her.

"Damn, New York. If looks could kill, I'd be one dead bitch, huh?" she laughed.

Messiah wanted to ice the bitch so bad but there was too much distance between them. He knew he'd never reach her before she shot him.

"You win this round," he stated, as Dee Dee got in the car.

"This round? Nigga, game over. Mwah!" She blew him a kiss as she backed out with the lick of all licks in her trunk.

The further she drove, the sicker Messiah got.

One million dollars...

———

When he got back to Goldsboro and told Lil' Earl, Knowledge and Tyrone, they laughed at him mercilessly.

"Yo, cuz. I shoulda warned you about that bitch," Lil' Earl said. "She been trying to get us to do the shit for months!"

"Why you ain't do it? That nigga had millions," Messiah stressed.

Lil' Earl shrugged. "All money ain't good money."

Messiah shook his head, still heated. "At least I got that nigga's Benz. I know I can get at least ten racks for choppin' it. But if I ever see that bitch again..."

PRESENT DAY

S pagoli sighed and paced. His frustration showing through like his sweat. He took off his tie and threw it on a chair. O'Brien was standing stock still, arms folded, with that unimpressed shit all over his face. "So, what's that got to do with the shooting at the club in Raleigh?" he asked.

Spagoli just rolled his eyes and looked at his watch. Did Spagoli make eyes at the one-way glass? He caught Spagoli's reflection in it over O'Brien's meaty shoulder.

He hit the cigarette, then exhaled slowly. "Everything."

"Meaning?" O'Brien uncrossed his arms and leaned on the table. He was trying to be menacing and failing.

When are these crackers gonna get it into their heads that he don't need to be scared into telling them everything he knew? He wanted to be there, but he wanted to do it in his own good time. He wanted to bring her out from behind the glass. He wanted to see her.

He flicked his ashes, then smiled slyly. "Let me ask you something, O'Brien. How many Q.B.C. shows are you familiar with on the tour?"

O'Brien shrugged. "Just the Raleigh one."

He laughed. "Then you've got a lot of work to do. Look up Baltimore, D.C., Richmond and Norfolk, Virginia. Then Charlotte, Greensboro—"

O'Brien impatiently cut him off. "What will I find?"

"Your answer."

"Don't be a smart ass."

"Bottom line? Every show has had a shooting incident, but ironically, no one ever gets shot. Do you know why?" he taunted.

"Why?"

"Because no one is being shot at. You see, police are against rap music in every city. They respond to any little incident with a strong show of force. Gotta keep the niggas in line, right?" He chuckled. O'Brien stared at him, unamused. Spagoli's back was still to him, hands deep in his pants pockets, looking at his shoes and rocking on his heels. *Go on, muhfucka. Look at her again, go on. I double dare you. I double fucking dare you.*

Spagoli kept looking at his shoes.

O'Brien's fingers snapped in his face, bringing him back to the matter in hand. Back on track. "Ok. I'm sure you agree in principal. My point is, when so many police show up in one place, it leaves a precious few for any other incidents, correct?"

O'Brien's eyes encouraged him on. He made the face you make when you're making the stupid kid in class feel even more stupid. "Every shooting was a decoy to get you pigs to come one way, while we did our dirt in another. Call it a head fake."

"What dirt?"

"Kane, pure and simple," he replied, looking O'Brien in the eyes. "Check for yourself. In every city Q.B.C. did a show, someone got murdered. Starting to get the picture now, cop?"

He smashed the cigarette in the ashtray while O'Brien wrapped his mind around what he had just said. At last, Spagoli turned around, his interest engaged for the first time in a while. His eyes drilled.

"So, who was murdered in Raleigh?" O'Brien probed.

He smiled. "Who else?"

FOUR YEARS EARLIER

Dee Dee had come up fast after the murder of her uncle. She used the money to buy several beauty supply stores and rental properties, but her biggest money maker was the legacy Peanut left behind. The dope game.

She didn't waste time either. She went to Peanut's funeral with the intention of meeting his connect. She wasn't disappointed. There was no mistaking who it was either, because she stood out like a diamond amongst glass. Her flawless skin tone looked dazzling against the black mourning dress she wore. She was also surrounded by three Colombian bodyguards who didn't blink.

Dee Dee approached her, offering her hand with tears in her eyes and her mascara running. "I want to thank you for coming to my uncle's funeral. I'm Dionna."

The vision smiled and took Dee Dee's hand. "I'm pleased to meet you after hearing so much about you. I'm Vanya."

Vanya put an arm around Dee Dee's shoulder as if it were the most natural move in the world, as if they'd been friends for a hundred years. Dee Dee liked the feeling of power it gave her. She had no idea it would be this easy to get in with Peanut's connection. She squeezed another couple of tears out, letting them sparkle on the end of her nose for a second before wiping them away with the handkerchief Vanya offered.

Dee Dee sniffed. "I—I miss him so much."

"As you should. You were his favorite niece," Vanya smiled.

"Will you be in town long?" Dee Dee probed. Vanya shook her head.

"Unfortunately, no. I only came to pay my respects."

"I see. Will there be a next time?" Dee Dee asked, pouring a little desperation over her expression. More tears at the corner of her eye. Wiping them quickly.

"Should there be?" Vanya quipped.

"After all, I'm my uncle's favorite niece."

Vanya smiled, telling Dee Dee that even at a funeral, she wasn't going to pass up a business opportunity. Greed always trumps grief...

Vanya looked at her watch. "My plane leaves in an hour. Perhaps you could ride with me to the airport," Vanya offered.

Dee Dee smiled inside. Exactly what she'd been fishing for. "Whenever you're ready."

In the Maybach Landaulet, Vanya didn't waste time getting to the point. "What makes you think you can fill your uncle's shoes?"

Dee Dee had prepared herself. "I learned from the best. I know his people, I know his moves, and I know the whole nine." This wasn't totally true, but Vanya wouldn't know the reality. Dee Dee had a fair handle on the score and was learning fast.

Vanya leaned in and wiped the residue of tears from Dee Dee's cheek with a soft stroke of her hand.

There was an expression on the beautiful woman's face that Dee Dee couldn't read. There were complex considerations going on behind her eyes, and for a heart-stopping second Dee Dee thought she'd overplayed her hand and that Vanya was going to tell her she was already considering business with Peanut's rivals.

But when the tears had dried, Vanya leaned in and put a gentle kiss on Dee Dee's lips.

"I have authority to make this deal, so please never make me regret using that authority. The ignominious end your Uncle suffered will be nothing compared to the agonies that will be visited upon you if you do. Is that clear?"

Dee Dee nodded, and for the first time today, she felt like crying for real.

The car pulled into the airport and the waters closed over Dee Dee's head.

DOWNTIME

P ower rubbed Egypt's back, she slowly relaxed and then embraced him. "What's the matter, ma?" Power inquired, hoping she would trust him enough to open up.

They were in the cabin of a yacht cutting through the serene blue waves of the Mediterranean. Duppy had charted the yacht for a day of downtime between TV appearances in Rome. Power picked some crystals of ice from the champagne bucket and crunched down on them between his teeth. It was hotter than a bad NYC summer. The sun was beating through the portholes, making the white sheets blaze like a thousand headaches. The ice cooled his mouth and soothed him.

"I'm...I'm okay," Egypt said, taking a deep breath. He could see the machinery working behind her face, trying to get her composure back.

"When you gonna trust me?" Power asked, watching her get dressed. By the time her blood red t-shirt was on and her white skirt wrapped around her waist, she looked a whole lot more composed.

"When you trust *me*," she said, running her fingers through her hair. "Seems like we've had this conversation before."

"Yeah, it does."

She checked herself in the mirror and Power saw her eyeing him in the reflection.

"I know who set you up," she said simply. Still messing with her hair in the silvered glass.

Power sat up, putting the champagne bottle down that was just about to make a journey to his lips. The bottle slipped in the bucket, the neck shifted at an angle and the golden liquid started to dribble onto the carpet. Power didn't give a fuck. "And you just *now* tellin' me?" He fizzed, vexation in his tone.

Egypt turned from the mirror "I'm trying to trust you."

Power was hot with anger, no amount of ice or champagne was going to cool him now. He got off the bed and looked through the gold rimmed porthole. The sea ran to the blue horizon as wide and deep as his displeasure. The hot sparkles of sunlight burned like the rage building in his gut. And then Egypt dropped the A-Bomb.

"C-Allah."

Power crashed his fist against the wood by the porthole, cracking the varnished pine of the wall. Blood welled on his knuckles, but he ignored it. "That bitch ass nigga did what?!"

"He wasn't trying to kill you. He feels like you didn't break bread when you blew up," she broke it down to him.

If anything, this made it worse for Power. Those niggas almost shot his brains out by accident. "I'ma show this nigga. Fuckin' coward ass nigga. Why you tellin' me?"

Egypt stopped at the door and looked back. "The Colombian," she replied, then walked out.

Egypt walked out of the cabin with a cold streak going down her spine. In her mind, she was back in her parents' house, the smell of blood and beer making her memory nauseous. She walked up the stairs to the helicopter pad on top of the yacht.

"Are you okay, Miss Powell?" her bodyguard asked.

"Fine," she replied, putting on her oversized Chanel shades.

Egypt looked out over the azure waters of the Mediterranean to where there was a hint of Italy in the distance. Downtime was over. More interviews and TV studios awaited.

Game face: ON.

The steady beat of the helicopter's rotors blew a breath of sea air all over her aching senses. She knew the information she'd given to Power would be acted on. She'd argued with herself for days after Vanya told her about C-Allah ordering the non-hit on Power and Kane. She wondered if she'd been used, wondered if The Colombian was testing her too; did he want to make sure the information got to Power, or did he want to know if she'd keep it from him? She couldn't exactly ask, so she went with her heart. She knew C-Allah would suffer for what he did, but even now she couldn't put up with the idea of Power being in that kind of danger. So, to hell with the consequences.

Game face on. For real.

"Yes...I'm just fine," she added under her breath, then climbed into the helicopter.

Power watched her fly off until he lost sight of the helicopter over the mainland. The sun was slanting towards the horizon and the late afternoon on the yacht, still hotter than Hades, at least promised a cooler evening in the lengthening shadows. That coolness outside wouldn't be matched inside him until he'd dealt with the information Egypt had given him.

It was in that moment he realized his feelings were falling into place. *I'm falling in love with her*, he thought to himself, then picked up the yellow satellite phone and stabbed in Kane's number back in NYC.

"Yo," Kane answered.

"I know who pushed that button."

TWO DAYS LATER

C-Allah cut through the Brooklyn traffic, weaving in and out, New York style. The sounds of hip-hop music pumped loudly through the speakers. He had been home for over a year and had hit the streets running. He was already moving heavy weight in Pittsburgh, PA and Columbus, Ohio.

He glanced over at the bad bitch in his passenger seat. Thin, but with a woman's shaping, and titties like the freshest fruit. Her skin was a golden-brown, like it couldn't make up its mind what it wanted to be, and this idea was carried through to her almost Asian eyes. Her head was topped with cornrow braids that curled like a snake across her scalp, down her neck and shoulders like a question mark. Her mouth was full and red. She looked like she'd been put together from five beautiful women and one skin.

It was crazy, he had met her before at Junior's—a spot he hit up religiously. She was sitting in a booth with another dude, but she kept giving him the eye when her man would turn his head. When her man got up to go to the bathroom, she waited until he was gone then slid over to C-Allah's table.

"You like cheesecake I see," she flirted.

"My favorite, "C-Allah replied.

"I taste delicious on top," she winked, dropped her number on a napkin and went back to her table giving C-Allah a full view of her juicy, two-melon ass.

Later that night, he called, and he found out her name was Cherry, which she said, "is why I taste so good with cheesecake."

"When I'ma find out?" he asked, feeling the stirring in his pants already.

"Whenever you want."

"Tomorrow night. I got a spot we can go to," he told her, and hung up with Cherry on his mind, draining the blood from his brain to somewhere more primal.

C-Allah's phone rang, but since he was driving, he put the call on speaker, smiling to himself when he heard Power's "Yo."

"What up, God?" C-Allah greeted him.

Power didn't answer straight away. The silence filled the car, and when Power eventually did speak, the temperature in his voice dropped below zero. "So that's how we do now? You really think it's that easy?"

Power's stiletto words sliced out through the speakers.

C-Allah laughed, but even to his ears it didn't sound authentic. He bit down and fronted. "I see you got my message."

"Nah, but you will get mine."

Cherry was asleep in the passenger seat, her breathing slow and regular, a pulse moving in her neck. At least she wasn't seeing C-Allah looking unsure. Power would pay for this. Pay for this hard. C-Allah got his voice under control. "Be easy, kid. If I wanted you dead, you would be. You just needed to be disciplined. You forgot who put you on? You runnin' all over the world, goin' platinum and shit, but you don't break bread? That ain't a good look," he said.

"I don't owe you shit. You introduced me. No more, no less," Power spat.

"Look kid, shit is real, aight? It's deeper than what you know. You never heard of True Allah?"

"Nah"

C-Allah spun the dials of the possible combinations to unlock this situation in his head. He looked around through every window. If there was a van heading his way about to spit the lead of retaliation, he was gonna be ready. He had a MAC-11 in the Benz' glove box. He thought about getting it out, but the noise of doing so might wake Cherry and he didn't need a bitch asking awkward questions in his ears right now. The road around the Benz contained the normal mix of cars, taxis and buses. Nothing out of the ordinary at all. C-Allah relaxed a little. There wasn't a drive-by about to develop.

The spinning tumblers in his head settled on a stab at appealing to Power's better gangsta...time for a bit of truth.

"Ask your man Kane. True Allah was my brother. Your man Kane killed him, yo. I've been wanting to get at that nigga for years! When you told me you were from QB and Kane was your man, I knew I could use you to get to him. But in the flow of things, I came to see you was a good dude. When I hooked you up with Duppy, I ain't expect you to blow like this. But shit ain't change. Your man gotta go. So this the deal. Since I fuck with you, God, fall back and let me handle my business wit' scrams. I'll let you live. Then boom, you'll eat heavy 'cause you'll be sold. It's a win-win. Or, you could die wit' your man," C-Allah explained.

If he'd read the situation right, Power would take the line of least resistance. He wouldn't want a war. He'd let Kane go by painting himself into the bigger picture.

But...

Power's laughter filled the car in surround sound. He laughed long and hard. He laughed until it irked C-Allah's nerves. He didn't care if he woke Cherry now. Fuck this shit. He'd done his best to help Power out here, but there was no return of respect. "You, you might laugh now kid, but on some real shit, you coulda been dead!"

Cherry was stirring now. C-Allah could see her rubbing her eyes out of the corner of his own.

"When them shooters came through, I told 'em not to hurt

you. I only wanted to scare you. I spared you nigga, laugh at that!" C-Allah spat as he pulled into the parking lot of his hideaway condo.

"You right, God. I did notice that you had me and Kane. We was slippin', I'll give you that, but you only get one shot."

"The God moves in mysterious ways."

"I couldn't agree more. Let me ask you something, you like cherries?" Power asked.

"Cherries?" C-Allah repeated, his fact a confused scowl. "What's that—?"

That was all he got out before Cherry put the gun to his head and growled, "Don't move."

C-Allah damn near shitted himself. Ice water dumped itself from his head down his spine and he had to force himself not to let his hands come off the wheel. Cherry reached her long leg out of her foot-well and placed her toes on top of C-Allah's, pushing them down on the brake pedal. The Benz slowed to a crawl. Cherry pushed C-Allah's hand on the wheel towards the off ramp.

"Mysterious, indeed," Power chuckled. "That's always been your weakness, God. Now it's gonna cost you your life."

The Benz came to the junction, Cherry indicated left and there was a deserted parking lot in front of a closed down liquor store. C-Allah half expected Power to be there waiting, holding his gun, ready for the end game. But there was nothing and no one there. The parking lot was windswept but empty. Even the streetlights near it, those that were working, seemed to have turn their backs on it. It was a dead space.

Well chosen.

"It wasn't just me!" C-Allah bust out. "Duppy supplied the shooters!"

"He'll be dealt with, too."

Buck! Buck!

Cherry put two bullets in C-Allah's brains, painting the dashboard, windshield and driver's side window a crazy shade of spaghetti red.

She hopped out of the car just as the SUV that had been tracking C-Allah the whole time skidded up. She jumped in and left the scene, looking back on C-Allah's body for the last time.

"Point blank range from inside the car. Clean hit," O'Brien stated as he and Spagoli stood in the open door of C-Allah's Benz, staring at the open-eyed death stare and blown-open head.

Police lights and yellow tape surrounded the car, while police and forensic technicians worked the area over. The thin grey daylight hadn't brought any respite to the wind that blew over the parking lot. Some sheets of newspaper had blown across concrete and caught on Spagoli's legs and flapped there like seagulls. He kicked them away onto the freshening breeze.

"We got a name?" Spagoli inquired.

"C-Allah Madison," O'Brien replied.

Spagoli walked around the car, wishing he'd brought a warmer jacket. Clouds were coming off the Atlantic, and although the day might warm up later, this soon after dawn, the East River was sending icy blasts across this part of town. Spagoli nodded and the breeze moved though C-Allah's car and ruffled the surface of his blood-spattered shirt. "I agree with you. This was a hit, but for whom?"

"Good question."

A short, stocky female detective walked up to Spagoli and O'Brien carrying a manila folder.

"Detectives. I thought you'd be interested in this" she announced as she handed it to Spagoli.

"What is it?" he asked, flipping it open.

"C-Allah Madison's phone records for the past three months. The number I highlighted should be familiar," she pointed out.

Spagoli scanned the page. It seemed as if every sixth call was the same highlighted number. He looked at the name.

"Paul Duppy?" he read aloud, his tone colored with confusion.

She smirked. "You must be getting old, detective. Duppy is one of the biggest names in rap."

"I'm a Springsteen fan myself. What does this Duppy do?" Spagoli inquired.

"He owns a major record label. His biggest acts are Q.B.C. and a singer called Egypt," she explained.

"Spoken like a true fan," O'Brien quipped.

"Please, R&B died with Whitney Houston," she returned, then walked away.

"Q.B.C....Q.B.C....where have we heard that before?" O'Brien pondered, looking at the phone records over Spagoli's shoulder.

Spagoli thought for a minute, then answered, "The Queens Boro cop murder...Officer named Boyd."

"And our old friend Jason Mitchell."

"Fine, let's pay this Duppy character a visit," Spagoli suggested. O'Brien nodded, then they walked off, leaving C-Allah's body staring off into eternity.

Running.

That's what Duppy was doing, not only physically, but mentally — his mind was always running. It never stopped, which meant he never stopped. His legs pumped like pistons as he jogged through Central Park. Anyone seeing a black man jogging in the park may assume he had stolen something, but the only thing Duppy had stolen was his own destiny out of the ghetto fate that society had waiting for him.

He stopped running but jogged on the spot, checking his phone to see if C-Allah had returned his calls. Nigga had been off the grid for sixteen hours now. Duppy wanted in on C-Allah's Ohio slice, and was willing to parlay with him. It was an expensive business trying to impress The Colombian, but he was willing to go deep wit' C-Allah, possibly fronting a lot of cash as a buy in. If he pulled it off and gave The Colombian a new profit stream,

Duppy could see the future would be a lot brighter for all of them and Duppy in particular.

But that muhfucka C-Allah was not picking up his phone. Maybe even not picking up his messages.

Duppy imagined C-Allah balls deep in a hotel room sniffing a line off some other finely tooled piece of ass. He looked at the overcast sky over Central park, the branches of the trees waving in the stiff breeze and a billion New Yorker's paying him no heed whatsoever. To them he was just another nigga in a tracksuit.

Duppy felt suddenly stupid. He looked around to see if anyone in the park was seeing him look stupid. And again, he might as well have been invisible.

Don't you muhfuckas know who I am?

He should be snorting a line off a beautiful ass, not bouncing up and down like a field nigga running from the overseer.

Duppy took off his sweatband and walked back to his car.

Fuck C-Allah. Fuck them all to hell.

TWENTY YEARS EARLIER

Paul Duppy was born and raised in Jersey City, New Jersey's Duncan Projects. His father was a handyman and his mother a cook at a local diner. He was a good kid in a bad situation because Duncan wasn't kind to good kids. It ate them up and spit out corpses or killers—doers or the dead. But Duppy was an exception because he was a born entertainer. He could sing, rap and dance, the latter of which he was especially good at. His moves drove the girls crazy. He owned the dance floor at any club or house party.

"Go Duppy! Go Duppy! Go Duppy!" the crowd would change, urging him on. And he fell in love with the roar of the crowds.

He went on to form his own group with another dude named Bruce and a female named Tatiana. Duppy and Tatiana rapped while Bruce sang. Duppy would choreograph their routines and every talent show they entered they won.

"Go Duppy! Go Duppy! Go Duppy!" He got used to the attention, even came to expect it.

Then one day...

"Yo, you cats are nice. I'm David Elms, A&R for Vodka & Milk Records! Give me a call!" a man told them, handing them a business card.

They were all excited.

Duppy was more a dancer and occasional rapper than Tatiana and Bruce. They were the lyric gods, but he could freestyle. And if they gave him lines, he could hold more than his own in the routines.

They'd just come off stage and the Vodka & Milk guy met them on the stairs before they made it back to the dressing room. Duppy remembered his face from the crowd. He had been loving the show, leaning on the back wall looking impressed, writing into a notebook, whispering into the ear of some crazy looking Cuban bitch. All hair and ass. But as they'd come off to the cheers from the dark club behind, the A&R man had met them alone. He'd fed them a bunch of authentic sounding compliments, talked meetings, getting back to them in the morning — and shouting *great look!* — at Tatiana.

"Vodka & Milk!" Bruce exclaimed, looking at the business card snatched from Duppy's fingers, trying to X-ray the money out of it. Vodka & Milk was the hottest label on the scene, and to get even a sniff of their farts was a big deal. But a meeting? This was a big deal thing.

"We about to blow!" Tatiana squealed, hugging Duppy tightly.

It was a heavy moment for Duppy, because once people found out about the Vodka & Milk connect, he knew these kids were heading for great things.

Especially D-Praved.

Shameek was a drug dealer, a middle of the food chain type hunter in the urban ecosystem. He was too big to be ignored, but not big enough to carry weight. He looked to Duppy's group to change all of that.

"You need a manager," Shameek told the three of them, catching them in the parking lot of White Castle as they walked out.

"Nah, we good," Bruce responded.

"That wasn't a question," Shameek returned firmly, looking Bruce in the eye.

Bruce dropped his head.

This is going to be sweet, Shameek thought to himself, because he knew Bruce and Duppy weren't street niggas.

Deep down, Duppy *wanted* to be a street nigga.

He loved the way they moved through the hood like dangerous, sleek sharks in a world of piranhas. The way their names rang bells and bitches were at their beck and call, because truth be told, the females at the clubs and all the house parties may have been yelling, "Go Duppy!" but they left with G's: Gangstas. Gorillas. Ghetto Gods. Duppy wanted *that* life, because it's a quirk in a man's nature to want what he can't have.

But Duppy was no fool, either. He knew Shameek wasn't a big name in the hood. He wasn't a gangsta; he was a thug. That meant he was tough, but not smart. Duppy knew Shameek only wanted a free ride while he and his crew did all the work.

"We already have a manager," Duppy announced to Shameek when he tried his shit again a week later at another club before they went on to do their set. The news of the Vodka & Milk interest was spreading faster than rats in a flooded basement, and those rats were surfacing all over town.

"Who?" Shameek spat back, with an incredulous chuckle. Duppy knew that hungry look on his face, planning to scare off whoever the manager was and take the spoils for himself.

This might be a problem for Duppy. There was no manager. He booked the clubs and greased palms, making up for the fact that he wasn't the most talented in the act by taking on the extra responsibility, but now he might have to find a real manager – someone Shameek couldn't scare easily. So, he reasoned, if he was going to lie, he might as well make it a big lie. The biggest.

"Wadoo," Duppy replied, straightening his face for maximum truth.

The look on his mug was like the sound of brakes being hit in a cartoon. Wadoo's name definitely rang bells like large cathedrals on Catholic Sunday. Wadoo wasn't only at the top of the food chain, he *ran* the food chain.

Play fair and you ate, but if you got on his wrong side, you were on the plate to be eaten.

It was almost a bullet proof lie.

Almost...

Shameek now knew there'd be no smacking up. Duppy imagined Shameek apologizing to the image of Wadoo for even thinking about smacking one of his acts up.

"Wadoo?" Shameek echoed, trying to hold his composure.

But Duppy heard his voice crack. "Yeah. Wadoo."

"Fuck outta here. Wadoo don't even know you little niggas. That's my man, all I gotta do is ask him," Shameek fronted.

But Duppy's lie had a built-in failsafe. He knew a man like Wadoo would never speak to Shameek, unless Shameek had cleaned his shoes and Wadoo was thanking him with a tip.

"Ask him," he said with a shrug, daring Shameek to do what he knew he couldn't.

Shameek's eyes wanted to smack the smirk off of Duppy's face, but Duppy was cool enough not to show the lie.

"I will, lil' nigga. I will. And if I find out you're lyin'..." Shameek warned, deliberately not making a threat just in case shit was real.

"You do that, my nigga. And hey, no hard feelings," Duppy winked as Shameek got in his car.

Shameek eyed him like a hungry grizzly, deterred by an army of park rangers. He got in his car and drove off.

Bruce turned to Duppy and spazzed.

"Duppy, what the fuck was that?! Wadoo ain't our manager. He don't even know we exist!"

"He knows," Duppy replied calmly, the confidence he'd come to be known for showing its arrogant head. Inside he was anything but, but he wasn't giving that away to someone like Bruce. If he could front on Shameek, Bruce wouldn't even blip the radar. He was talented, but really had no idea about the realities of their situation. Duppy's mind was racing at a zillion miles an hour.

The lie about Wadoo was out in the wild now. He would have to do whatever it took to either make it a reality or make sure Shameek never got to discuss it with the gangsta. The lie was Duppy's. He didn't need any of this shit from Bruce, but he was getting it anyway.

"All I gotta do is ask him."

"But what if he says no?" Tatiana probed, because she could see Duppy's logic.

"He won't," Duppy assured her, already trying to formulate a plan.

Bruce shook his head. "Even if he does, which he damn sure ain't, I don't want to be in business with a dude like that, Duppy. That muhfucka had Rico and them murdered last year for selling in Kerry Woods," Bruce objected.

"Yo B, the industry is full of cats like that," Duppy returned.

"Yeah, but Wadoo will own us. Fuck that, I ain't wit' it."

"So, what you sayin' Bruce?" Duppy questioned.

"Just what I said. I want to be an *entertainer*, not some thug's puppet! We go to Vodka & Milk and get a deal, cool. But if you plannin' on going to Wadoo—"

"Bruce, you heard what Shameek just said. If we don't go to Wadoo, Shameek is still going to extort us. Wadoo don't need to play us. Who knows, he may even help us," Tatiana reasoned.

"Yeah, yo, I guess you're right," Bruce sighed with resignation. "This is too much for me. I'm out."

Bruce turned and walked away.

"Bruce!" Tatiana called out.

"Let him go. Fuck that, we don't need him, yo," Duppy said, knowing that they certainly needed Bruce's lyrics. He'd worry about Bruce later. There were bigger problems to fix first.

"Vodka & Milk Records wants us as a group. We can't blow this chance," Tatiana pleaded. Duppy gave her a hug.

"Don't sweat it, baby girl. We'll still make it. I'ma holla at Wadoo. He'll hold us down," Duppy assured her.

"Okay," she sniffed.

Duppy's dream of being a star died that day, but his reality of making stars would be born that night.

CLUB HYSTERIA

It was the biggest club in Jersey City. Housed in an old warehouse, it was huge, almost the size of a football field. Everybody who was anybody partied there, from ballplayers to real ballers. The parking lot was almost cleaner than an exotic car dealership. Everything was $100,000 or more. The stars were out, and Wadoo ran it all.

Wadoo wasn't only big in the game, he was a big dude. An ex-boxer, he parlayed his Vegas connection with the mob into a connect with their heroin pipeline. He never looked back. He came home to Jersey and proceeded to put together a team with a reach as far as Baltimore.

"Peace, beloved," Wadoo greeted a celebrity as he entered the VIP area.

Everybody knew Wadoo, and he was about to meet one more celebrity.

The line outside wrapped around the corner as a stretch, cocaine-white Maybach pulled up to the front entrance. All eyes were on the Maybach door as the driver walked around and opened it. Out stepped a navy-blue Gator boot followed by the other, worn by none-other than Duppy.

He stepped out in a rented Armani suit, dripping with fake diamonds on his ring finger, ears and wrists. He looked like a million bucks even though he was flat broke. He had spent his last dime on a Maybach, suit and Tatiana, who stepped out in a Versace dress that was as bootleg as Duppy's diamonds. But she looked too good for anyone to notice. Her resemblance to Halle Berry was so uncanny, people in line thought that was who she was—a fact that Duppy planned to use to his advantage.

"We love you, Halle!"

"Let me get your autograph, Halle!"

The crowd yelled out. Tatiana smiled and waved.

"Are you sure this is going to work?" she asked through clenched teeth.

"It already is," Duppy offered. His confidence shifted from *steal it* to *king it* until he made it at almost every step. His plan was crazy, but it had merit. The thing that would kill it stone dead however, had nothing to do with Wadoo, and everything to getting in the front door. Once inside, the plan could pretty much take care of itself.

Getting inside Club Hysteria was the *hard* part.

Duppy and Tatiana stepped up to the entrance rope. If the bouncer knew they existed, he didn't offer even a flicker, let alone remove the red velvet rope from where it was clipped to a gold post.

Duppy cleared his throat. *Come on muhfucka. Come the fuck on.*

"You ain't on the list," the bouncer's mouth was as unyielding as the arms folded over his massive chest.

"You ain't even check," Duppy responded.

"I don't need to, I know. Kick rocks!"

"Yo, you talk to Wadoo nephew like that?! You got a lotta balls! Where that nigga at? Tell him Duppy out here and I bet he smack the shit out of you for disrespecting me!"

The flex in the bouncer's jaw and the tick in his neck told Duppy he was not ready to go to ask. But Duppy knew this was his only chance so he held his ground.

"My man, if you knew like I know, you'd get the fuck outta my face," the bouncer growled.

But Duppy shot right back, "If you knew like I know, you'd take your big ass in there and tell Wadoo his fuckin' family out here! The same nephew he expectin'!"

The bouncer grilled Duppy, and Duppy grilled him right back. They eye-boxed each other for a few moments, then the bouncer said, "You better be who you say you are because if you ain't—"

"I am," Duppy cut him off arrogantly.

The bouncer unhooked the rope. "Come on."

Tatiana stepped through first, followed by Duppy. As soon as he stepped inside and saw the famous, the infamous, and the notorious rubbing elbows and popping bottles, he knew he was home. There was no way he wasn't going to live this life.

"You see what I see?" he whispered to Tatiana under the music.

"What?"

"The future," he smiled.

They entered VIP to find Wadoo with a bad bitch on both sides of him, and another bad bitch sitting next to the chill as shit NBA player Brandon Christopher. Wadoo looked up as the bodyguard approached with Duppy. A slight frown creased his brow.

"Hey boss, this kid claims he's your nephew," the bodyguard spat, grilling Duppy hard.

"Nephew?" Wadoo laughed. "Nah."

The bodyguard grabbed Duppy so hard by the collar, he damn near lifted him off his feet with one hand. Tatiana let out a slight yelp.

"What I tell your ass?!" the bodyguard bassed.

"Yo, Wadoo! All I need is five minutes! Five, I swear!" Duppy yelled as if his life depended on it, because quite frankly, it did.

Wadoo eyed him with an amused expression and glanced at Brandon. "What do you think?"

Brandon shrugged. "Hear him out."

"Okay. Bo, let him go," Wadoo said. Reluctantly, Bo did as he was told.

"My name is Duppy, and this is my partner Tatiana. We're—"

"I know who you are. You've been winning all the talent shows around J.C. I thought it was three of you?" Wadoo inquired.

Duppy felt ten feet tall when Wadoo said he knew them. "It was. We're all that's left, but we're all we need. We're gonna put J.C. on the map," Duppy announced proudly.

Wadoo nodded. "Congratulations. But what's that got to do with me? And keep in mind you've got about a minute left."

"The next Michael Jackson is living right under your nose and I'm going to find them for you," Duppy stated confidently.

"I thought you were a rapper?"

"Nah, I'm a producer."

Wadoo nodded, then sipped his drink. "You know if I say no, my man Bo is gonna take you out back and beat the shit out of you for wasting my time, right?"

Bo looked at Duppy and flexed his neck, getting loose for the ass whooping he was itching to deliver.

"I know."

"And you lied anyway, saying you were my nephew."

"How else was I going to get to you?" Duppy smirked.

"Tell you what...I'm going to see what you're made of. See if you got what it takes. If you bomb, Bo's gonna keep that ass kicking in his back pocket just in case," Wadoo explained.

Bo patted his pocket.

"Got it right here, boss," he chuckled. Duppy made a fist and spanked his own hand. *Yes indeed!* Duppy could see that despite his better judgment, Bo the bouncer liked him too.

"I appreciate that...Unk," Duppy winked.

Out of the corner of his eye, Duppy saw Shameek on the other side of the velvet rope.

"Yo 'meek! What up? Come here real quick," Duppy called out.

Shameek's eyes got big as soccer balls seeing Duppy with Wadoo. His face was a complex mix of stay or go. In the end, his move was decided for him when Wadoo's eyes brushed him from across the club. Now he had no choice. Duppy laughed to himself.

"Come on," Duppy repeated, then turned to Wadoo "That's my man right there. Can he enjoy this moment with me?"

Wadoo laughed. "Sure, why not?"

The bouncer let Shameek into VIP.

"Wadoo, this Shameek, better known as D-Praved. D, this Wadoo," Duppy introduced like he knew Wadoo for years.

Shameek replied, "P-peace Wa."

Wadoo nodded, seeing Shameek was star struck. Duppy gave Shameek a hug then whispered in his ear, "No hard feelings, my nigga. Holla at me, I got a job for you."

Shameek was thrown by the offer at first, but when he found out Duppy was serious, he became one of Duppy's most loyal label execs, rappers and goons.

TWELVE YEARS LATER

"If you can call this livin'," Egypt's Uncle Joe spat with disgust. They were under an elevated section of the L.I.E. fires burned in oil drums. In the dust and garbage there were knots of homeless bums, like walking piles of rags. Even though there were seven or eight guys there, none of them were interested in anything other than themselves. Not one was near enough to talk to anyone else. They all sat yards apart in their own island worlds of addiction or mental infirmity.

Egypt looked around, her emotions as silent as the calm, grey skies.

Joe looked at her and said, "Pick one."

"For what?"

"Just pick one."

Egypt stared at the human wreckage. She could have picked any one, they were all washed up trash, and there wasn't much to tell them apart. Finally, she settled on a fat white hobo sitting against a freeway pillar. His face was ruddy in the firelight, his eyes dead, his mouth moving like he was sending prayers to himself. The homeless bum shifted his ass on the dusty ground and looked straight through Egypt as if she wasn't there.

"Him."

"Okay," was all Joe replied, then began to approach the man with Egypt in tow.

The bum watched them walk up. His dead eyes began to show signs of life as they approached, and he held out a grubby hand, covered with a fingerless glove.

"Spare a dime?" he croaked, his voice sounding as gritty as broken glass. Egypt could smell him now. The tang on the still air was of rotting flesh and thousand-year-old sweat.

Joe ignored his request, looked at Egypt and asked, "Does he deserve to live?"

Egypt was confused.

Joe had told her nothing about why he had brought her here. He'd just said to get in the car and come for a ride. The journey out of the city had been a one-sided conversation. Egypt listened and Joe talked about the business. Since the murder of her parents, Uncle Joe had taken over moving the heroin from supplier to the streets. It had been a business her Daddy had built and ultimately died for. No one had been found responsible for her parents' deaths, but Joe and his crew hadn't given up looking. Now Egypt was seventeen, and it was time for her to see if she had what it took to join the family crew for real. Egypt didn't know if she had it in her to deal drugs and run pushing teams, but if it made it more likely she would find her parents' killers, then she was better inside the crew than out of it. But how did she get into it? She guessed that Uncle Joe was showing her tonight.

"Does he deserve to live?" Uncle Joe repeated.

"I-I don't know him," she said, still confused, but unwilling to back down now.

"Look at him. If he died, who would care?" Joe pressed, pointing at the bum, who was now getting as confused as Egypt, not really happy with his position below them, so he got to his feet. The man, not grasping the gravity of the situation said, "The Lord loves me."

Egypt, beginning to understand, shrugged and said, "No, I guess not."

"Then do something about it."

Joe pulled out a .25 automatic and handed it to her. It fit perfectly in her hands. She took it and looked at the man. The man, now seeing that the situation was more serious than he thought, began to try to struggle to his feet but he was so big, he couldn't.

"Are you people crazy? I ain't did nothin'!"

Joe smiled and replied, "Exactly."

Egypt aimed the gun at his face. In that moment, she knew what this was all about.

The Switch.

The family business wasn't just about pushing smack and making scores, it was about brutality and it was about bringing fear to the enemy— an enemy who would stop at nothing to muscle you off your patch. *Even kill yo ass.*

The men who had killed her parents had *The Switch.*

They had at one time in their lives had to find that switch. The switch that turns you from victim to killer. One day those men might be standing in front of her, and she would have no time to make the choice but to flick it. She would have to end them. But before that, she would have to know that she *could.*

Joe had brought her out to find out if she had *The Switch.* For him it would be to see if she had what it takes to represent for the team. Egypt knew for her it was more than that. Much more.

Looking down the barrel at the fretting fat man, frantically grabbing at the concrete of the pillar, trying desperately to claw a hand up, made her realize how pathetic he really was and his fear of losing something as worthless as his life made her laugh.

The Switch was there and Egypt had just flicked it with that laugh.

When Joe heard the laughter, he looked at her and nodded. His face told her that the trip out and the gun in her hand hadn't broken her, but had in fact made her certain, stronger... And as she laughed at the pathetic bum he would know then that Egypt was naturally cold-blooded. Just like she needed to be.

The hobo saw it too.

In the vast second before his last breath of his last day on earth, he saw in her eyes what she truly was.

Pure evil.

"Nooooo!" he bellowed, trying to cover his face with his arm.

Buck! Buck!

Both shots hit him in the forearm, sending blood spurting out. The pain made him jerk his arm away, exposing his face. Egypt didn't hesitate.

Buck! Buck! Buck! Buck! Click!

She emptied the clip in his face. Once in the cheek, once in the forehead and chin and once in the eye. The eye shot exploded the socket and finally put an end to the agony his whole sorry existence had been. His body slumped over and didn't twitch. Egypt looked around and saw the other bums had moved away. Other than that, no one even paid attention to the cold-blooded murder.

Joe looked at her, "how do you feel?"

She allowed herself to feel, then replied, "I don't."

He nodded. "A killer is like God. We allow people around us to live. We alone understand the power we have over life and death. You surprised me, baby girl. I didn't think you had it in you."

Egypt smirked. "Now what?

"Now I'ma teach you the game."

And he did. He taught her everything. He not only taught her to shoot, he taught her how to break down, clean and repair guns. Uncle Joe even made sure Egypt got lessons in self-defense, from jujitsu to karate. And when it came to drugs, she could cut cocaine and heroin like a chemist. He immersed her in the game, preparing her mind and body. Her end of the bargain was to go to school and get good grades, something she didn't understand at first.

"Why I gotta go to school?" She asked one day where they were counting money.

Joe looked up from the money machine as it spat out another bundle of cash. He stacked it with the rest.

"You know everything already?"

Egypt shrugged. "Everything I need to know."

"If you did, you'd know why you have to go to school," he quipped playfully, without smiling.

Egypt sucked her teeth. "Shit stupid."

"Keep countin'."

And then came the boys. At seventeen, she had three bodies under her belt. But she was still a virgin. Truth be told, she was scared of dick. Go figure. Anyway, her first one found this out the hard way.

"You know I love you, right?" he charmed one day while they were kissing on his living room couch.

His parents weren't home and he'd brought her to the house on the promise of a movie, but Egypt knew all he could think about was the sweet virgin pussy between 17-year-old legs. If he was any more transparent he would have been a ghost.

"I love you, too," she replied. It didn't matter that she knew what his real motives were, she was in love. *Eye-crossed puppy love*, her Uncle Joe might have called it, but she was feeling it real.

In her eyes, he was the finest man in the world. He looked like a young Denzel Washington, with soft, curly hair that she loved to run her fingers through, and a mouth she could kiss all night.

His name was Ray and he knew Egypt was on him. He had it all planned out. Ray leaned in and kissed her again, passionately. Egypt returned the kiss just as passionately. He thought it was on. He tried to lay her back on the couch.

She stiffened and broke the kiss.

"Why you not down?"

Her feminine feathers were nervous and ruffled.

He smiled soothingly. "Relax ma, we good. I just want to take our love to the next level."

She took one look at the oversized bulge in his pants and replied, "I-I-I'm not ready."

"I thought you loved me."

"I do," she answered quickly, as if eager to prove it.

Her apparent eagerness made Ray's dick hard. He ran his fingers over her cheeks then hit her with the oldest line in the horny teenager handbook: "If you loved me, you'd let me love you."

"But..." was all she got out before his lips were smothering her, not with a kiss, but basically a muffle to silence her protests.

At first, she went with the flow, allowing him to lay her back on the couch, but when he began to unbutton her pants, she broke the kiss again.

"No, I–"

"Just chill."

"Ray, stop."

"Come on, baby," he growled, the frustration in his tone, obvious as he tried even harder to take off her pants.

"Stop!" She yelled, pushing him hard in the chest.

The blow hurt his pride more than his person. "Fuck that!" He spat back, slamming her back against the couch, adding, "Yo, come help me with this bitch!"

That's when two of his friends Tony and Mark burst out of the closet.

Egypt had hit her head on the exposed wooden arm of the couch, so she was a little dazed, but seeing the two boys coming at her, grabbing at her legs and arms, her agile mind became lucid quickly.

"You were going to run a train on me?!" she screamed at Ray, feeling her little heart breaking for the first time.

Ray simply laughed as he unbuttoned her pants. "Was?! We are!"

She let out a laugh that caught the three boys off guard. Then she went into action...

Egypt grabbed the middle finger of Mark's right hand, the same one that was grasping her wrist and bent it until it snapped like a twig and touched the back of his hand.

"My finger!" he screamed like a bitch.

At the same time that she was breaking his finger, she poked her finger in Tony's right eye, blinding him for life in that socket. Blood poured out of the useless orbit. He fell back, holding his leaking face.

Shit happened so fast, Ray didn't have time to react. He still had his pants around his thigh, hard dick in his hand, which Egypt promptly put her foot on. He damn near passed out as he crumpled to the floor. Egypt slowly stood up and looked at the three of them squirming.

"You crazy bitch! Look what you did to my eye!" Tony screeched like a hysterical banshee.

"Crazy? Oh, you want crazy?" Egypt stared and the look on her face made Tony regret he even opened his mouth.

She grabbed a solid ceramic longneck goose off the mantle, gripping it by the neck and began beating Tony's face in until it was just a bloody pulp.

Then she beat Mark. Then she beat Ray. By the time she was finished, she was covered in as much blood as they were. She stood up, breathing hard.

"Now...we're going to have some fun."

With that, she rolled them all over on their stomachs and pulled their pants down around their ankles. Three black asses smiled up at her. She pinched her nose.

"Damn, one of y'all need to wash your ass. So you wanna fuck, huh? Okay, let's fuck," she announced. Then she flipped the ceramic goose around, gripped its body and plunged the head and neck deep in Ray's ass. He didn't even have the energy to cry out. He lifted his head, opened his mouth—nothing came out—then he passed out.

He would need 30 stitches to sew his asshole up.

Egypt stepped to Mark. He tried to scramble away. She kicked him in the ribs, and he stopped. She gripped the goose like a knife and stabbed him over and over in his asshole.

He would need 60 stitches.

Tony, knowing he was next, looked over his shoulders, tears running from his only eye. "Please..."

"Sure," she winked, then penetrated his asshole. But to her surprise, there was no resistance.

She laughed.

"Damn, you already been tampered with, huh?"

He didn't need any stitches.

After that, they would see her in school and drop their eyes. They never told anyone, because they were afraid to admit they got beat up and raped by a girl. Egypt would smirk to herself and keep it moving.

Egypt sat on the bed, looking at Vanya for a reaction. Vanya snuffed out the cigarette, allowing the silence to dictate the rhythm.

"So... are you going to tell me how you knew?" Egypt probed.

Vanya smiled.

"Let's just say nothing happens without a purpose. Your uncle is a well-known individual."

"I know."

"Now it's your turn to answer a question?" Vanya remarked.

Egypt's expression said she was listening.

"Do you want to meet The Colombian?"

"Hell yeah."

A beat.

"Are you sure? Because once you do, it's like an initiation. A lifetime initiation," Vanya cautioned her.

Egypt thought about it, then asked, "What's in it for me?"

"You'll find out who killed your parents and you'll be family. Nothing can touch you."

Egypt nodded. "Then hell yeah. When do I meet him?"

Ten minutes later, she met The Colombian and it... blew her mind.

ROCK BOTTOM

Spagoli stepped into the living room, slamming the door behind himself, grumbling, "fucking nigger!"

His wife, Gina, heard him from the kitchen and cringed. She knew to keep her mouth shut.

Spagoli entered the kitchen, stood in the doorway and glared at Gina.

"Hi-hi honey. How was your day?" she asked. She cooked at the stove without turning around.

"How do you think it's been? Everywhere I go at work, people know! I'm fucking blackballed! Ironic, huh? I'm blackballed but you're the one that licked black balls," Spagoli raged.

Tears welled up in Gina's eyes as she turned around.

"What do you want from me, Frank?! I made a mistake! I offered you a divorce but you said no!" she screamed.

"What? So you could collect alimony for being a whore?!"

"That's it! I'm leaving!"

Smack!

"Oh my God!" Gina screeched and spun away. As she fell backwards into the stove, her arm fell flat against the burner. Her sweater caught on fire as she dropped to the ground.

"Frank, help me please!"

Spagoli was stuck. Everything had happened so fast. One minute she was standing there, then the next she was a ball of fire, writhing in agony on the flour.

"Frank!"

The pain in her second scream finally spurred him to action.

He grabbed the pan full of water out of the sink and splashed it on her. The flames hissed and twisted, but only went out on her extremities. There wasn't enough water, so he began to stomp the flame out, adding insult to injury by stomping on Gina in the process.

By the time the fire was completely out, not only did she have third degree burns over half her body but her ribs were broken by his attempts to put her out.

"C-c-call the ambulance," she groaned, barely conscious.

He looked into her face and saw his future.

This was her way out. She would tell exactly what had happened to her. Everyone knew about her affair and would think he had tried to kill her. Even if he beat an attempted murder charge, Spagoli knew his career would be over. He'd be stuck behind a desk. He knew he had to do something...

And then it hit him.

"Hold on babe, I'm calling them now," he assured her, as he grabbed her phone and walked out of the kitchen.

He scrolled through her phone, hoping the number was still in the phone, but as soon as he found it, the anger consumed him. He knew it by sight because it had been a part of the investigation. Spagoli paused for a moment, until his mind convinced him that this was the only way.

He dialed.

"Bitch, didn't I tell you not to call me again?" The gruff voice on the other end answered.

Spagoli felt a sick thrill hearing this man talk to his wife like that, but he was too gone to worry about it.

"This isn't Gina, it's Spagoli."

Silence.

"Hello?" Spagoli said, hoping this man hadn't hung up.

"Yeah, I'm here," he answered.

Was that amusement Spagoli heard in his voice? "I... I've got a deal for you."

"I'm listening."

"I'm not discussing it over the phone."

A pause to ponder. "Let's meet tomorrow."

"No," Spagoli quickly cut him off. "It has to be now at my house."

"Your house?"

"Trust me, it'll be worth your while."

"I'm on my way."

Click!

Spagoli was heated that he didn't even have to tell him where he lived and it made him imagine the things he had probably done to his wife.

"This bitch deserves this," Spagoli grumbled to himself, trying to convince himself that what he was planning was unwarranted. But deep down, he knew he'd burn in hell for this. He just had no idea whose hell.

Spagoli walked back into his kitchen. Gina's eyes pinned on him as soon as he entered.

"Who were you... talking to, Frank?" She struggled to ask.

He couldn't even answer. He just dropped his head.

"You didn't call an ambulance, did you?"

"No. No I didn't," he answered.

A tear rolled down her soot-colored face. The burns made her face look like a ghoul.

"So, you're going to just let me die?"

"I'm...I'm sorry."

"No, you're not. I never meant to hurt you, Frank. I know I don't have any excuses for my actions, but do I deserve to die for them?"

Spagoli wanted to relent, but the overriding need within that was only concerned with self-preservation wouldn't let him. "You-

you're going to tell them! Tell them it was my fault!" he said coldly.

"No, no I won't. It was an accident. I know you didn't mean—"

"I-I can't trust you, Gina! How can I believe you?!" Spagoli remarked.

Gina closed her eyes. "I swear."

"I... I can't."

Spagoli walked out and sat on the couch. He couldn't bear to look at her. For a few minutes, she called his name until she realized he wasn't going to answer. Then her sobs tortured his conscience...but not his will.

The knock came twenty minutes later.

Spagoli opened the door and Blunt stepped in. He was a big black dude. He had to be, since his occupation was a bodyguard.

Blunt sniffed the air.

"Something burning?" He asked.

Spagoli didn't answer as he closed the door, then he turned to the huge black guy.

"What up?" Blunt inquired, looking at his watch, then adding, "I don't make it a habit of talking to the police."

"I'm sure," Spagoli replied sourly, then continued with, "I was thinking maybe we could help one another."

"Help?"

"The investigation."

"I'm listening."

Spagoli glanced back toward the kitchen.

"You and your boss. There's a lot of info going around."

"I'm not my boss. What's in it for me?" Blunt pressed.

"I'll make sure your name doesn't come up," Spagoli offered.

Blunt smiled. "Wow, you must really need me, huh?"

Spagoli didn't answer. He just wanted to blast that arrogant smirk off Blunt's face.

"Okay, I'll bite. What do you need?"

Spagoli paused, then sighed and replied, "in the kitchen."

Blunt followed Spagoli into the kitchen, when he saw Gina just lying there, half conscious. His eyes bugged. "Whoa! You tried to burn up your wife?!"

"It was an accident," Spagoli said with irritation masking deep anxiety.

Blunt laughed in his face. "Then you should've called an ambulance. Why did you call me?" he challenged.

"You wouldn't understand! It-it...I didn't mean to—it doesn't matter, are you in or not?"

"In what?" Blunt wanted to know.

"I need her taken care of."

"Taken care of? You mean *killed*?"

Spagoli nodded.

Blunt sighed. "Then I need more sweet talk. Sing, copper," he said taunting him.

Spagoli was bowing, but he knew he was fucked. If Blunt would've told him to suck his dick, he would've done it. Anything to save his own ass.

"Name your price?" Spagoli replied, broken.

Blunt scratched his chin, contemplating it. "I'll take the gift that keeps on giving."

"What the hell are you talking about?!"

"I just bought you. When I call, you come. When I ask, you give. When I say how high," Blunt concluded, then pointed at Spagoli.

"I jump," Spagoli seethed, his jaw tight.

"Exactly," Blunt nodded, then looked down at Gina, adding, "You got a sleeping bag?"

Half an hour later, Blunt was driving out of the city and reminding himself he'd need to get the car detailed first thing in the morning. The stench of the burnt woman was seeping into the leather, and the next person to get in would think he'd been having his own personal hog roast in there last night. As that person may well be his employer, and the car belonged to him, Blunt figured getting the car cleaned up was one of his better ideas.

Blunt checked the mirror, which was angled to see what was happening on the back seat. Gina wrapped up in a sleeping bag, was semi-conscious, her blackened lips moving. The crust that the skin and hair on the right side of her face had become, crackled crisply as she moved her head. Her eyes opened and he saw her looking at him in the mirror.

"Just shoot me," Gina croaked, her voice dry from so much gasping and wheezing.

Blunt heard her, but acted like he didn't. He was too busy contemplating how small the world really is...

"Yo thun, bitch got that jungle fever," Duppy remarked as he and Blunt sat at an outdoor restaurant in midtown Manhattan. Blunt glanced around and caught the woman who he would soon find out was called Gina, looking at him from another table. He smiled to himself because he was used to the attention of white women. His dark complexion and hulking, muscular build made him a white woman magnet. She wasn't bad looking by a long shot. She had that classic Sicilian, olive skin.

"Yeah, I see her," Blunt acknowledged.

Blunt got up and headed for her table. Gina looked away, demurely. "You waiting on anyone?" He asked.

"He just arrived," she shot back.

Blunt smiled and sat down. The first thing he noticed was her wedding ring. "Should I be worried?" he inquired.

Gina glanced at her ring and shrugged. "Not particularly."

"My name's Jaylan. Jaylan Blunt."

"Gina Spagoli."

They shook hands, allowing the shake to become a kiss on her palm instead of the back of her hand.

"That's different," she remarked.

"It just means you've already got me eating out of the palm of your hand," Blunt charmed.

She giggled. "You're incorrigible."

"So let me ask you something. Are we going to waste time beating around the bush or get down to what's on both our minds?" He asked directly.

Gina leaned on her palm. "What is it do you think is on my mind?"

"You're thinking about me putting this big black dick down your throat, then bending you over and fucking you until you cum screaming," Blunt replied.

By the time he was finished, Gina was hooked. She had that smile on her face and hotness in the eyes that told Blunt that she was at risk of sliding off the seat on a tide of her own juices.

"Wow. You don't mess around, do you?" She smirked.

"Life's too short."

"I agree."

"Then why are we still talking?"

As soon as they entered the hotel room, Gina was all over him, tonguing him down and unbuckling his pants at the same time. When his rock hard ten-inch dick popped free, it hit her in the forehead.

"Oh my God! I can't take all of this!" Gina gasped.

"You can and you will," Blunt grunted as he grabbed a handful of her hair, tilted her hair back and filled her throat full of dick. The feel of his big black dick in her throat made Gina gag, but as she pushed it down further by grabbing at Blunt's hips, he could tell she was loving it, gagging or not.

"Yeah, you nasty white bitch, I knew you wanted this dick! Eat it!" Blunt demanded. Feeling himself about to cum, he pulled out and jizzed all over her face.

"You got me so wet," Gina gasped, licking cum from her lips.

"Let me see," Blunt demanded, turning Gina to the wall and pulling up her skirt.

He pulled her panties to the side and slid his whole swollen shaft up in her to the balls. She let out a scream of pleasure, cumming hard and making her pussy even wetter. He began to pump her furiously, making Gina try to get on her tip toes to get away from his back strokes.

"Oh my God. I'm squirting!" She squealed, seeing the thin stream of liquid shoot out of her.

Her knees were buckling.

"Pl-please, no more," she groaned.

Blunt laid down on the bed, put her legs over his shoulders and began to lick and suck until her body trembled like electricity had been shot in her. She tried to climb away, but Blunt cuffed her thighs and made her cum until tears of joy came down her cheeks.

After that, she was his. She would call him constantly. Her name became a joke between Blunt and Duppy, which was why Duppy knew her name when Spagoli first questioned him. Their affair went on for a few months before Spagoli and O'Brien were in a stake out outside of Duppy's Brooklyn brownstone.

Spagoli was drinking a coffee trying to stay awake.

"This fucking nigger's got it made. Dancing his way to millions," Spagoli spat, shaking his head with disgust. When the familiar gold Accord pulled up, he couldn't believe his eyes. His stomach retched and he damn near threw up. His heart sank to his knees as he watched his wife step out of the car, looking around as she approached Duppy's door.

"And not only that, look at this white slut. Look at her, she can't wait to get that black—"

Spagoli punched O'Brien in the face.

"Shut up," Spagoli barked so loud, his voice almost reached Gina down the street.

O'Brien was more surprised than he was hurt. He rubbed his jaw, eyes wide and glued to Spagoli.

"What the fuck is wrong with you?!"

Spagoli's heart was beating a mile a minute. He got out of the car and stalked off in the opposite direction. O'Brien, bewildered, got out and jogged behind Spagoli, catching up with him as he rounded the corner.

"What the hell?! We're on a stake out!" O'Brien blasted him.

"That was my fucking wife!" Spagoli screamed, on the verge of tears.

O'Brien's jaw dropped. "Jesus...I... I don't know what to say."

Spagoli paced furiously back and forth, then started back towards the brownstone. "I'm going in."

O'Brien grabbed his arm. "Are you crazy? We'll be throwing away months—"

Spagoli snatched away. "You think I care?! I'm going to kill him!" Spagoli was heartbroken, so even though his words were venomous, his insides were jelly. O'Brien just let him burn off the steam.

"I can't believe this!" Spagoli growled.

"You want to call it a night?" O'Brien asked.

Spagoli shook his head. "No...I'm okay...I'm okay."

Quietly, they went back to the stake-out car.

After three hours, he watched her come out again. Her walk was definitely different. Nude legged, she walked pussy-sore. A tear traced Spagoli's cheek. He was forever humiliated and he had Blunt to blame.

Yet now, since the accident in the kitchen, he was forever in debt to him.

Blunt drove, the faint smell of burnt flesh wafting through the car.

"Please..." Gina sobbed.

Blunt just laughed and turned on the radio.

TRACK 5

"Where did you go?" Kane questioned Egypt, when she returned to the hotel.

She had just returned from her scheduled rendezvous with Spagoli in the park and crept in through the back exit. She tried to make it up the hotel's back staircase, but Kane caught her. He had no business being on the stairs, and so it was obvious to Egypt he'd planned to head her off at the pass.

"I... I had the munchies," Egypt lied, adding a sweet smile, it was an obvious lie. She wasn't carrying any munchies. She could see that Kane knew that too.

"What did you buy?" Kane said, blocking the way on the stair.

"I ate it," she tried to walk away, but Kane grabbed her arm.

Egypt snatched away from him. "Don't do that."

"And if I do?" Kane smirked.

Egypt itched to show him, but she decided against it, she couldn't risk this getting out of hand, not when the operation was starting to bear fruit. "Look, I'm tired. I—"

Kane stiffened and reached into his pocket, Egypt prepared herself for Kane to bring out heat, but all that was in his hand was his phone. "So, you didn't go to the park? This isn't you?" Kane said, handing her the phone.

Egypt looked at herself, sitting in the car with Spagoli. The picture was taken within twenty feet. She wondered how he had gotten so close.

Egypt looked at Kane, and he was smiling triumphantly. Her quick mind automatically thought about killing Kane right there in the stairwell, but there was a surveillance camera in the ceiling corner above them. CCTV had a habit of getting back to the people who needed it the most and Duppy was sure to have people here who would gladly hand it over to him.

So instead, she handed Kane back his phone. "Okay. Now what?" She said, a smile that didn't reach her eyes, playing across her face.

"That was one of the cops that snatched Messiah up. You know how it looks to find you in the dark with the police? Makes you look like a rat," Kane said, coldly. He wasn't angry so much as someone who looked as if he were calculating a risk and return strategy.

"What do you want, Kane?"

"What makes you think I want something?"

"Because if you didn't, I'd already be dead. I know how QB gets down," she replied.

Kane chuckled. "What up with you and Power?"

Now it was her turn to chuckle, perhaps this was fixable after all. "Really? Pussy, Kane? You catch me talking to the police and all you can think of is fucking?"

Kane instantly got heated; Egypt had calculated right. Kane was a man who didn't like his gangsta being questioned. "Bitch, don't be cute. This ain't just about pussy, the pussy is personal. What I really want is for The Colombian to go through me instead of Power."

"So, you want his woman and his money?" She smiled. "I got you so worked out, I'ma gonna put a tick next to your name."

Kane moved quicker than she was expecting. He put her against the wall and pushed up. "You know his woman?" He charmed, then tongued her down.

She embraced him like the chameleon she was. Once he broke the kiss, he caressed her cheek, then said, "Meet me in my room."

PRESENT DAY

"That's when shit started to get ugly," he said, as Spagoli walked back in.

O'Brien watched Spagoli. The Italian looked like he'd been hollowed out and the hole filled up with shit. He raised a questioning eyebrow.

"I'm okay," Spagoli assured him, lighting a cigarette and smoking it like it was the last one he might ever taste.

O'Brien looked at him skeptically for a moment, then nodded.

"So that's when things started to break down?" O'Brien turned back to the subject of the interview. He rolled the next part of the story through his head like a horror movie where he was one of the stars. "No doubt. But war is more accurate. At first, it was subtle, but the rift just got wider, and wider, and wider..."

INTRODUCTION

"Yo, yo, hold up. Take that, again from the top," Kane told Power through the monitor as he sat behind the mixing board in his swivel chair.

Power was heated. He had already done seven takes, and he'd rather be using his mouth on Egypt than the mic. "What was wrong with that?" Power questioned.

"Flat," Kane clicked in.

"Flat?" Power rolled his eyes. "I ain't singing."

"It need more energy. You sound dead, yo!"

That's when Egypt blew him a silent kiss through the glass from behind the mixer. That was exactly what Power needed. Power dropped the lyric once more, putting so much energy into it, the whole place was rocking.

Egypt stood up and clapped like a crazy Kermit. Power caught Kane's face dropping at Egypt's antics. Power turned his finger in the air to tell Kane to run the beat again. And this time, he killed the beat with his swag. He knew exactly where the energy for that last take had come from. It had come right outta Kane's face at Egypt's expression of love and respect for Power. It looked like a burning thread was cutting through his heart.

Power sighed as he took off the headphones and walked out of the booth. He didn't want to face it, but it seemed he and Kane were going through déjà vu...

"Nigga ain't even from the Boro, Fi!" Kane slurred before putting the bottle of E&J to his lips and devouring a greedy gulp. Ty Five$ nodded, but didn't say anything because he knew Kane was drunk. He also knew drunk lips speak the truth of how a person really feels. But Ty Five$ couldn't front, Power may've been new to the Boro, but he fit right in.

Real recognize real, Ty Five$ thought to himself.

But for Kane, it came down to one thing:

Tanika Freeman.

To Kane, she was the baddest bitch in QB. Her skin was the same texture of honey with eyes as green as emeralds. She kept her hair in a wrap or Chinese bobs with what ghetto girls called baby hair. She wasn't super thick, but her petite frame was curvaceous in the correct places.

Kane had a crush on her since she had started fucking, but she wouldn't give him the time of day. Even when he started to get money and all the young bitches were on his dick, Tanika still acted like he didn't exist.

"Man, fuck that bitch," he would growl whenever she rebuffed his advances. It became an obsession on Kane's part, until Power came to the Boro.

Power, Kane and Knowledge had walked up in the party in the Rec Center. The place was packed and tension was thick, because both sides of the Boro were at the party. It was only a matter of time before some shit popped off. But in the meantime, bitches were everywhere, shaking ass in poom poom shorts, begging to be fucked.

"Ay yo! I'm fucking four bitches tonight!" Knowledge cracked, giving Kane dap.

"Man, I done fucked most of these bitches anyway," Kane commented dismissively. Power spotted one chick in stretch pants that made her bow-legged stance stand out.

"Yo, who dat?" Power questioned.

Kane followed the finger. Once he saw who it was, he sucked his teeth and waved her off. "Man, that's stuck up ass Tanika. Bitch ain't about shit," Kane replied.

"Say no more. Watch me bag this hole," Power spat arrogantly as he bopped off to show and prove.

Kane knew he would Crash and *Burn*. "Bitch 'bout to front on thun."

But Kane's self-assured smirk quickly faded as he watched Power approach Tanika. When she glanced over her shoulder, her face was twisted up in a stank expression for having her conversation interrupted, but once she laid eyes on Power, her face lit up with a sexy, ghetto smile.

The smile that broke Kane's heart.

———

"What's your name?" Power asked.

"Tanika. What's yours?"

"Power."

"You ain't from the Boro," she remarked, giving him flirtatious eyes.

Power nodded and brushed something from her sleeve that wasn't there in the first place. "Nah, I just moved here. You wanna dance?"

Tanika shrugged, like she was nonchalant, but he could see through her eyes deep down into her excitement. And when she replied, "I don't care." Power knew he'd stuck his landing.

———

They moved to the dance floor with Kane's eyes glued to them.

Knowledge saw Kane was in his feelings, so he said, "Man, fuck that. Let's go outside and burn somethin'."

Eventually, Kane allowed Knowledge to lead him towards the door. He didn't need to burn anything because he was already on fire. He just needed a chance to vent his negative energy. It wasn't long before he found his opportunity. A dude from the 48th side of the Boro was coming in the door. Kane bumped him hard as they passed each other.

"Ay yo, nigga, you—" the dude started, but never got a chance to finish.

Kane smacked the shit out of him. The dude wasted no time going for his gun, just as Kane went for his.

"Muhfucka," Kane grunted.

Two people saw the exchange and dove out of the way, causing a domino effect as Kane and the dude exchanged gunfire while diving for cover at the same time. Guns came out everywhere and suddenly the Rec Center was the 4th of July in Tennessee.

"Muhfucka," Power barked, grabbing Tanika and getting low. She buried her head into his chest, and even in the mayhem of screams and shots Power liked the feeling. When he saw a break in the crowd, he dragged her towards the door.

Kane fired indiscriminately, hitting two dudes and killing one. He saw Power and Tanika duck for cover, running out of the center. Something primal within Kane made him swing the gun around and aim it at Power.

It was for pure satisfaction, even though his conscience could never pull the trigger. He swung the gun away from Power, then aimed at the crowd.

Power and Tanika rushed out the back exit and didn't stop running until they were back on 12th street. Her heart was beating a mile a minute. Power looked back and laughed.

"Welcome to the Boro," Power chuckled.

Tanika's emotions were so hyper, she felt compelled to grab Power and kiss him passionately. He grabbed her ass and pushed her against the wall, tonguing her down. He slid his hand into her tights and began fingering her on the spot. His two fingers slid in easily because her pussy was already sloppy wet.

"Come on, let's take this to the spot," Power told her, taking her hand.

He took her to the roof of the building aka "Pebble Beach," where he and the crew usually took bitches or went to smoke. The city was alive with light, the river a shimmering lake of white fire. The bridge over the waves were as solid and as hard as Power's desire. And with that as the backdrop, Power bridged the distance between her pussy and his dick.

Laying her down, stripping her to the waist and pulling her shirt up, he exposed her two full C-cup breasts. As he positioned himself over her, she grabbed his dick to put it in herself and gasped.

"Uh-huh, that's gotta be illegal," she protested, trying to scoot away.

"Chill ma," Power replied, kissing and sucking on her neck. "I'ma gonna take it slow."

"You better," Tanika answered with more sass than necessary. Her face showed her fear and desire were raging in different directions.

Power slid it in her halfway, she dug her nails in his back.

"That's enough," she groaned, squeezing his girth with her pussy muscles.

Power began to move back and forth with only half his shaft. As he stroked, he slid deeper and deeper until his balls were slapping against her ass and her eyes were rolling up in the back of her head.

"Ohhh, baby, you so deep," she moaned, finally getting used to his size.

"Show me you can take this dick," Power grunted.

Power put her legs over his shoulders and began long dicking her vigorously.

Her moans of pleasure could be heard all over the Boro.

And in the middle of that, Knowledge and Kane came bursting onto the roof, running and out of breath.

The first thing they saw was Power fucking the shit out of Tanika.

For Kane, it was like seeing someone fucking his wife. He was sick. Power looked back and smiled.

"Yo, this pussy bangin'. Y'all want some?"

Knowledge grabbed his dick. "Hell yeah!"

Kane was too stuck to answer.

"No, Power, don't do me like that," Tanika whimpered, but her pussy was too wet to make good decisions. Power kissed her forehead while bringing her to a second orgasm and replied, "Come on, ma, don't be like that. You like me right?"

"Yeah."

"You wanna be my girl?"

Tanika nodded.

"Then don't tell me no," Power spat coldly.

"O-okay," she sniffed, tears welling.

Power banged her until he came on her stomach then got up, looked at Kane, and said, "It's all yours."

Kane stared down at the girl he had been trying to make his own for so long. Seeing her almost totally naked, waiting to be fucked like a common whore had him so upset. He wanted to pull out his gun and blow her brains out.

Instead, he pulled his dick out and made her give him brains.

"No, uh-uh," she tried to resist at first, but Kane rubbed his dick across her lips, pulling her head back and forced it in her mouth. He fucked her face while Knowledge bent her over and beat her pussy from the back.

The next day, when Kane saw Tanika, she was no longer the bad bitch he had a crush on. She couldn't even meet his eyes, but he pulled her aside and told her, "Yo, ain't nobody gonna put you out there like that."

Her expression told him how grateful she was. "Thank you."

Kane felt that he'd grown into a giant overnight and Tanika was just another ant crawling over the NYC slime. But that recognition wasn't enough closure for Kane. He wanted more than just the realization that he was over this bad bitch.

"You wanna burn something?" he smiled.

"Sure."

They sat in a project back staircase and blew a blunt.

Tanika said, "Kane you nice. I shouldn't have been so stuck up wit' you."

This made Kane laugh darkly in his head. What she didn't know was the blunt she was smoking was laced with Angel Dust. Kane was only pretending to hit it, but was making sure she got it all.

Within minutes she had the Angel paranoias and her eyes were flickering.

"You hear that?" Tanika asked, listening hard.

Kane smiled to himself, knowing it was kicking in. "Yeah."

She jumped up and looked around.

"Yo ma, you better look out! Look!" Kane clowned, but with a straight face.

In Tanika's mind, zombies were growling and coming near.

"Oh my God, they're coming!" She screamed. She pushed herself back against the wall.

"Take off your clothes, it'll make you invisible."

Tanika didn't hesitate. She stripped down, including her socks and ran out of the building. Kane laughed himself teary eyed.

Revenge is sweeter than pussy.

From that one blunt, Tanika's mind was gone for the rest of her short, sad life. Tanika was in and out of the mental hospital. No one ever knew what really happened to Tanika. Power suspected it was because of Kane, because whenever he and Kane would see her walking around muttering about zombies coming for her, Kane would laugh and say, "Yeah, bitch ain't boss no more, huh?"

She ended up jumping off the roof of her building, because her mind told her the whole city was underwater and she wanted to swim in it.

Power never forgot it, remembering Kane's remarks.

PRE-HOOK

"Y ou fuckin' Kane?" Power confronted Egypt as they left the studio, chewing down on the deferasirox capsule for his thalassemia he'd forgotten to take this morning because he was so wired. He didn't need his condition getting in the way of this.

She looked at him and knotted her eyebrows, hand on hip. "Why? You jealous?"

"You playin' a dangerous game," Power warned her, swallowing the bitterness of the dry medication.

"Who says I'm playing?" she replied, then turned and walked away towards her car, the back door of which was being held open by her bodyguard. Power didn't even know why she had starting traveling in a separate whip. Things were not as they should be. She was spending time with Kane and not always returning Power's calls. He didn't want to get so hung up on a bitch, but this pussy was worth the problems...for now.

Power watched her with murder in his eyes.

He jumped in his whip and pulled away from the sidewalk. Several minutes later, his phone rang. It was The Colombian.

"We need to talk," the voice said. "There have been developments."

Damn straight there had been developments. Mostly Kane *developmenting* all over Egypt. Power pushed the unwelcome thought from his mind and glanced at his watch.

"Gimme an hour."

The Colombian clicked his tongue with annoyance. "Now."

Power was taken aback. "Must be serious."

"Very."

"Aight, I'll be at the spot in fifteen."

"I'm already there."

When Power walked into the bistro, The Colombian looked more agitated then he ever had. He shook Power's hand, pointed to the seat and then said without any sugar coating, "Duppy's snitching."

It hit Power like a hammer, his ass hovered over the seat as his knees locked, freezing with the shock. "What?!"

"You didn't know?" The Colombian questioned, looking Power in the eyes.

Power shot right back, like, "You tryin' to play me?!"

The Colombian smiled, then seemingly relaxed. "Just checking. I needed to see your expression. Now sit. Please."

Power's knees started to unstick, and he splashed-down across from The Colombian.

"My expression?" Power questioned.

The Colombian smiled. "To see if you already knew that Duppy was a rat. If you did, then I'd have considered you a bird of a feather."

Power decided to let the disrespect of The Colombian even thinking he was on the take with Duppy slide. He wanted to find out what The Colombian knew. "How you know he is a rat?"

"I have my ways. The question is, what are we going to do about it?"

Power sat back and pondered the question, stroking his chin. "If we kill him, then we lose our cover for the operation," Power said.

"Indeed. Plus, we'll expose our hand. Do you know how

Duppy came to my attention and why I chose to deal with him in the first place?"

"No."

The Colombian sat back, lit a cigarette and replied, "Then listen up. I think you'll find this interesting."

HOOK

Duppy was on top of the world. Wadoo had put him in touch with several hip-hop labels who loved his production skills. Requests for beats began to roll in. On top of that, Tatiana's single, "Do Me Boy," was beginning to make noise.

"I think you should let Tatiana sign with Vodka & Milk," Wadoo suggested, one day when he and Duppy were reclined in Wadoo's penthouse apartment in New York City. They were 42 stories up, with a view of all of Manhattan. It was like Bladerunner with the lights on.

The view alone had Duppy's dick hard. He looked down at the tiny cars and the even smaller people. He felt like a God who could send a lightning bolt down from the heavens and fry any one of those heads. Then the idea hit him, maybe he could send out lightning bolts into those heads, just not to fry...

"I think we should start our own label," Duppy replied.

Wadoo took a toke on his cigar and looked at Duppy.

"Our own label? Who's gonna run it?"

"Me," said Duppy putting his hands and forehead against the cool glass of the window. His mind expanding to the size of the sky. Everything was clicking into place. He couldn't fail.

"You don't know how to run a label."

"Then I'll learn," he answered, enjoying the soothing chill of the glass against his skin.

Wadoo got up, opened the balcony door and he and Duppy ambled outside.

The spring heat wasn't oppressive, and this high in the sky, the breeze felt better than the window had against Duppy's skin. Wadoo wasn't a man who made rash decisions. He needed to be coaxed, and Duppy could see he'd got under the Wadoo's skin with this idea. Vegas was rolling by in the gangsta's eyes.

Wadoo flicked his ashes over the edge of the building and watched his debris pollute New York. "That's really not a bad idea. Reason being, I need another way to launder some bread. What can you do with a million dollars?"

Duppy kept breathing like he was offered him this amount of big faces every day and replied like it was just another fucking Tuesday: "Take over the game."

They both laughed.

Duppy gave Wadoo dap and the deal was sealed.

Duppy wasted no time putting together his label. A million dollars rented a nice slice of office space in Chelsea Market, and Duppy signed Tatiana as his first artist. She was ecstatic, when he brought her to the office, sat her down and pushed the contract across the football field desk. "Oh my God! For real?! Thank you!" She squealed, wrapping him in a tight hug.

He chuckled. "If you choke me to death, I won't be able to do anything six feet deep!"

She let him go. "Sorry! I was just so excited!"

Duppy stepped to his bar in the corner and poured them both a drink. He handed her a glass, then held his up for a toast.

"To the Grammys! You're going to win for Best New Artist."

They clinked glasses, then drank. Another deal in the hand. The streets.

"We've come a long way, huh?" Tatiana commented.

"No doubt."

"I wonder where Bruce is."

Duppy shrugged. "Probably working at UPS."

They laughed. Duppy stepped closer to Tatiana, as he sat his glass on the coffee table. "But for us... nothing but good shit in the future."

Duppy caressed her cheek but Tatiana took a step back, giving a nervous giggle.

"Damn yo, one sip got you trippin', huh?"

"Nah ma, I'm just sayin'. You said you're excited, right? I just want to see how much."

Duppy leaned in to kiss her, but Tatiana leaned away. "Now you really trippin'," she remarked.

Duppy wasn't feeling her rebuff, but to be honest he was used to it. He had long since had a crush on Tatiana, but she had never given him the time of day. She appreciated him as a friend and loved his musical skill, but she didn't see him like that. Duppy chuckled but underneath, his aggravation was rising. He had the label, the Chelsea Market office and now all he needed was... "Trippin? Nah man, I'm definitely not trippin'. You know I've had feelings for you for a long time, Tati. And now that we about to blow, all I know is I always want you by my side."

She stepped closer to him, heightening his expectations, caressed his cheek softly and replied, "Paul... you are a really nice guy and a good friend but I just don't—"

Duppy didn't want to hear it. He put a palm over her mouth, but she gently took his fingers and pulled his hand away. "Duppy baby, please. I don't like to say no, but, I gotta. I love you like a brother...but only a brother, dig?"

Duppy let go of her hand, and burned his eyes into her. She near flinched. "Nice guy? Yeah. I've heard nice guys finish last."

"No, don't act like that. I didn't mean it that way."

"But you said it. So, let's talk business. This label is ready to make you a star. Are you ready?"

Her face showing, she was glad to be back on track, Tatiana's excitement bubbled back to the surface. "Hell yeah, I'm ready!"

Duppy looked her in the eyes.

"Then take off your clothes."

Tatiana's jaw dropped.

Duppy nodded coldly. "As people always say, there's more than one way to skin a cat. Today, you're the cat. You want this deal... show me how much."

"Nigga, fuck you," Tatiana huffed, then turned and headed for the door.

"That's exactly what you're going to do if you want this deal. If not, go back to the projects and see how far you get. What are you going to do, get a G.E.D.?"

Tatiana paused at the door, hand on the knob, the door slightly ajar. He knew that deep down, she knew he was right. Tatiana had dropped out of high-school to pursue her dreams of being a singer. "If you walk out now, what kind of future will you have?" he said as her hand paused on the door handle. She looked back at Duppy and that's when he felt the sexiest thrill of power in his entire life. It was the thrill that jacked straight into his heart and veins, becoming his one true God in that moment. A tear dropped from Tatiana's cheek as she closed the door and with just the tiniest of sobs and catching of breath in her throat. It was the sound of defeat and resignation, and Duppy was as hard as stone in his pants.

Fuck every bitch that ever said no.

She walked back up to Duppy and smacked the shit out him, then calmly began to remove her clothes.

Duppy wasn't taken by surprise by the slap, he could have stopped it if he wanted, but he liked seeing how broken she was that she would overstep that particular line. Duppy's heart was beating like a thousand wasp wings in his chest, their stings gleaming. His mouth was dry but his dick was so zinging with the electricity of power, he could have illuminated every strip-light in Manhattan just by dropping his pants.

Tatiana's golden hued skin tone, free of blemishes and completely naked made him stretch his neck, rolling his head around on it, raising him up, taller, widening his shoulders. Wadoo had changed everything with the money. Duppy really was a God now. He was also the lightning bolt. "Now get on your knees."

Tatiana never broke eye contact with Duppy, she wasn't giving in that easily. As she sank to her knees, her eyes mocked him, telling him without words this was consensual rape.

He thought about slapping the bitch, and even raised his hand. But a God didn't have to give satisfaction to no one, and he wasn't going to show this little skank that she had got under his skin. "Close your goddamn eyes and open your mouth," he said lowering his hand.

She did as she was told. He slid his throbbing dick in her mouth and began vigorously fucking her face. "Yeah, bitch. I win! I'ma make all you bitches pay for your bullshit," he grunted as he rammed his dick down Tatiana's throat.

Since he had been a kid, he never got the girl. He was always the oddball, the guy the females didn't take seriously. Now that he had power, he was going to wield it with an iron fist. Starting today.

Duppy pulled his dick out of her mouth and came all over her face, further humiliating her. But he wasn't done. "Turn around and bend over," he demanded.

Tatiana no longer had any fight left. He knew she was complying just to get this done. Her body was there, but she had shrunk inside herself. She turned around and got down on all fours like a dog. Duppy forced her face down into the carpet as he shoved his dick into her dry pussy.

"Oh bitch, you ain't wet? Don't worry, you will be."

Duppy pulled his dick back and peed all over her ass and pussy, then rammed it back inside her. The force of his entrance made Tatiana gasp.

"Yeah, bitch, I knew you wanted it. Now fuck me back."

He slapped her ass hard over and over until her ass reddened and she began to thrust and throw it back. Her pussy got wetter and wetter, then her body betrayed her anger and came all over his dick.

"Damn, this pussy good. See it ain't so bad. Daddy gonna take care of this pussy. I'ma make you a star."

Tatiana sobbed as Duppy slowly inserted his dick in her tight asshole.

"Ple-Please, don't," she cried, before she was blinded by the pain of penetration. "It's hurting...puh...puh...lease you can do anything you want Duppy, but please don't duh...do that."

Duppy loved hearing her beg, and he rammed his dick into her puckered asshole with full force. Her knees almost gave way, and he repositioned her with his hand on her hips, giving her another slap for the badness of it. Her sniffles and whispers had him in a zone, stroking her strong and steady, gripping her ass cheeks and watching his dick sliding in and out.

"Tell me whose ass is this," Duppy gritted.

Tatiana didn't respond.

Slap!

He reddened her ass cheek again, this time a back hander from the rock on his finger leaving a thin bleeding line on her skin.

"Tell me!"

No response.

Slap! Another slice.

"Tell me!"

"Yours!" She cried out, her resistance broken by the pain. The blood smeared and spurred him on, deeper and harder.

Hearing her admit that this ass was now his sent Duppy over the edge and he exploded inside of her, cumming until his knees gave out and he laid on the carpet. When he had caught his breath, he said, "Go get me a rag."

Dutifully, Tatiana did as she was told and went to his private office bathroom. Duppy laid back with his hands behind his head. He watched her return, her eyes looking anywhere but at him. He pulled her down on to her knees and instructed her to clean him off. "You lucky I ain't make you do that with your mouth," he growled.

Duppy stroked her head like a pet as she cleaned the mess of jizz and shit off his dick. "You belong to me now, you understand? I'm going to make you bigger than Madonna, but you'll always be my bitch. Got it?" Duppy stated.

Tatiana looked at him and smiled a smile that didn't reach her eyes.

"Yes, Daddy," she replied, but he could see in her soul that she hated his guts.

He didn't care. It made his ownership of her all the sweeter.

For the next year, Duppy proved true to his word. Tatiana became a household name. Her first album went double platinum.

She was nominated for a Grammy, but she didn't win, which caused an uproar on social media because everyone felt she got robbed. That made her the people's champion. Tatiana was on the cover of *Billboard*, *Rolling Stone* and *VIBE*. Her face was known to the world. To all outward appearances, she was now a star, but she didn't feel like one. She felt like a whore. Duppy used her in every way he could while maintaining the facade that shit was all good. The worse Tatiana felt, the more she drank, until her soul went numb and drinking wasn't enough.

"Yo, you turnin' into a fuckin' cokehead, Tati," Duppy sneered, as he walked into her dressing room in Madison Square Garden. Tatiana sat at the makeup table, an ounce of coke on a mirror in front of her as she glared at Duppy with a glass-eyed gaze.

"So? All you care about is my voice and my pussy," she spat back.

"And both of those are getting sloppy, too."

"Go to hell, Paul."

"All I know is you better get it together," Duppy warned, then walked out, slamming the door.

His warning only made her want to go harder. Tatiana stuck her face in the pile of cocaine and inhaled until she felt like her head would explode. She heard a knock on the door, then her assistant Maxine stuck her head in. "We go on in five," she announced, then closed the door without waiting for a reply.

Tatiana looked at herself, but her shame couldn't take its own reflection. "Fuck!" she screamed, grabbing a ceramic ashtray and smashing the mirror with it.

Her reflection fractured into a broken jagged edge prism. She took another hard snort then sashayed out the door with coke on her nose.

The show was an absolute disaster.

Her voice cracked on every high note. She forgot the lyrics to two of her hits and berated the crowd when they began to boo her dismal performance.

"Fuck you, pieces of shit! You think I give a fuck about you?! I'm Tati, bitches! Boo all you want!"

She ranted for a full three minutes before Duppy couldn't take it anymore and had security escort her off the stage.

"Get off me, muhfucka!" Tatiana screamed, as one of the guys scooped her off her feet. She kicked so hard, one of her thousand-dollar Louboutin's flew off her foot and was caught by a girl in the front row. The girl posted it on eBay after Tatiana's death and got thirteen thousand dollars.

"Take her to the Maybach," Duppy ordered. Once they placed her in the car, Duppy climbed in and then instructed Jaylan to drive off.

Slap!

Duppy backhanded the blood out of Tatiana, knocking her into a fetal ball on the floor of the Maybach.

"What the fuck is wrong with you?!" Duppy spat, then punctuated his words with another slap.

Tatiana screamed up at Duppy, "Beat me, nigga! You can even kill me! I don't care! It's over! I'm done, you hear me? I'm done!" Tatiana cried.

Hearing those words shook Duppy to his core. Tatiana was his bread and butter. He had other artists, but none were close to Tatiana's level of success.

"Done? Bitch you ain't done 'till I say you're done!"

Tatiana laughed through her tears. "Joke's on you! I don't want this anymore! I don't care, Paul! I'd rather be a broke bitch on welfare than to let you use me ever again!"

The timbre in her voice told Duppy that she was dead serious. He knew threats wouldn't work, so he softened his approach. "Tati, listen. I know shit has been crazy, but don't quit. If you want me to fall back, cool, but the world loves you, baby." Duppy begged.

Tatiana cried harder, shaking her head. "I-I-I can't do this anymore, Paul, I can't," she sobbed, and Duppy could tell that she was through.

That was the first moment he thought about killing her. He didn't want to kill her for personal reasons. It wasn't about her rejecting him. No. He simply did the math in his head. Alive she was worth millions, dead, she could be worth billions. Especially now with this total breakdown on the stage in Madison Square Garden. Duppy's conniving mind spewed possible scenarios while one popped out like a light bulb being turned on...

Suicide.

"Okay baby, I understand. Just... let me see you upstairs. You're upset and I'm worried about you," Duppy intoned, sympathetically. He spoke loud enough to make sure Jaylan heard and could attest to, which he later did.

"O-okay," Tatiana nodded.

When they arrived at her penthouse, Duppy made sure when he walked by the door man, he said, "I'm worried about you, baby. I'm scared you may do something crazy."

The doorman would later note how tender Duppy was with Tatiana. If only he knew what was going on in his demented brain.

Once they reached her suite, Duppy poured her a drink. He slipped two Xanax pills from her medicine cabinet. He already anticipated telling the police she was on antidepressants. "I gave her two Xanax pills. I thought it would make her sleep, but when I woke up..."

She took the drink and knocked it back. Duppy refilled her glass.

"Paul, why did you do this to me? Did you have to have me that bad?" Tatiana questioned.

The honest questioning in her gaze made Duppy look away. "I've always loved you, ma. I guess I got carried away," he admitted.

Tatiana sobbed. "You didn't love me, Paul. You just love control. You wanted to be in control."

He gave her another taste. "Maybe you're right."

After the third drink, Tatiana began to nod, the tears receding into the haze of alcohol and the kicking in of the pills.

"It doesn't matter anymore...nothing... matters," she mumbled, as she drifted off.

Duppy looked at her sleeping face and for a moment, his heart wouldn't allow him to follow through with his plan. She looked so innocent, so vulnerable, like when they first met in high school. Quiet, but her presence always lit up the room, and when she sang, even the rowdiest thug could be brought to tears.

"Why couldn't you just love me?" Duppy asked her sleeping form.

But she hadn't, although that didn't stop his desire from becoming infatuation, then obsession and then demonic possession. His twisted soul knew, by killing her, she would always be his and he'd reap the rewards as well.

After all, you're nobody until somebody kills you...

He scooped her into his arms and picked her up.

"What are you doing?" Tatiana questioned softly, more asleep than awake.

"Taking you to rest," he replied, more truthful than she would ever know.

He carried her out onto the balcony, the wind whipping all around them. Duppy looked down 27 stories. The kiss of the breeze on Tatiana's cheek woke her up.

"Where—?" she started to say, then she saw the tears in Duppy's eyes and her heart instantly understood.

"Oh," she gasped.

"I'm sorry," he sniffled, as he let her go over the balcony.

He watched her drop. In his mind, he would forever see her eyes large and luminous, locked on his as she hurtled to her shattering death. Her eyes would never let him go. Her eyes would always haunt him.

When she hit, it seemed to explode in his head as well as boom in the air. Her body hit the roof of a car, smashing the windshield and setting off car alarms up and down the block. He even heard the doorman exclaim, "Oh my God!"

Duppy took a few Xanax in order to go to sleep, which was a part of his strategy. He laid down and drifted off to sleep quickly, before he was awakened by the sound of the police ringing the bell. Once he let them in, it all went according to plan.

"She was on antidepressants. I gave her two Xanax pills. I thought it would make her sleep, but when I woke up..."

Everything was going according to plan. The media ate it up. "Young R&B diva kills herself" read the next day's New York Times. The streets wept. The world mourned and the police swallowed the story whole.

Except for her.

"Hello, Mr. Duppy. Do you mind if I ask you a few questions?"

Duppy would've thrown any other Federal agent out, but Vanya was too beautiful to resist. "And you are?" He questioned, extending his hand to shake hers.

When she tended hers, instead of shaking her hand, he kissed it.

"Mr. Duppy, you realize I am a Federal agent," Vanya said, flashing her badge.

"You're also beautiful. Please, have a seat," Duppy offered, as he resumed sitting behind his desk.

Vanya sat down. "Just a few questions about Miss Marlow's death."

Duppy dropped his head. "Yeah, yo... her suicide broke my heart," he replied.

Vanya eyed him steadily. "I didn't say anything about a suicide."

Duppy quickly lifted his head and met her gaze. "I don't understand. The police ruled it—"

Vanya cut him off. "New York State ruled it a suicide. I'm Federal."

Duppy kept his cool, but inside his heart was banging. "Is there a problem?"

"That's what I'm here to find out. You were the last person to see Miss Marlow alive, correct?"

"I already told the police that."

"Yes, I'm aware of that," Vanya replied curtly, as she jotted notes on her pad.

Her standoffish attitude was beginning to irk Duppy. Up until that point, the police had been deferential to his celebrity and sympathetic to his story. Now, Vanya was coming at him hard.

"Am I missing something? I mean, correct me if I'm wrong, but I am the man who lost his best friend here, right?"

"And biggest money maker. Let's not forget that," Vanya added, with a smile too sweet to be sincere.

Duppy shifted in his seat. He was thinking quickly, trying to imagine where this was going, and what this FBI bitch wanted. Man, she was an angel to look at, but there was a devil heart beating in that chest. He could feel it. She was every kind of trouble wrapped up in pretty paper. Showing attitude wasn't going to get him anywhere with this woman, so he tried to be smooth. "Money isn't everything."

Vanya looked around at his spacious office, designed right out of *Architectural Digest* and chuckled. Duppy's office had moved from Chelsea Market to downtown off the back of Tatiana's success, and pretty soon if her death was anything to go by in terms of sales, he'd be able to buy the building.

"Really? Is that why you're sitting on the 40th floor of a suite that cost more each month than some people make in a year?"

"Look, Agent—"

"Green."

"Green. I don't appreciate you coming in my office treating me like a suspect. I—" Duppy said, keeping it civil, but Vanya cut him off.

"But Mr. Duppy, you *are* a suspect," Vanya answered.

Duppy's stomach dropped, but he kept his composure. "Then this conversation is over. Talk to my lawyer."

Vanya shrugged. "Suit yourself, but we both know you don't want to lawyer up. Not now. Not with the media all over this case. Imagine if it leaked that Duppy was under investigation for the murder of Tatiana. Not a good look, huh? Lawyer up and that'll be tomorrow's headline, I guarantee!"

Duppy glared into her poker-faced expression. His gut was saying there was more to it, but he couldn't put his finger on it. "What kind of game are you playing, Agent Green?"

"The kind that costs lives. Care to wager?"

"You come in here, accusing me of murdering someone I really cared for, someone I—"

"You do understand calculus, don't you, Mr. Duppy? I happen to be very good at math. I love math, especially calculus, because calculus can help solve very complex real-world problems. Problems like if a person jumps off a balcony 27 stories in the air, taking the rate of gravity and velocity into account, they would've landed very differently depending on if they were standing, dived over or were simply...dropped," Vanya explained, maintaining eye contact.

No words passed for several moments, as the two of them kept a steady gaze. Duppy finally broke the silence.

"What... do... you... want?"

"Not what, who."

"I'm listening."

"The Colombian," Vanya answered.

Duppy scowled, confusion written in his brow. "Who?"

"You never heard of him?"

"No."

"That's the most truthful thing you've said all day. Don't worry. He knows you. You have heard of Baby J, correct?"

"James Manfred. He owns a label in Chicago. What about it?"

"He's my in to get at The Colombian," Vanya replied.

"And this Colombian, should I assume he does what Colombians are known for?" Duppy questioned.

"As long as we aren't talking coffee," Vanya quipped.

Duppy nodded. "So, what do I have to do?"

"Have Wadoo introduce you. We know that Wadoo is being supplied by The Colombian as well."

"You seem to know a lot."

Vanya smiled. "More than you will ever know."

"So, what about—"

"Tatiana? What about her?" Vanya winked, then stood up, adding, "I'll be in touch."

She walked out, leaving Duppy relieved and scared to death at the same time.

VERSE

Power sat back, hit the blunt and took in everything the Colombian told him. "So, Duppy been workin' for the goddamn feds the whole time?" he said, the word of Duppy's betrayal twisting in his mind.

The Colombian nodded. "Exactly."

"But...you knew and he's still livin'?" Power probed. He still couldn't get away from the idea that The Colombian was testing him in some way. Because if Power had found out that Duppy was selling him out to the Feds he'd have iced him without breaking a sweat.

The Colombian laughed. "Sometimes it's better to let a rat live; then you can feed him poison and watch him die."

They both laughed.

"Yeah, I guess you right. But now, I think we need to make a move," Power suggested.

"I couldn't agree more. Set it up."

"You already know."

After Power left, the whole thing was still nagging at him. Something just wasn't right, but he knew who he needed to talk to.

Egypt slid her little black dress off her shoulders. Her sensual movements seductive enough to charm a snake. And he was a snake that enjoyed being charmed.

"Damn ma, you shoulda been a dancer," he grinned, sitting back and enjoying the show.

Her dress hit the floor and her perfect, naked body made him instantly hard. She spread her legs and wound her hips so sexily. He swore he could feel the grip of her pussy already. Her eyes locked on him and she touched herself in the way he knew he would be doing soon. She stroked two fingers between her legs against her pussy. He could hear whispers of flesh as the fingers brushed against her pussy lips. The words they spoke in the silent room were calling him forward.

"You ready for me, baby?" Egypt cooed.

"Bring yo' sexy ass over here."

She smiled, the tip of her tongue between her teeth, and came over to him. She dropped to her knees and began to unbuckle his jeans. She still didn't break eye contact once. She didn't need to look to work on his belt.

His dick popped out, heavy and hard.

"Damn boy, how that thing fit in those pants?" Egypt smiled slyly. She leaned forward, eye contact maintained, taking a year to slowly approach the swollen head of his dick. After a century of anticipation, she ran her tongue along the head. It felt like she was moving ice across the hood as her breath backed up the movement of her tongue. He groaned and lifted his lips, wanting to go fully inside her mouth. She pursed her lips and placed a firm kiss down on him, before just as slowly parting her lips millimeter by millimeter until she finally allowed him inside her mouth.

"That shit feel good," he said knowing it was the understatement of his life, but it was all the words he had as his dick reached the back of her throat and pulsed there.

She bobbed her head a while, and then seeming like she was

giving up the best thing she'd ever tasted, she brought his dick out, to where it where it rested on her chin. "Oh yeah, you ain't seen nothing yet," she snickered before taking the whole thing back into her mouth, relaxing her throat this time until she had taken all nine inches.

His toes curled in his Jordans as he bit down on his bottom lip and grabbed the back of her head. He began to slow fuck her face. Her wet mouth felt like a pussy, and as he put a palm beneath her chin he felt his dick bulging her throat below.

Shit. This bitch was the real deal.

"Fuck," he growled. "You a beast."

He could feel her smile on his balls.

Egypt deep throated him until his dick started to twitch, a sure sign that he was about to bust. Egypt stood up, straddled him and slid his dick deep inside herself.

"Shhhit," she gushed, her pussy sloppy and dripping against his full penetration. He grabbed her ass and massaged her cheeks as he long dicked her hard and steady.

"Who's your Daddy?" He grunted.

"You are," she sang.

"Who?"

"Youuuu," she screamed.

He worked his dick as deeply as it could go, making her cum a second time before he scooped her up and laid her on the floor. He cocked her legs over his shoulders and stroked her vigorously until she clawed at the carpet.

"Oh yes, Daddy, that's my spot!" She squealed.

"Show Daddy you can take this dick!"

She began to push back, stroke for stroke, their slapping skins sounding like applause.

"I-I can feel it in my stomach."

"Turn over on your stomach," he told her.

Egypt turned over, touting her ass in the air and looking back over her shoulder.

"Like this, Daddy?"

He answered with the force of his penetration, taking her breath away with one stroke. Egypt was loving every minute of it, as he pounded her, thrust after thrust, making her cum again, back to back.

"Cum for me, Daddy, please," she begged.

He was in a zone. Her pussy had him fucked up. He was so turned out, he was ready to marry it.

"You better not ever give this pussy away," he grunted. He made the face that would tell Egypt that he was dead serious. Now he had plowed this field, only he would be able to plant the seed there. This was a new feeling for him, so definite and consumed by one bitch. This girl was worth the feeling, he knew he'd never want to fuck another pussy as long as he lived. And if she wanted to live, there'd never be any other dick better for her than his.

Whoever wanted it.

His body became a spasming thing and with a rising, tingling rush he came deep inside her, hoping that one day a third person would grow. He had to shake his head at that. Man, he was getting lost. "Damn," he sighed.

Several seconds of bliss later, they heard a knock at her door.

"Don't answer that," he told her, because they both knew who it was.

"I have to."

Reluctantly, he rolled over. She got up and put on a robe and went to the door.

Egypt didn't need to look through the spy hole to know who was out in the hotel corridor. He knew she was there, and she knew his knock. This could go one of two ways, it could be war or it could not. There would be no middle ground. These gangsters don't have light and shade, they don't have maybe's and nearly's. It was all or nothing with them, and it was all or nothing right now.

Sometimes when you reach a crossroads you have no idea which road to take, Egypt thought, sometimes you just have to strike out and make the best of it. The only option that wasn't open to her was going back down the path already taken.

She took a deep breath, then opened the door.

It was Power.

The smell of sex hit Power like a punch in the face.

His stomach got queasy, but he refused to show her she had hurt him. He walked into the hallway of the suite. He could see through the door to the bedroom that the bed had not been disturbed. This had been an urgent, improvised fuck, and the trail of Egypt's clothes leading to the suite's lounge area told him everything he needed to know.

Egypt might be in a robe, but she was completely naked beneath. Her big eyes were giving nothing away, and she offered no explanation, so Power went with his gut. No point denying the obvious. "You get around, huh?"

"You coming in or not?"

Power eyed her hard, then stepped inside. She shut the door, then turned to him. Her robe hung open now, exposing her nakedness underneath. She wasn't trying to hide anything.

"Yo, I gotta talk to you," Power said, keeping hold of himself. If he had to front this out he would.

"I'm listening," she replied.

Kane stepped around the corner, wearing only his boxers and a shit-eating grin.

Power's world shifted like the deck of a liner hitting an iceberg. Power just held the breath inside that was threatening to blast out his rage like the heat from an opened furnace.

"Peace, God," he greeted Power, nonchalantly.

Power looked from Kane to Egypt.

"At least you kept it in the family," Power said, his jaw set, doing a good job of masking his anger and pain.

"Ay yo, ma, you good?" Kane questioned.

"Yes," Egypt replied.

Kane walked back into the bedroom. Egypt turned back to Power.

"So, talk."

"It's about Duppy."

"What about him?"

Power hesitated, looked toward the bedroom, and then stepped closer to her, whispering, "He's a rat."

Egypt looked at him. "Are you sure?"

"The Colombian is." Power just wanted to back hand the bitch but kept what cool he had.

There were bigger games being played around them. He could deal with this situation later.

"So, what are we going to do?"

"I need you to find out what he knows."

"And then?" She pressed.

"We'll handle the rest," he assured her.

Power started for the door. He stopped then turned back to her. "You're playing a dangerous game, ma," he said then left without waiting for her reply.

"You have no idea," Power thought he heard her say as he closed the door.

Never go back.

BRIDGE

While Kane and Power were burning up the charts, they were burning down their relationship. At first, the beef was subtle. Slick little words masked as jokes, jokes that became sharper and crueler as the beef gained steam, until one day, it exploded.

"Everybody throw your guns up! Throw 'em up!" Power screamed to the capacity crowd in Vegas.

They screamed loud, some caught nose bleeds.

"Who wanna hear this raw shit?" Kane barked.

The beat kicked in and the crowd exploded, rapping along as Kane and Power spat their hottest tracks. Drunk, Kane substituted one line with an ad-lib.

"I fuck so many bitches, I'm fuckin' Power's bitch too!"

Power didn't hesitate. He punched Kane dead in his mouth and they went straight at each other's ass. The crowd, thinking the fight was a part of the show, roared with approval.

"Ay yo! Power and Kane fightin'!" Messiah yelled when the rest of the crew finally turned their attention to the show. Knowledge and Five$ all ran on stage to break up the fight. It wasn't easy, and Five$ got a broken nose for his trouble. With maximum effort and two of the road crew joining them, they were finally able to pull them apart and drag them backstage.

"Get the fuck off me!" Power bassed, snatching away from Five$.

"Nigga, you a pussy! How the fuck you gonna catch feelings over a bitch!" Kane spat.

"Muhfucka this ain't about no bitch, it's about you! You always wanted to be me!" Power shot back.

"Be you?! Who the fuck is you?!"

Power laughed derisively. "I'm the nigga who made you!"

Kane laughed at him, but then Messiah held him back.

"You bitch ass nigga, you made me?! You made me? Then make another me, 'cause I'm out!"

"Fuck you waitin' for?!"

"And I'm takin' the name! You ain't even from the Boro!" Kane spat.

"Q.B.C. ain't shit without me. Ask Duppy."

Both men went their separate ways in more ways than one.

OUTRO

The realization hung in the room like cracked math as Spagoli and O'Brien's faces showed they'd unlocked the algebra of betrayal. "So... you're telling me that Power thought Duppy was snitching and it was you the whole time?" Spagoli laughed.

He smirked. "Like I said in the beginning, no man is safe."

"So, is that why Power had Duppy killed?" O'Brien asked.

He shook his head. "No, he had Duppy killed because he thought Duppy was me."

"I don't understand," Spagoli said, his face telling him the pieces of the story in Spagoli's head still weren't fitting together.

He looked past the detectives at the one-way mirror. He saw not the woman beyond it, but saw his own face clearer than he'd ever seen it in his life. Was it the face of a rat? Was it the face that would betray everything he stood for? *What was all this shit about in the end?* He thought. *Just pussy and saving my ass.*

Is staking Power out for the vultures to feed on the actions of a man with gangsta pride? Any other beef and he'd have just shot the muhfucka in the face.

Why not now?

He stared into those eyes looking back at him from the glass. The eyes that burned from the face that had burned Power.

He looked from O'Brien to Spagoli, and fixed on the WOP with a look of pure steel. "You don't understand?" asked Kane. "Don't sweat it man. You will."

TRACK 6

When the breakup of Q.B.C. went viral, their fans went crazy. No one could believe it, until Power confirmed it on the radio during an interview in Cincinnati. "Yeah yo. Things ain't always what you think. Sometimes, situations can't be helped," Power remarked.

"Well, the word is that the singer Egypt is at the bottom of this. It's been said that you, Kane, and even Duppy—"

Power cut the interviewer off. "You can't believe everything you hear. Bottom line, groups break up all the time. It ain't that serious. Let's talk about my solo album!"

Deep down, the question burned him up because it was true. He finished the interview, then he went straight to the airport and flew his ass back to NYC. He didn't even go to his own crib. He went directly to Egypt's spot.

Egypt answered the door then let him in.

"I ain't catch you at a bad time, did I?" he asked, sarcastically.

"No. I'm alone," she said truthfully. She'd been feeling low for weeks now as the cancer between Kane and Power had grown from a small tumor of hate into a terminal disease. The radio interview had been playing on every news show and every rap station from the moment the words had left Power's lips. TMZ had been ringing her phone off the hook. It wasn't just the fans who were in mourning. Egypt felt broken.

"I know you heard the interview," said Power.

"Yes, I did."

"So, what are you going to do?"

"Do?" She echoed, fully understanding his question but her face betraying that she was dreading the answer she knew she would have to give.

Power's jaw flexed with aggravation. "You know what the fuck I'm talking about."

"Power, I—"

"Are you rolling with me, or what?" He demanded to know.

Egypt blinked back the tears. "Believe me, baby, I wish I could. But I can't."

"Can't? Or won't?" Power bassed, stepping closer to her.

The tears broke free. There was no way she could tell him that Kane had her painted in a corner. That he knew she was a cop and that he was not working with her. Her heart may've been with Power, but her common sense was with her own sense of survival.

"I... I just can't," Egypt sobbed.

Power started to storm out, but something gave him pause. She knew he loved her. That much had been made clear on the yacht floating in the Mediterranean, but she also knew Power's gangsta pride wouldn't allow him to express it aloud, even now. The fact she knew how much he truly loved her, and that he saw the bind she was in with Kane as a kind of rejection. It was turning his pain to rage.

He stopped at the door. "Nah, fuck that," he spun back and stormed towards Egypt, adding, "You choosing that nigga over me?!"

"No baby, it's not —" was all she got out when Power back handed her to the floor.

"Please, don't," she cringed, throwing up her hands expecting another blow. But the back handed slap wasn't from anger, it was from his broken heart. She could see pieces of his heart snapping off in every movement of his eyes. Power took hold of her wrist. She could've easily reversed the hold Power had on her as he snatched her up from the floor, but in a way, she felt like she deserved to be hurt too because she had betrayed their love.

"You want him that bad?!" Power barked, as he snatched her dress up and ripped off her panties.

"You-you don't understand," she sobbed.

"I'ma make you understand, bitch." Power unhooked his belt, pushed his jeans to the floor and stepped out of them, his dick swinging free, growing and stiffening. He picked her up by her ass checks, lifting her off the ground and making her wrap her legs around his waist as he sat her on his dick.

Upon penetration, she moaned. Almost as if the shame felt good, as if the hurt in her pussy and in her heart were linked and complimented one another. She clung to him, throwing her arms around his neck and burying her head in his shoulder. "Oh God, why are you doing this to me?" She trembled.

"'Cause you mine and always will be," Power gutted as he pounded her pussy, grudge-fucking her. She felt the vengeance in every stroke. Every thrust, Egypt felt in her stomach as a piece of Power's absolution and his forgiveness. Power fucked her with violence, but there was love returning as he kissed down on her neck. Her whole body shivered as he hit her spot over and over.

"Who fuck you like this, huh?"

"Nobody!"

"Can he fuck you like this?"

"No baby, only you, only you." She whispered in his ear as she came a second time.

Power couldn't hold back anymore. He exploded inside of her, his knees giving way and his breath coming in short sharp bursts.

He put her down gently, all the violence dissipated, as they both panted, willing their heart rates to slow.

She cried heavily then as he took her to the bedroom and they made love, slowly and calmly, the broken pieces coming back together.

Then Power told her exactly what he was going to do to Kane.

Power exhaled smoke from the blunt and passed it back to Five$. "So you in this wit' me, thun?"

"Yeah, yeah, God. It's whatever wit' me. I fuck wit' you so you already know what it is," Five$ said, giving Power dap.

Power was back in the projects, on the roof. Just him and Five$, drinking, smoking and watching the sun go down. Power wasn't bothered by randoms when he came back to the Boro. Everyone was cool with him. Project peoples were as cool as fuck, but this wasn't just a social visit. He had wheels he wanted to put in motion.

"The nigga think it's a game. Bottom line though, he ain't gonna let me get near him. So, I need you to set it up."

Five$ stopped mid-puff. "Set it up?" he echoed, sounding unsure.

"Yeah. I thought you said you was down. What up, you scared?"

"Nah, nah, fuck nah. I'm just sayin', nigga ain't no dumb muhfucka. He know you my man. Why not just get a bitch to rock him to sleep?" Five$ suggested.

"'Cause that's our MO. He'll see that comin' a mile away. The only bitch that could pull it off is Egypt," Power replied, bitterness lacing his tone.

"I don't know, Power. This whole other level shit."

"I just need you to tell me where it's gonna be. Just text me. That's it. No one will ever know," Power assured him.

Five$ hit the blunt and thought about it. "Just text you?

Power took the offered blunt and nodded. "One text."

"Aight my nigga...I got you," Five$ said, then they shook hands. The sun had gone, and now it was full night.

As Five$ sat in the back of the Uber ride heading home, he thought about everything Power had said. Seeing Kane die wouldn't have bothered Five$ one bit. Kane had always looked down on Five$, ever since they had been kids and were stealing from the corner bodega.

He and Kane were about eight and had just started their shoplifting crime spree. They would go in supermarkets, stuffing candy and cookies in their coat pockets and pants, then run all the way home to QB and eat until they couldn't eat anymore.

On this particular day, it was no different. They went in the store with every intention of filling their pockets, but Carlito, the store owner was watching them. He knew from the minute they walked in that they were there to steal. As soon as they made their move, he was on them.

"Hey! What are you doing?" Carlito barked.

Five$ got scared. He dropped everything he had, but Kane didn't panic. As soon as Carlito tried to grab him, he bit the shit out of Carlito's hand.

"Holy fucking Christ!" Carlito bellowed, the pain intense enough to bring tears to his eyes.

Kane darted by him, pockets full of stolen candy bars, and took off out the door. Five$ tried to follow but was too slow. Carlito grabbed him by the throat with his good hand and slammed him hard against the racks. Candy bars fell around Five$'s ears like a Vegas jackpot.

"You little piece of shit," Carlito spat.

He was enraged because Kane got away, so he took it out on Five$, kicking him in the stomach. Five$ circled up in the fetal position. "I'm going to kill you! You steal from me?!"

Carlito spanked Five$'s ass for good measure. The stinging pain zapping through him. Carlito raised his foot to stomp on Five$. Five$ was so scared, he peed on himself there and then on the shop floor. "Please don't kill me, mister. I-I-I was hungry," Five$ sobbed.

Carlito snatched him up by his arm and pointed in his face. "Who was the other boy?! Huh? You tell me or I cut you up in little pieces!"

Five$ had never been so scared in his life. "He-he-he lives on 12th street!"

"Come on! You show me now!"

Five$ knew he was wrong, but he walked Carlito right up to Kane's door, pee dripping from his pants, leaving a trail of shame. Carlito took him up the stairs and knocked on the door, shaking the boy by the shoulder and cuffing him upside the ear twice. Every head on the street was turned on Five$ and his plight in Carlito's grip. Five$ felt like the whole world was watching his humiliation...

(Later when Carlito walked back to his bodega, with the five dollars he'd got from Five$'s Momma to cover the theft held high, it gave Five$ the hood name he would wear for the rest of his days. Getting that hood name was the only good thing to come outta that day.)

After a minute, Kane's mother answered the door. For a second, her face showed only confusion and then her eyes settled on Five$ and recognized him.

"Your son stole from me!" Carlito bellowed.

Kane's mother pointed at Five$. "He ain't my son!"

"Not him! Him!" Carlito barked and indicated beyond the door into the building, to where Kane was sitting on the couch munching on a candy bar, watching TV. He had been so taken by surprise, that his mouth stayed wide and the piece of candy he'd bitten off slid slowly down his chin.

Kane's mother could spot guilt in her son from five hundred yards away. She went right up to Kane's ass, whooping him right in front of Carlito and Five$. And she didn't stop until Kane was crying the same as Five$.

After that day, Kane always called Five$ a rat, clowning him unmercifully for his eight-year-old mistake. He would never let him live it down. Having Kane out of the way made Five$ agree to help Power.

But he also feared Kane, and he knew, if anyone ever found out he had something to do with Kane's death, he was a dead man himself. That was a chance he wasn't willing to take just to stop being bullied. It was like one of those pharmaceutical commercials where the medicine cured a minor problem, but the side effects included even worse problems. So, Five$ jumped the fence on Power and called Kane.

"Yo."

"It's Fi. What up. Meet me at the spot."

Click.

The call was short and sweet. Five$ conveyed the fact that the issue was urgent because he told Kane to meet him at an out of the way diner in Long Island.

Five$ was already there when Kane pulled up and parked. Five$ got up, leaving his coffee undrunk and his sandwich untouched. He'd ordered it out of habit before he'd realized that he was too wired to have an appetite. He got up from the table, went outside into the warm night air and got in Kane's passenger seat.

Kane pulled away. The city shimmered like a mirage. Five$ felt as thin and transparent as the windshield looking out on the scene, but there was no way he was going to not tell Kane what was going down. The memory of the Carlito incident be damned.

"What's good, yo?" Kane questioned, as he made a left turn against traffic.

"Shit is crazy thun, word... I just left Power," Five$ admitted.

Kane looked at him. "Yeah? And?"

"The nigga in his feelings over this shit, thun...We planning to kill you," Five$ informed him.

Kane chuckled. "Oh word? That bitch ass nigga think he can murder me? What else he say, Fi?"

Five$ pulled out a cigarette and lit it, then replied, "He don't want you to leave Q.B.C. It's a brand now. He wants to take over."

Kane made a left that got Five$'s attention. Five$ looked up and saw that they were in a cemetery. The graves and monuments loomed. Angel wings riding over smooth marble, family mausoleums faced with shadows that could have hidden anything. "What up thun?" Five$ questioned, trying to mask his anxiety.

But Kane only smirked. Five$'s could smell his own fear. It wasn't just the atmosphere of the cemetery that was chilling him. Kane's face was fixed forward. He had that *always in control* look that marked him as the coolest of operators. Kane pulled the car over, looked at Five$, and said, "Come on." Then he got out of the car, not waiting for Five$'s response. The arrogance of knowing his order would be obeyed.

Five$'s guts ran liquid. He knew if he didn't front this right, Kane would know he had some kind of guilt in his mind. But if he did get out, there was no telling what Kane would do. He took a deep breath and climbed out of the Benz. For a second, he couldn't see where Kane was, but then he picked up the glow of a blunt like an ember in the shadows beneath a tree. Kane was waiting for him.

Five$ walked over, trying to keep his face from showing the fear he felt inside.

Kane sucked on the blunt, and exhaled, but didn't offer it to Five$. "Tell me somethin' thun, why did Power feel like he could bring something like this to you?" Kane asked.

Five$ felt the rug being pulled from beneath him. How could he have been so stupid not to see this coming? He made up some shit on the spot, and it sounded exactly like he had just made it up on the spot. "I—um—yo, the nigga was just smoking in his feel—"

Five$'s stomach turned like a sick cat.

"Stop stuttering and answer the fucking question," Kane growled, his voice taking on an ominous edge.

Five$ lit a cigarette to buy time, but the hand shook as he raised it to his mouth.

"Thun, I swear I would never—"

Smack!

Kane smacked the shit out of Five$, sending the cigarette one way and spittle another. The sparks of ash looked like drunken fairies falling to the ground. Without hesitation, Kane pulled his .50 and put it in Five$'s face.

"Why did he tell you, Fi? You better not lie," Kane warned.

Five$ was damn near in tears. "I don't know, Kane, I don't know."

"You used to talk shit about me to him, didn't you?!"

Five$ hesitated to admit the truth. Kane put the cold steel to his face and cocked the hammer. "Sometimes thun, but it wasn't like that. It was just some bullshit!" he stammered.

Kane smiled, then slowly lowered the Eagle. "See? That wasn't so hard. You must think I'm slow. Nigga, he woulda never said no shit like that to you if he ain't think you felt the same way," Kane pushed the point home by putting the muzzle directly against Five$'s forehead, as if it could suck the truth out of his brain.

"My word thun—"

"Shut the fuck up. Your word ain't shit. So, what up, what's the plan?" Kane wanted to know.

"He...he wanted me to just hang with you then text him and let him know where you are," Five$ answered, squeezing his eyes shut, thinking the next thing to happen would be the top of his head flying away and his brains falling on the gravestone like pieces of confetti.

But the shot never came.

The Eagle came away from his forehead. He heard Kane clicking on the safety and the rustle of clothes as he put the gun into the top of his pants.

Kane nodded and thought to himself *no one knew that I'm talking to the feds. The feds didn't even know that there is a plot on my life.* How he could use both those facts to his advantage came at him in a rush and worked up a smile on his lips. Kane pulled Five$ up by his sweatshirt and all but threw him back in the car. Squealing out of the cemetery like the stone Angels were coming to life and fixing to take him, Kane raced through the darkness trying to plan out the next move that would be his best tool.

Then, he stopped the car in a dead part of town, smiled and told Five$ what he wanted.

He could see from Five$'s expression that the nigga couldn't believe his ears. "Follow through?"

Kane nodded. "You rock Power to sleep thinking that shit is all good. I'll tell you when and where to text him, you understand?"

"Yeah, yeah thun. I got you," Five$ replied.

"You handle this nigga and I won't forget how you held it down. But if you fuck up, nigga, I'ma kill your whole goddamn family," Kane bassed like it was the real deal sermon talk.

"I got you, thun," Five$ vowed.

Kane looked him in the eye and replied, "You better."

LONG LIVE THE KING

I *t's good to be the king...*
These were the words that went through Duppy's mind as the news of Q.B.C.'s breakup blew up the hip-hop world. Sales for both of their first two albums catapulted them into another stratosphere, as people tried to grab hold of the past and preserve the classics. Duppy talked up that Power was working on a solo album and fielded questions from the press as if it were some kind of secret. Adding a layer of bullshit and mystique never did sales any harm with product. Power was a product like all the others.

Duppy did another interview over the phone, the fifth that morning. The media was sucking on Duppy's titty and he was squeezing them only the best milk of information. "Mr. Duppy, how are you going to keep the peace when both of these acts are on your label?" the reporter questioned.

"I'm keeping these guys separate. No tours together, no videos. It's going to be rough, but we all about the money, not war. Anyone that doesn't understand that has no business in the building."

"What about Egypt? It's been reported that she is the reason for the break up?"

Duppy chuckled. It was a feeding frenzy and Duppy felt like the Emperor of Sharks.

"Egypt is the cause of a lot of things, but the break up isn't one of them."

"One more question—"

"I'm sorry. I have to go," Duppy replied then hung up on the phone right before his secretary stepped into his office.

"Paul, Ménage is here," she announced.

"Who?"

"Ménage."

Duppy had been so caught up in the morning of interviews and Q.B.C. bullshit, he couldn't remember anything about anyone called "Ménage." His expression was blank.

The secretary sighed and flicked a picture up on her phone. Two thin girls, one blonde, and one redhead. Finely tuned bitches with more hair than talent. "The group you set up for your four thirty. The white girls."

Duppy's expression brightened. He'd invited them to a meeting on the strength of their picture rather than the sound of their demo. Anyone can be taught to sing, but it was a real talent being pretty. "Oh yeah, yeah. Send them in."

Moments later, three white girls walked in. There was the redhead and the blonde he was expecting, who were singers, and their manager, a brunette.

"Good afternoon, Mr. Duppy. I appreciate you arranging this meeting," the manager smiled, extending her hand.

Duppy nodded, smiled and shook it. "Please, call me Duppy."

"Lisa," she replied.

The three women sat down, the girls looking around the room with its expensive furniture, framed platinum discs and its own bar. Their eyes lit up like a kid's first trip to Disneyland. Lisa was remaining cool and professional. *I'm gonna enjoy breaking **that** down,* he thought.

"So, what do you think?" Lisa questioned, gesturing to the girls.

Duppy nodded. "Nice look. They complement one another aesthetically. Nice balance, contrast."

"What did you think of the demo?" the blonde asked, but Lisa shot her a look that said, *I'm doing the talking.*

Duppy smiled subtly at the eye check. "I loved it, you both have beautiful voices," he lied. He'd had one of his people listen to it for him and they'd given him a *so-so*, but the girls themselves deserved...a closer inspection.

"Do I hear a 'but' in there?" Lisa probed, doing her best to keep her anxieties in check.

Such was Duppy's standing in the rap business now, that any meeting he took with a prospective artist was a big deal. You had to be very *very* good to get through his door, or very *very* easy on the eyes.

Duppy chuckled. "No buts, only ands. And I want to see this group do big things!"

The two singers looked at each other, wide-eyed, barely able to control their excitement.

"So where do we go from here?" Lisa asked.

Duppy shrugged. "That depends on you. How far are you willing to go to be stars?"

"Whatever it takes," the redhead gushed.

"Anything," the blonde added.

"Glad to hear it." Duppy turned from the girls to their manager, leaning back in his chair and stroking his chin. This pause seemed to stretch into infinity, the manager shifted uncomfortably in her seat. Duppy smiled. "Lisa?"

Lisa blinked. "What are you asking, Duppy?"

"I'm asking you the same question I asked them. How far are you willing to go to be a part of the project?" Duppy asked, looking Lisa in the eyes.

And then he shut up.

Duppy had used this tactic many times before. They say cream rises to the top, but so does scum. Did he feel uncomfortable pitching what he was about to pitch? Not one bit. It worked with

Tatiana before her unfortunate date with a hotel balcony and destiny, and since then, the conveyor belt of desperate young hopefuls who would bend any which way to get his business had continued. He'd long since let go of any chitter-chatter from his conscience. Bitches wanna work? Bitches gotta pay.

Duppy stayed silent. It was always a killer move. Let the bitch try to make sense of his behavior. He enjoyed watching them squirm as the sexual subtext swam like electric eels below the surface of his silence.

"I'm...um...not sure what you mean," Lisa stuttered.

Duppy smiled. *Oh yes you do he,* thought but said. "Can you dance?"

Lisa's face creased with concern. "Dance?"

"Dance," he offered like he was talking to a child. "You know, move your body. Matter of fact," Duppy continued, pulling up their demo on his phone then playing it through the surround sound system in his office. "I want to *see* you perform."

The blonde and the redhead didn't hesitate. They both got up and began to do their routine, but Duppy held up his hand and hit pause on his phone. With faces just as tattooed with confusion as Lisa's, the girls came to an uncertain stop. One began to speak, but Duppy shushed her with a finger to his lips. This was almost his favorite part. He pointed at the manager. "No, no, wait a minute. Lisa, I want you to join them."

Lisa just looked at him. "But... I'm not a performer."

Duppy shrugged. "We all must perform sooner or later. Didn't Shakespeare say all the world is a stage?" he drawled. Duppy had never seen *Hamlet* in his life. Someone had repeated that quote once to him once and it stuck. He didn't always use it in the right context, but he did like to use it in situations like this. Especially when the stage was soon to be his dick.

The look in his eyes confirmed for Lisa the disgusted feeling that was playing out on her face. This is what he meant by *how far was she willing to go?* Duppy liked it when that penny dropped with a near audible *clunk.*

Slowly, she stood up, then joined the group. Duppy restarted the demo and slid a smile across his face the size of and as dazzling as, a fully pimped Lincoln Continental.

Lisa's steps were awkward, but she looked determined to do her part, her face shadowed by deep concentration. Duppy stopped the music again. Three sets of eyes flicked towards him, not knowing what might be coming next.

"Wait, wait, this isn't working. I need an exclusive performance. Something only my eyes can see. Do something to make me feel you," Duppy told them.

The blonde and the redhead got it right away, then looked at each other, then back at Duppy. They began a sensual striptease. Duppy restarted the demo and watched as they discarded their clothes like professional strippers.

Lisa stopped dancing, her anger overtaking her willingness to play along. "This is bullshit! This isn't a fucking meeting."

Duppy laughed in her face. "You want this deal or not? Ladies?"

"Yes!" the blonde and redhead sang in broken unison. By now neither were wearing panties, already naked from the waist down.

"Fuck you!" Lisa spat, with every ounce of venom her battered self-esteem could drag up, then turned for the door.

"Million-dollar deal, but fuck it, I can always get another manager. Take care, Lisa," Duppy taunted.

Lisa paused, her hand on the door knob. Duppy wondered if she'd been asked to prostitute herself before. He assumed so given her reaction. Bitches often knew the score when they came up to his office to do business, especially if their underwear they put on was anything to judge. Duppy decided to tell Lisa exactly what was at stake if she left the office.

"If you walk out, honey, it's back to the 9 to 5 grind. I guess you saw these girls as a chance to escape that for you. So, what am I doing other than exploiting another exploiter? Welcome to the food chain. In or out Lisa, I haven't got all day," Duppy finished coldly.

Lisa took a deep breath, let go of the knob and turned back to the room.

"You're an asshole," she remarked.

Duppy laughed. "It's your ass I'm more interested in right now. Ladies, help Lisa get in the mood."

The redhead and the blonde knew where they fit into the situation, and so they moved toward Lisa. At first her body froze as they began to caress and stroke her. A tear balanced on the lid of her eye before making a slow path down her cheek. The girls were getting more involved. Putting their hands inside Lisa's clothes and down inside the waistband of her skirt.

Duppy clicked his fingers at Lisa. "Enjoy it bitch. I hate to see an unhappy employee."

Lisa closed her eyes, began to sway to the music, and hesitantly her hand began to move over the redhead's titties. Duppy was happy to see that she was complying fully now. The sheer power of the moment had Duppy hard as a rock.

"Now, it's my turn to perform," he said slowly. He stepped from behind the desk and the girls automatically engulfed him in kisses and strokes. They were a little scrawny for his taste. The redhead was tomboy skinny and the blonde had no ass, but big juicy titties. Pleasingly however, their bodies went in and out in all the right places.

Lisa, by contrast, may have been the coldest but she had the baddest body. She was heavy-chested with long shapely legs.

Duppy was in white girl heaven, snowed in. Lisa hung back, a rough gem of resentment still waiting to be cut into the diamond of her submission. "Bitch, get over here," Duppy demanded.

Lisa approached him, uselessly covering her titties, even though her skirt was off and Duppy could see everything in the store. When she was close enough, Duppy grabbed her by the hair, snatched her head back then tongued her down. The redhead grabbed his dick, sunk to her knees and began licking the blonde's pussy in a matter that showed they had done this together before.

But the energy in the room swirled and centered on Duppy and Lisa.

Duppy was bent on breaking any woman that told him *no*. He would rationalize to himself that he wasn't a rapist, because no man would want to own up to that. He saw this situation differently—and seeing it differently made him ok with it. It wouldn't stand up in court, and so that made Duppy think it was consensual in a way. Not that anything that happened in his office would ever get to court.

The way Duppy rationalized it to himself was that every woman freely gave what he demanded. They simply started out not wanting to. If anything, he was a rapist of their will. In that sense, he was like a serial killer. Tatiana had whetted his appetite. Controlling her was like his first drug, and now he needed a shot constantly.

Lisa was just another hit from the same pipe.

"Get on your knees," Duppy grunted, pointing to the floor. Lisa got her knees.

By that point in the situation, she had become totally pliant, almost welcoming. She dropped to her knees and took out Duppy's dick, licking her lips at him as she did it. When his long fat dick came out, her eyes grew wide.

"Damn," she gasped.

"You ever fucked a black man?" he questioned.

Lisa shook her head.

"Then you're gonna *love* this," he snickered, then let loose a stream of a liquid she was not expecting. A stream of humiliation, the harsh liquid of degradation.

Lisa howled and tried to move her head, out of the way, but Duppy had a firm grip on the top of her head.

The other two females were recoiling, taking steps away. Duppy pointed at them and they froze where they were when the look in his eyes nailed them. Lisa started sobbing, big tears running from her eyes. She was wiping at her mouth to get rid of the taste. Her brunette hair had gone into dark rat tails with the soaking, and her shoulders were shivering.

Duppy, satisfied with Lisa's submission, turned the stream onto the redhead. When the force of the stream finally subsided, he pulled the back of her head towards him and shoved his dick in her mouth.

For the rest of the afternoon all three bitches squirmed underneath him. Submissive to his every whim and filthy desire. But this was easy. They wanted the contract and so would do this without feeling it. What Duppy really wanted, he knew, was to thoroughly humiliate Lisa but at the same time make her love doing it.

"Bend her over the desk," he told the blonde and redhead, and just like devilish minions, they hurried to do his bidding.

Lisa didn't resist. There was nothing left to resist. Gone with her pride was her inhibitions. As she was bent over the desk, Duppy could see her pussy was throbbing to be used. Whatever her head was saying, her body was betraying her, and Duppy would make sure her mind caught up with her body. The redhead and the blonde both held one of Lisa's arms by the wrist, pinning her to the desk. Duppy slid off his alligator skin belt and wrapped it around his hand slowly, with all the arrogance of a matador about to dispatch the life of a bull. He eyed her pretty pink ass with just enough of a bubble to be considered phat, then squeezed her checks.

"Say my name," he said. The growl of passion at the back of his throat seemed to make Lisa shake with a mixture of fear and anticipation.

"...Duppy," Lisa answered, her voice weak with lust.

Smack!

The first strike seemed to crack and sizzle as it instantly turned her pink cheek red and tender. She half-moaned-half-groaned her mind and body trying to process pain and pleasure at the same time.

"Say my name!"

"Duppy!"

Smack!

The other cheek jiggled and reddened just as quickly as Lisa howled. But her pussy was so wet, juice ran down her thighs.

"Wrong!"

Smack!

"Daddy!" she squealed, her pussy cumming all over itself.

Duppy smiled, then lowered the belt to his side.

"Now you get it," he replied, before using the wetness of her pussy to lubricate his dick, then slid balls deep into her tight asshole, inch by agonizingly pleasurable inch.

"Oh God!" Lisa gasped, squirting, trying to escape the sensation, but the other two bitches had her securely pinned.

"Yeah, bitch, say my name!"

"D-D-Daddy, it hurts," she groaned, her asshole getting wetter with every stroke.

"Shut the fuck up and take it like a big girl," Duppy spat, long dicking her until he pulled out and waxed her back with his cum...

After that he smashed the redhead and the blonde. When he was completely spent, and his dick raw, he put them out. He took a shower in his office bathroom, the water washing away their juices, his piss and cum. He watched the filth running down his body, along his legs, over his feet and down the drain in the same way he had taken their dignity and submission. As he stepped from the shower, he felt a thousand feet tall. He sat back at his desk, naked and lit a blunt.

Close to nodding off, he heard a knock at his door.

"Who is it?" he called out, irritated for being disturbed.

Kane walked in. Duppy picked his robe from the floor and covered his nakedness. Fuck Kane and his arrogance.

"Damn, this shit smell like pussy," Kane remarked.

"The best way to relax," Duppy said regaining his composure. While Kane went to the bar and pulled a bottle of Henny from the shelf, pulling the cork out with his teeth.

Duppy could have shot the disrespectful nigga right there. But

Kane equaled dollars, and he could buy a thousand bottles of VSOP for the money he made Duppy's label every day.

Kane took a long thirsty slug, and then sat down on the chair on which only a few hours before held Lisa's ass cheeks. It suddenly occurred to Duppy that Kane was probably sitting down in a drying residue of his piss. That made up for the Hennessy and the spat cork. *Fucking justice, nigga.*

"Look at you, kicked back in your robe like you the black Hugh Hefner," Kane said, then they both laughed. But Kane didn't know Duppy was laughing at him sitting in piss.

Kane pulled out his own blunt, lit it, and then kicked his feet up on Duppy's desk.

"That's a five-thousand-dollar desk," Duppy deadpanned, wondering if it was worth telling Kane what he was damaging.

"Shit, all these records I sold for you, I bought this desk," Kane shot back playfully, adding, "I want everything."

"You are Q.B.C. now that Power is solo."

Kane's face shaded serious and put the bottle down. Duppy narrowed his eyes and looked at Kane — was this going to be bad news?

"No, I want it on paper, I want the rights. All of them. Every song, every lyric. Everything. The publishing. I want control."

Duppy swiveled in his chair. "I see. What's in it for me?"

"Twenty five percent."

"Twenty five?" Duppy echoed with a chuckle, adding, "Like I said. What's in it for me?"

"I don't jump ship. You know this is our last album."

"True."

"Lock us in for another five albums, plus whoever else we bring," Kane offered.

Duppy thought for a moment. Running calculations in his head, the girls from Ménage now just a distant memory and a musky aroma in the air. He finished the numbers and started negotiation. "Sixty percent."

"Fifty. Take it or leave it." Kane had the look of a man who wasn't going to go any higher.

It was a risk, but if it locked in anything Kane produced on his next five albums, then Duppy figured he could make that work. And who knows, Kane might bring him more pussy that wanted to be famous...*fringe benefits.*

Under those circumstances, everyone wins.

Duppy reached across the table, and then he and Kane shook hands. "I'll have my lawyers get on it."

"Say no more," said Kane with a smile.

A week later, the deal was final... and the contract for Duppy's life was sealed.

"Yo Fi, where you at?" Kane said, as he sped alongside the West Side Highway in his brand-new Porsche.

"At the crib. Why, what up?" Five$ answered.

"Tonight's the night, my nigga. I'll be at Club Griselda at 11pm. I'll be in a white Maybach, got me? The white stretch Phantom, aight?"

Five$ sat up. "You're going to do it, aren't you?"

Kane heard the gears clicking in Five$'s head, even over the phone. He grinned at Five$'s confused silence. And then, as if putting in the final piece to the jigsaw from Hell, Five$ began "But the Ph..."

"Yeah. That's right." Kane cut him off. "You not as stupid as you look, Fi'."

Another silence, as Five$ came to terms with the truth. "Aight, Kane. Say no more."

"You do everything we talked about, thun, understand?"

"Done." Five$ sounded like an eight-year-old, one shamed for ratting on his friend to Carlito. Kane saw the years rushing back through him, and it felt good. "And Fi, you fuck this up, I'ma fuck you up."

Click!

As soon as Five$ hung up, he called Power.

"Yo," Power answered.

Power was at a new and upcoming strip club in Atlanta called Gold. It was rumored to be owned by a legendary gangsta bitch out of Jersey, but no one had seen her in years. Out of the blue, she had gotten in contact with Power through The Colombian.

When Power answered his cell, he was getting a lap dance by a gorgeous Dominican dancer.

"It's now or never, thun, you ready?" Five$ asked.

"Just tell me the time and place," Power answered.

"Club Griselda. 11pm tonight. Sharp."

"One!"

Click.

Power turned his attention back to the dancer. Her ass was phat, like a real stallion the way she moved it. Power was ready to see what else it could do.

"Damn ma, you makin' a nigga want to take this to a whole 'nother level," Power crooned smoothly, running his hand down her back. The Dominican looked over her shoulder mouth parted, tongue glistening over the glittery sheen of her lips.

"Oh yeah? What level is that, papi?"

The accent was Spanish, but it didn't come from the dancer. Power looked up and smiled, seeing Griselda approaching across the floor on six-inch heels. For a lady who had five years on his mom, Griselda was still *all* woman. She had a figure that would shame an hour glass into shyness, and she moved it like she rolled along on wheels. A brunette mane of weave exploded from her head and fell around her shoulders and down the back of her vintage velvet fishtail dress all the way to the small of her back. A cleavage that would sink a baseball team on a raft shimmied as she moved towards Power and the Dominican.

"You slippin', Power. Never let your attention be distracted from your surroundings," Griselda jeweled him.

"Facts," Power nodded.

Griselda said something to the dancer in Spanish and she sashayed away.

Power stood up and gave Griselda a hug. "What up, big sis? I love the spot."

Griselda flicked her cigarette ash then hit her cigarette. "I hate it, but there's always a method to the madness."

They both sat down. A waitress instantly appeared. "Bring me a bottle of whatever he's drinking," Griselda told her.

She nodded and hurried off.

While Griselda ordered, Power studied her profile. She was beautiful. The hint of grey in the hair beneath the weave was the only indicator she wasn't an inexperienced bitch. She'd come up the hard way in a man's world and had carved her place in it with audacity. She was a legend. She was Roland Father, aka R-Daddy's, right hand. She had been off the radar for a few years, but now she was back, although Power found it strange that she was running a strip club.

She turned her attention to Power. "So, tell me. You want to be a rapper or you want to be rich?"

"Do I really need to answer?" Power replied.

Griselda laughed and hit her cigarette. "Then listen to me: fuck that rap shit. I hear you and your man is beefin' over that bitch, Egypt. Don't. She ain't no good. She the police."

Power's ears perked up. "The police? Like a snitch?"

"Nah, nigga. Like a badge-wearing police officer. She's out of Chicago, but the feds deputized her to go after The Colombian," Griselda explained.

Power couldn't believe his ears. "Does The Colombian know?"

Griselda looked at him and guffawed. "Is all you Queens niggas this slow? Of course, he knows, but there's a way to handle it. There are major consequences for shooting a cop. Besides, it's better to let them think shit is sweet."

Power downed his drink. "I can't believe this shit."

"Why? Because you love her?" Griselda offered with a smirk.

Power shot her a look.

"What, you think I didn't know baby boy? It's written all over your face. Hell, you fell out with your mans over her. Of course, you love her," Griselda said.

Power shook his head. "Me and Kane was bound to fall out sooner or later," he replied.

Griselda drew her cigarette deeply, considering Power with all the wisdom of her years to back up what she was saying. "Love is a weakness the strong can't afford...especially gangstas," she sighed with a wistful eye.

Power was reeling. Griselda had no reason to lie. She was on the level. Trust. But he couldn't yet process what she had told him about Egypt. He squashed the feelings down into his gut where they festered, but allowed him to change the subject. "Can I ask you something? Is R-Daddy..."

"Dead?" she added, anticipating his question. "Yeah, unfortunately."

"That's what muhfuckas thought the first time," Power reminded her.

Griselda looked at him. "This time... I was there. He's dead."

She looked off in the distance, as if she were fighting back tears. But after she hit the cigarette, she was back to her cold, gangsta self. "Anyway, bottom line is the game is wide up. niggas done got soft. You can make a name for yourself if you smart and The Colombian says you are... Are you?"

"No doubt," Power replied, firmly.

Griselda nodded. "Then peep game. Lay low, handle your business and I'll be in touch. You fuckin' wit' a vet now, baby boy," Griselda winked, then walked away.

Power watched her bop off. She may've been a dyke, but she was still a bad bitch. Power sat back and contemplated the situation. Griselda was a legend. Her man R-Daddy was one of the greatest hustlers in the game. But he knew associations of that magnitude came with a price.

"Fuck it," he mumbled to himself and pulled out his phone.

After three rings, the phone was answered. "We got him," Power spoke like he was focused and tight, but inside his heart, ice was growing with hard, sharp spikes.

DOUBLE FACED JACK

"Yo, bruh, don't be late. 11 on the dot," Kane said to Duppy. Duppy could hear Kane was driving, and that his foot was hard on the gas. "I'll be there." he replied, and Kane was gone to the sound of his speeding car and the click of the line going dead.

Duppy and Egypt were in the studio listening to some tracks for her upcoming album. "Who was that?" she asked.

"Kane," he answered, hitting the play button to resume the music. A sweet neo-soul style track filled the room. Duppy began nodding to it.

"I don't like it," Egypt remarked.

"Are you crazy? This shit is hot! It has that ill '90s type vibe," Duppy remarked.

"This isn't the '90s," she snapped back.

Duppy shook his head and started another track. It had more of a millennial feel, but still, Egypt wasn't satisfied.

"No."

Duppy sighed and stopped the music. "What's wrong, Egypt? You've said no to every track I've played."

"I'm just... I've got a lot on my mind."

Duppy reached out and touched her knee. "Talk to Daddy," he said.

Egypt angled her body away from his caress. "My Daddy's dead."

"Ouch! Wow, I thought you were my baby girl. But I guess its Kane's turn now, huh?" Duppy spat sarcastically.

Egypt looked him in the eye and said, "You can't hurt me with words, Duppy. You should know that by now. Kane is strictly business."

"So, you're not fucking him, Egypt?" Duppy probed, knowing the answer.

"Fucking is my business," she said, getting up, reaching for a VSOP and pouring herself a double hit into a glass. She drank it and immediately poured another, enjoying the heat scorching down into her belly.

Duppy shook his head. "You're one of a kind, ma."

Egypt didn't respond. Her mind returned to the place it always returned to: Power. She missed him like crazy, but she knew they could never go back to the place they once were at. Too much had transpired. Power felt like she had betrayed him by choosing Kane over him, not knowing the choice wasn't hers —it was an order to not bring about a bigger betrayal of herself. She was a part of a bigger plan, one that would change the street game for years to come. She refused to let her heart get in the way of that.

"Yo, Egypt. You heard what I said?" Duppy asked with irritation. He had called her twice.

"No, I'm sorry. I was thinking," she admitted.

Duppy sighed. "Look, it's clear your head isn't in this today. Let's just pick it up tomorrow. I've got to go meet Kane," Duppy said, looking at his watch.

He stood up, but Egypt sat back down, making it clear she didn't want to go with him.

"You staying?" he asked.

Egypt nodded.

He leaned down and kissed her on the cheek. "You'd be happier if you weren't so beautiful," he said, then exited the room, leaving her to contemplate the meaning.

———

Duppy sat back in the Maybach going through his emails. He found one from Lisa, talking about Ménage's first photoshoot. He grinned to himself because he hadn't thought about the girls since their romp in his office.

"Ménage plus one," he said to himself, the grin turning to a full-on laugh.

In the front seat, Jaylan Blunt operated the intercom. "You need something Duppy?"

"A time machine, so I can go back and do these hoes all over again," he said, holding up the attached photoshoot picture on the phone. Jaylan looked at it reflected in the rearview mirror, and Duppy saw that Jaylan's eyes were smiling as much as Duppy was laughing. Jaylan was an excellent procurer of bitches for Duppy, as well as bodyguard and driver. Duppy made a note in his head to give Jaylan a nice bonus at the end of the week. Jaylan's loyalty meant a lot in a world where trust was rarer than blue diamonds.

Duppy focused back on Ménage. He fully intended on making the girls stars because he knew he could make a lot of money off them. But they were also freaks, which promised he could use them in more ways than one. He looked at his watch.

10:48pm.

"How much further?" Duppy asked Jaylan.

"We're almost there, sir. Traffic is real heavy because of a Knicks game," Jaylan answered.

"I hope the Knicks won," Duppy said, looking out at the nighttime streets sliding by. He sat back and poured himself a drink then toasted himself. He was on top of the world. His label was the biggest rap label in the world, and with the addition of Ménage, he would be moving into the mainstream world with a big impact.

Duppy expected the world to bow down. He expected the industry to crown him king. He expected to be a billionaire by the time he was 50, but he didn't expect for the Maybach door to open and...

LONG DIE THE KING

"Here comes the Maybach," the driver of the stolen Maserati said. The guy next to him cocked his weapon and pulled the ski mask over his face.

The other passenger in the backseat pulled the sawed off fully automatic AK-47 onto his lap and spat, "Power said don't miss!"

"We won't."

As soon as the Maybach pulled up in front of the club, the Maserati skidded up onto the sidewalk, scattering the screaming crowd and plowing straight into Jaylan as he opened the door for Duppy. Jaylan didn't die straight away as the crumpled metal of the door sliced into his chest. His head bounced off the edge of the Maybach roof, cutting a deep gash and cracking his skull like a robin's egg.

Out of habit, he had reached for his gun as soon as he'd heard the screeching tires. As the Maserati crunched on at full speed, breaking every one of his ribs against his spine, Jaylan's arm snapped and broke off at the elbow. It was the same arm that held the gun that shot Gina—poor burned Gina, the woman who had loved him—in the face. It was the same arm that had picked up the shovel that then poured earth onto her body in the shallow grave.

The nose of the Maserati lifted, scraped on, and tore the door of the Maybach off completely. Jaylan went down in the mess of metal, his head popping finally, as it was caught between the Maserati's tire and body work, twisting his neck like a toy.

Duppy was thrown back in the Maybach, head crashing against the side door leaving him almost upended, ass high, legs spread, dazed with a thin trickle of blood coming out of his mouth where he had bitten through his tongue.

"What the—?" was all he managed before two shadows appeared in the hole left by the torn off doorway.

The first bullets from the sawed-off AK-47 ripped up Duppy's legs and buried themselves in his crotch. The shells minced the dick and balls that had cum all over Lisa. Spitting and slamming upwards the bullets tore through his belly, ravaging the bladder that had pissed in Lisa's face. Duppy tried to hold up the hands that had dropped Tatiana from the hotel balcony, but the palms were peppered, fingers flying off like bark from a wood chipper. Then the bullets burst like stuttering icepicks into the black heart that had driven his desires. Up further, they cracked into his chin, smashing the teeth encapsulated in the mouth that had delighted in humiliating Lisa and the girls of Ménage. Then finally, they caved in the eyes and skull, liquidizing the brain beneath that had thought-up every scheme to apply his twisted desires in the sick power exchanges of his business.

Duppy's near fingerless hand fell down, as the blood pumped from the holes in his body, there was one last sigh from his ruined lungs, a twitch of confused nerves and then he became still.

The shadows put five more slugs in him just to make sure.

"Fuck!" the driver gasped. The gunmen were walking away from the two bodies, clearing their weapons and giving each other dap for a job well done. They got into the back seat of the Maserati just in time to shut the doors before the driver slammed the car in reverse and fish-tailed it into a one eighty, putting his foot on the gas hard.

"Fuck wrong wit' you?!" the one gunman barked.

"That wasn't fuckin' Kane!" said the driver. Knuckles glowing, hands tight on the steering wheel.

"So?!"

"So? Nigga we was supposed to kill Kane! That was fuckin' Duppy! We killed Duppy!" the driver agonized.

The shooters sat back stunned. They hadn't waited to see who was who. Their only concern was not completing the job. Now, they was stuck by the implications of the situation.

"Goddamn," one groaned.

"Fuck my life," said the other.

They skidded up to the second stolen car they had parked two blocks away. Once they made the switch, they rode in silence.

Finally, the driver heard from the back seat, "You gonna call Power?"

Before he could answer, his phone rang. He looked at it.

"It's Power," the driver said.

They knew they had fucked up, but they knew they had to answer the call. The driver answered.

"All niggas look alike or something?" Power questioned, as he sat in the hotel bed, staring at the TV screen. The killing was already all over the internet.

Speculations abounded. The Illuminati was implicated. Conspiracy theorists had a field day, but none of them understood the irony that one of the most famous people in the rap game was a victim of mistaken identity.

"Nah, yo. Shit was crazy," the driver stammered.

Power shook his head, the myriad of consequences moving

through his head like sparks off a grinder. "Don't sweat it. I need to holler at you so I can pay you the rest of the money. Meet me at the spot we talked about," Power instructed.

"We on our way," the driver said, hanging up the phone and adding, "out of town!"

"What he say?"

"Meet him at the spot so he could pay us the rest of the money. Yeah right! We outta here!" the driver hissed. He then punched the gas to further make his point and lit out away from the city forever.

Meanwhile, Power paced his hotel suite's bedroom floor.

"What's on your mind, papa?" the Dominican stripper pouted, laying in the bed, naked and breathtakingly sexy.

"Not now," Power replied coldly. Right away, he put two and two together. He picked up his phone and called Five$...

No answer.

He called again.

No answer.

He texted him: *call me.*

Five minutes later, there was no response. That's when he started to worry.

ACE OF SPADES

The funeral was like a rap video extraordinaire.

Everyone in the industry showed up. Phantoms, Bentleys and Bugatti's lined the cemetery, as everyone who was anyone came to pay their respects to Duppy. The media was in full force with cameras and reporters everywhere, but they really went crazy when Egypt stepped out of the Rolls Royce Wraith escorted by her bodyguards and Griselda.

"Egypt! Egypt! Is it true you were the last person to see Duppy alive?"

"Did you know about Duppy's street ties?"

"Why is Griselda Marcos, reputed gangster, here with you?"

"Egypt, what do you know about Duppy's death?"

Egypt maintained her composure, dressed in all black, oversized Chanel shades and a Jackie O-like expression. She stepped through the barrage of questions like a specter through a wall of words.

Power stood off to the side and watched her every move, her style, sticking him in his heart with every measured step.

How did I get so far gone? Power thought to himself. Egypt had him fucked up, but his pride wouldn't let go of itself and allow him to embrace her despite her flaws. To him, she had betrayed him and no man can live with that.

Egypt looked up, breaking the spell of cool she was casting, as if she could feel Power watching her. Their gaze only held each other for a moment, but to Power's heart, it felt like an eternity. She looked away and then disappeared in the crowd. Griselda eyed Power and nodded. He returned the nod, then slid off.

Many tears, real and contrived, were shed as the reverend preached Duppy's eulogy. He extolled him to the heavens as if he were a lawyer trying to get his client through the pearly gates. Power stood silently, watching. Across the horizon of the coffin, across the expanse of the grave, stood Kane. He was looking at Power wearing a knowing smirk that Power wanted to smack off his face. Beside Kane stood Messiah and Knowledge, both glaring at Power. They were all strapped on both sides, but no one wanted to be the one to set the spark to the smoldering beef.

Once the funeral was over, Kane approached Power, with the twins out of earshot, yet still close enough to be a problem if Power decided to act up.

"What up, thun?" Kane greeted, but didn't extend his hand.

"You already know," Power replied, maintaining eye contact.

"Shame what happened to Duppy, huh?"

"Yeah, no doubt."

"I wonder who would do that? It's crazy," Kane shook his head, then looked at Power, adding, "You have any idea?"

"Not the slightest. Is there a point to this conversation?" Power asked pointedly, wanting to get past the bullshit.

Kane looked at him and gave him a wicked grin. "Speak to Fi lately?"

BOOM.

That's when Power knew.

He kept his poker face, but inside he was breaking like a jigsaw thrown at a wall. He knew Kane had beat him to the punch. Power's actions may have had Duppy killed, but Kane had set him up to die, knowing the hit was meant for him.

Power began to reach for the heat below his jacket, but Kane clapped him on the shoulder, stilling his hand. "Stay focused, thun. Murder is like a virus, anybody can catch it," Kane said, his eyes showing he knew Power wouldn't pull out the gun there and now. That shit was for later.

Then Kane walked off with the twins in tow, through the trees and into the sunlight.

NO MORE ACES

"Did you say Griselda Marcos?" O'Brien probed.

Kane shrugged. "Yeah. The dyke bitch that ran with R-Daddy. I guess she's one of The Colombian's lieutenants or something," Kane explained.

O'Brien and Spagoli looked at one another.

"Why didn't you mention her sooner?" Spagoli questioned.

"'Cause she wasn't a part of the story until now. But she's irrelevant. The key is getting The Colombian. Do you know why he chose to use the music industry to front his business?"

"No, why?" O'Brien replied.

Kane smiled. "CDs"

A beat.

"CDs?" O'Brien echoed.

"C.D. Compact discs, or at least that's what everyone thought. In actuality, the CDs were compressed cocaine."

Spagoli's mouth dropped. "Compressed..."

Kane nodded.

"The veneer is laminate, but the actual CD was made of cocaine. Uncut. You press up a couple million of those and no one will ever know the difference. We weren't selling records, we were selling drugs," Kane revealed.

"But what about all the people who bought your CD? They got coke?" O'Brien asked.

"No, the CDs in stores were legit. It's the CDs we only broke that were the dummies. Check Duppy's records. You'll see."

"But now that Duppy's dead, how do we connect The Colombian to the coke," Spagoli said, speaking his thoughts aloud.

"That's not my problem. I held up my end of the bargain, now it's your turn," Kane replied.

O'Brien and Spagoli looked at each other and smiled, matching shit-eating grins.

"You want to tell him, or should I?" O'Brien quipped.

"Be my guest," Spagoli answered with a chuckle.

Kane sensed something was wrong. O'Brien turned to Kane and said, "Well...It's true that you held up your end. You are a man of your...word," O'Brien snickered at the irony of his praise, then continued, "And yes, we are going to hold up our end as well. You won't get any state charges. But as far as the feds..."

As soon as his voice trailed off, the door opened and Kane's whole stomach dropped when he saw her walk in. All the while he thought it had been Egypt behind the glass, the cop fuck bitch whore. Watching Kane rat to save his ass, but it hadn't been Egypt at all.

The woman who walked in like she owned the fucking joint was unknown to him.

"Who the hell are you?" Kane growled, trying to sound tougher than he actually felt.

"Didn't these gentlemen tell you?" she replied, the smirk on her face simple but sinister.

Kane looked at Spagoli. "What the fuck is going on?"

Spagoli shrugged. "We're done here. Ask her."

With that, Spagoli and O'Brien walked out, closing the door behind them. The woman's heels clicked against the linoleum floor as she approached Kane.

"Who—who are you?" Kane questioned, his bravado swallowed.

She perched on the edge of her desk and flashed her badge. "FBI, and you my friend, have a date with destiny."

"Look... I can tell you everything," Kane offered, but she just laughed in his face.

"You already did. You told them, they told me. You have nothing to offer but your soul and that's worth less in today's mad world."

"This is some bullshit," Kane spat.

"I hope you packed underwear because this is going to be a long trip," she smiled sweetly at Kane.

"What is this shit? Who are you?" Kane whined, feeling the whole weight of the world falling away from him, leaving him empty and alone.

"Me? Oh, just call me Vanya. Everyone else does."

And the room darkened around him, right then and there.

Kane sat in the back of the sedan, sick to his stomach. He had violated every code of the streets, and he still had nothing to show for it.

"I-I can't go to jail," Kane whined like a bitch. Suddenly, he was looking through the years at Carlito and Five$ standing in the doorway of his apartment, and his Momma was coming at his eight-year-old self in a rage. Kane's bladder was fixing to let go all over again.

Vanya glanced in the rearview mirror as she drove. "Doesn't seem like you have much choice."

"Muhfuckas find out I'm a rat, I won't last a week," Kane predicted.

"Should've thought of that before you became a rat."

"I've got money. Millions. It's yours. Just...please."

Vanya laughed. "Are you trying to bribe me?"

"Nah, yo. I'm just trying to help myself," he replied.

"You already tried."

"Look man, I'm desperate and you're a Federal agent. There must be something we can work out," Kane reasoned.

Vanya eyed him through the rearview and replied, "What makes you think I'm a Federal agent?"

Kane stopped. "Huh? Because you said you were."

"You believe everything a person tells you?" Vanya laughed.

Kane felt the situation had shifted, but he couldn't explain how. "You walked in and showed me your badge."

Vanya reached over the seat and tossed her badge in his lap. He looked down at it, metal glistening in the moonlight. His mind did a backflip when he read the insignia.

Disney World Security.

"Ain't no goddamn way," he mumbled, realizing he had been set up.

"Way," Vanya snickered.

"But the police, O'Brien and Spagoli—"

"Spagoli owed us a favor."

"Us?" Kane echoed.

"Oh, I'm sorry, I guess I should introduce myself properly. Vanya is just what people call me...sometimes. In reality my name is Xavier, or you can call me The Colombian." Kane's mind was blown because it was a woman's face but The Colombian's voice.

Vanya laughed, then said in The Colombian's voice, "Still haven't put two and two together? Can't believe your own eyes? Here, let me help you."

Vanya slowed the sedan down and pulled into the parking lot where C-Allah had been ended. She reached into her purse, took out her makeup kit and opened it. She pulled out a fake mustache and goatee and adhered it in place. Next, she placed the thicker eyebrows over her perfectly arched ones. Right in front of Kane's eyes, she transformed from a beautiful woman into a handsome man. Kane's mind was more than blown, it was devastated.

"What the... fuck? You a bitch?!" Kane stammered, feeling the piss starting to well between his legs.

"Bet you never saw that comin', huh? The richest player in the game is really a woman," Vanya laughed, then added, "But that's not the crazy part. The crazy part is how you used to look at me."

Kane glanced at her and their eyes met in the rearview. "I don't know what you're talking about," he lied.

Vanya snickered. "Sure, you do. I used to see you looking at me when you thought I wasn't looking. You had a crush on me, didn't you?" Vanya teased.

"Hell no!" Kane roared. The cable ties holding his wrists and ankles digging into the flesh, drawing blood. Kane was leaking all over...

"You're lying. I could see it in your eyes. They were saying, "'Damn, he a pretty muhfucka.' You wanted to fuck me."

"No."

"Yes, you did!"

"Even if I did, you a woman!"

Vanya laughed. "Yes, but you didn't know that at the time. You thought I was a dude. Guess you never thought you'd be attracted to a man, even if that man really is a woman. Don't worry, your secret is safe with me," Vanya assured him.

Vanya started the car up again and headed out of the parking lot, up the on-ramp to the L.I.E. and burned away into the afternoon. Kane was a scared mess of blood and piss, uncomfortable in the backseat, running through any possible option of escape in his mind. But he came up with nothing. He was as nailed as he'd nailed Power. There's nothing he wouldn't have given now to be back in QB with Power, on the roof, hitting a blunt and necking Henny. How far he'd come. How much he's lost, how...Kane looked up. They left the expressway behind many miles ago and now were rolling through the leafy roads of Long Island's Gold Coast.

"Where are you taking me?" Kane said, trying to pour some

small sliver of dignity back into his voice. He was done with whining like a bitch.

"Where? We're here. Look around," said Vanya, whose face was that of Xavier replied.

That's when Kane noticed they were turning into The Colombian's estate, the moon reflected off the fountain in front of the gate. The gate swung slowly open with the sound of money and power.

Vanya drove them inside.

"You don't have to do this," Kane pleaded.

Vanya stopped the car, then looked over the seat at him. "I'm not going to do anything."

Two big bodyguards came out of the house and opened the door. "They are," Vanya winked, as the two bodyguards snatched Kane out of the car.

Kane tried to put up resistance, but both men were as big and black as gold-trimmed Hummers, so his movements were as futile as the flapping of a fish in a bear's mouth. They dragged him up the steps into the neo-classical mansion, through the stone pillars on either side of the door, across the cool marble floor, past oil paintings and Chinese vases on plinths. They turned right and took him through a door and bumped him down wooden stairs into the basement. The basement was lit by naked bulbs, the walls were raw brick, the corridor down which they dragged him dusty. Kane could taste the concrete dust they were kicking up in his mouth. It had the graveyard flavor of death.

They took him into a small room with barely enough light to see and slammed him to the floor. The force of impact knocked the wind out of him. The two bodyguards then turned and walked out.

"Fuck," Kane coughed as he struggled to catch his breath.

"What up, thun?"

Kane heard the voice before he saw the face. Power stepped out of the shadows of the room. "Checkmate, nigga," Power chuckled.

Kane looked up at his old friend and recognized a new enemy. "Yo, Power, I know shit been crazy between us, but we still Q.B.C., thun! We a team," Kane pleaded.

Power laughed. "Come on, yo, I know you can think of something better than that."

"It's the bitch, right? Egypt? You can have the bitch, yo, she the police! I caught her coming out of the hotel one night when we were in Raleigh and I followed her and she was meeting with the police! I threatened to tell, and that's why she fucked with me, yo! The bitch a snake."

Once Kane finished, Power said, "I know snakes. Egypt laid wit' you Kane, because she had no choice. You think you exposing Egypt to me, but in reality, you exonerating her." Power spat on the concrete floor like he was getting something bad and troubling out of his gut. His hooded eyes cleared. "It doesn't matter, yo. This was all a long time coming. You were never my man," Power said quietly.

Power took a knife and cut the cable ties around Kane's ankles, but not before Kane had flinched like a bitch when he saw the glint of the blade.

"Get up, snake." Power said, closing the knife and dropping it into his pocket.

Kane struggled to his feet. He looked at Power's hands, expecting the knife to have been replaced by a gun. But they were empty.

"You ain't got no gun," Kane commented, almost surprised.

Power shrugged. "Why would I? I don't need a gun to kill you."

Kane laughed. "Come on Power, you ain't built like that. You can't handle me head up," Kane snarled pitifully. "That's why you got me tied up."

Power sighed, got the knife out again and cut Kane's wrists free. Power smirked, shrugged and put his hands up. "Who said I have to handle you?"

He made a hissing noise with his tongue and two sets of red eyes appeared on either side of him. They looked demonic in the dark, but as they crept forward and began to growl, low and menacing. Kane's nuts shrunk in their sack.

Two sleek, black Rottweilers stepped out of the shadows, fangs bared and drooling. "They got a taste for snake," Power said with a million-dollar smile.

"Yo, Power, I'm sorry man," Kane bawled.

Power chuckled. "Yeah. You are. Kill!"

As soon as they heard the command, both animals leapt at Kane. One went at Kane's throat. The throat that had spoken the orders to have Duppy killed. The throat that had blackmailed Egypt into Kane's bed. The other leapt towards Kane's nuts and the shriveled dick in his pants—the dick that had fucked Power's girl.

Kane's cries told Power all the bitch had been brought out of him with one bite. He didn't even bother to stick around for the rest. As he walked out, all he could hear was the sounds of Kane's screams and the dogs' ravenous growls of feasting.

"From the cradle to the grave," Power chuckled.

TWO MONTHS LATER

T he crowd in Brazil was losing its minds because Egypt was
in rare form.

She had packed the soccer stadium to capacity and kept the
crowd on their feet for two hours. Egypt was working it.

After Duppy's death, she started her own label, Egyptian
Records, backed by a shell corporation that was owned by Vanya.
Vanya aka The Colombian had the world fooled. She moved as a
man with the subtleness of a woman. Griselda was her lieutenant
that ran a team of bad bitches coast to coast that no one knew
worked for The Colombian. Meanwhile, Egypt branched out from
music to movies and fashion. Her name was big, but she still
couldn't stop thinking of Power. Chicago PD thought she was still
working for them too, believing she'd deliver them The Colombian at some point. She wasn't yet ready to disabuse Malone of
that notion. He sure as shit thought she was a good cop now. She'd
testified incognito in the trial for Detective Spagoli's conspiracy to
murder his wife. Egypt wished she'd been able to hook the worm
as he'd gone down for life without chance of parole. If there was
one thing she hated, as she had smiled ironically at herself many
times, was a dirty cop.

Ever since the disappearance of Kane, Power had been M.I.A.

Her heart was broken, but she was slowly getting over it. Slowly that is, until that night in Brazil. She had the crowed mesmerized.

"Are you having fun yet?" Egypt squealed to the multitude of fans. A roar of approval erupted from the fifty-thousand voices.

"Do you wanna hear 'Street Love'?"

The crowd went wild, but it wasn't Egypt who yelled it out. The voice caught her by surprise. She wasn't expecting to hear it. And then Power stepped on stage and Egypt didn't know who screamed more, her heart or the crowd. He walked up to her smiling and his dimples made her panties wet.

"Y'all ready to turn up?" Power barked at the crowd.

The crowd yelled so loudly, it sounded like a building exploded as the music kicked in and Power began to rap. He pulled Egypt close, driving the ladies in the crowd crazy, making them wish they were Egypt as he rapped his verse. Egypt was in a special zone. So many men had come and gone in her life, but Power definitely had her heart.

For Power, he knew he had finally found that ride or die chick to hold him down. Every thug needs a lady, and she was definitely the lady for him, but there was one piece of business to take care of.

After the show, they went back to Egypt's dressing room. The energy was palpable, but the anxiety was just as thick. Power had brought a silver guitar sized flight case with him. He placed it carefully at Egypt's feet. But Egypt wasn't interested in the case.

Yet.

"Where have you been?" Egypt asked.

"Vanya had me overseas, setting up shop. The game is about to change and I'ma be a big part of that," Power explained, slipping a deferasirox capsule between his teeth and biting down.

"You could've called!"

"Ma, you know where we stood. You chose Kane over me," Power answered, remembering the pain of that time.

"Baby, I—" Egypt started to say but Power silenced her with a shake of his head.

"No, you don't have to explain. Kane told me everything. About the hotel and the police and that you're a cop," Power revealed, looking her in the eyes but keeping a blank expression.

Egypt returned the gaze then looked away. "So now you know."

"I can't say I blame you for not telling me."

Egypt leaned against the wall and folded her arms across her chest. "So where do we go from here?" she asked.

Power shrugged. "That depends."

"On what?"

"If I can trust you."

Without hesitation, Egypt replied, "With my life. I've been looking for a man I could trust my whole life and now that I've found you, I'm not letting you go so easily."

Power smiled. "Only time will tell because... I have something to tell you."

"What?" Egypt responded.

"It's about your parents, ma...Griselda told me who murdered them. It was Vanya."

Egypt's mouth dropped.

Power bent to the flight case and clicked the catches open, lifting the lid. In the black foam interior was a wicked looking AXMC multi-caliber sniper rifle.

Egypt's eyes were wide as hub caps. "What the fuck...?"

Power hefted the rifle up and put it in Egypt's hands. "You're gonna want to learn how to use this, and I know the guy who's going to really enjoy teaching you how to."

KINGSTON IMPERIAL

Marvis Johnson — Publisher
Kathy Iandoli — Editorial Director
Joshua Wirth — Designer
Bob Newman — Publicist

Contact:
Kingston Imperial
144 North 7th Street #255
Brooklyn, NY 11249
Email: Info@kingstonimperial.com
www.kingstonimperial.com